PRAISE FOR
LEO, Inventor Extraordinaire

"Luke Cunningham has created an amazing world filled with cool inventions, brain teasers, and humorous adventures, all centered around a boy genius who somehow has to find a way to save the world from an evil toy company. And maybe find his family along the way. *LEO, Inventor Extraordinaire* is a book all kids should read, with a hero we all can root for."

MICHAEL STRAHAN, two-time Emmy winner, TV personality and host, and Super Bowl Champion

"In *LEO, Inventor Extraordinaire*, Luke Cunningham has created an utterly engaging and charismatic protagonist and an absorbing mystery filled with spectacular inventions, vivid action, an occasional life lesson, and a hearty dose of humor."

CLINTON KELLY, TV personality and host

LEO

INVENTOR EXTRAORDINAIRE

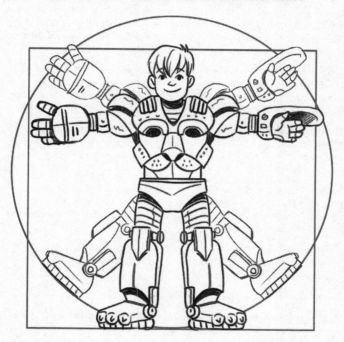

LUKE CUNNINGHAM

ZONDERKIDZ

ZONDERKIDZ

LEO, Inventor Extraordinaire
Copyright © 2021 by Luke X. Cunningham

Requests for information should be addressed to:
Zonderkidz, *3900 Sparks Dr. SE, Grand Rapids, Michigan 49546*

Hardcover ISBN 978-0-310-77000-8
Ebook ISBN 978-0-310-77002-2

If you'd like to learn more about the art that inspired this story and how it connects to the Renaissance, please check out @Leo.Inventor.Extraordinaire on Instagram.

Cover direction: Cindy Davis
Cover illustration: Tim Lane
Interior illustration: Theresa Chiechi
Interior design: Denise Froehlich

Printed in the United States

21 22 23 24 25 / LSC / 10 9 8 7 6 5 4 3 2 1

For Finn.
Heroes are ethical.
Be a hero.

PROLOGUE

The Academy of Florence was a bad place to ask for directions.

Five miles from a two-lane highway that ran parallel to the icy Arno River was a covered bridge. The bridge was barred by two sawhorses and a hand-painted sign that read WARNING, BRIDGE UNSAFE. If someone were to get lost and cross the bridge by accident, and they kept driving another five miles, they might see the soaring pillars of the Academy of Florence—its towering roof throwing the rotunda into deep shadows, the gold dome of the library winking in the fading light, the whole property ringed by a wrought iron fence and guarded by two huge, snarling bears. If they continued past the gate, they might see a statue of Gaga MacKinnon, the wealthy candy heiress who founded the academy as a free boarding school for gifted students. It was a strange, imposing place that seemed to shout *go away*.

The Academy of Florence was a bad place to ask for directions.

But it was a great place to hide.

CHAPTER 1

It was Christmas morning, and snow fell fat and slow outside the Academy of Florence.

Inside, the main hall was decorated with red ribbons and fresh pine boughs that smelled crisp and sappy. A tall Christmas tree, covered in colored lights, stood twinkling in the vestibule. All the students were searching for the Christmas pickle that was hidden somewhere in the tree's branches. Everyone except Leo, who was staring at the corner, getting ready to collect a spiderweb.

"What's he doing?" someone whispered behind him.

"Ah, he's just zoning out like he normally does. Forget that space cadet and let's find that pickle!"

Leo Briga was used to the comments behind his back. Although thirteen years old, he was small for his age, with a large, round head that seemed too heavy for his thin neck. His short blond hair stood up defiantly no matter which way it was brushed. Though Leo spent so much time alone with his inventions that he rarely felt the need to brush his hair.

He knew there was no point in searching for the Christmas pickle. Savvy would find it any second now.

As if on cue, Savvy yelled, "I found it! I found it!" and held the pickle over his head as he danced around the tree.

All the other children pouted.

"Not again!"

"How come he finds the Christmas pickle every year?"

"He cheats!"

"I do *not* cheat," Savvy said. "I'm just smarter than you." But Leo watched as Savvy slipped something small from his palm into his pajama pocket.

Savvy was the same age as Leo but looked at least two grades older. He had wide shoulders and moved like an athlete, confident and quick. His chestnut hair was always falling into his eyes, where he would flip it away with practiced nonchalance. Savvy's left eye had been slightly disfigured since birth, leaving his pupil a feline shape. When someone annoyed Savvy, he'd tuck his hair back so he could stare them down with his cat eye. And that was exactly what Savvy was doing right now—staring at Francis, who had accused him of cheating.

"Just kidding, Savvy." Francis skulked toward the fireplace.

Leo had to admit it was a little suspicious that Savvy had found the pickle every Christmas since he had transferred here. Even in a school filled with exceptional kids, Savvy stood out as smart and charming.

Before Savvy arrived, Leo didn't have many friends. He'd mostly been the weird kid who was constantly getting into trouble over the state of his room. Even worse, Leo was a "lifer," which meant he was one of the students who lived at the Academy of Florence and had no family to go home to. Some lifers had left homes they'd rather forget. Others had left homes they'd never wanted to leave. In Leo's case, he had been the youngest lifer ever, left at the academy as a baby; he never even knew his parents. The school was all he had.

Two years ago, on Savvy's second day at the academy, Savvy was making his classmates laugh around a cafeteria table when he motioned for Leo to come over.

Leo had been eating at another table. Alone.

"Hey, dude."

Leo looked around. "Me?"

Francis leaned into Savvy and nudged him. "Don't bring that lifer over here. Have you heard the noises coming from his room? He stays up all night with the lights on because he's scared of the dark. Not to mention that he can't even ride a bike, he smells like pennies, and he *always* has scabs on his arms."

Dominic piled on, "One of his pets is a psycho. He's such a nerd that his initials are L-A-B."

Savvy smiled at them but still made space for Leo to pull up a chair next to him. The other boys cringed as Leo dragged his seat over to their table. It squeaked loudly on the newly waxed floor.

"It's Leo, right?" Savvy asked as he flipped his hair back.

Leo nodded and took a seat.

"Cool. I'm Savvy. We're playing a game called Chain, and it works like this. First, pick a category. In this case, Dominic picked animals. Then someone says a word in that category. The person next to them has to take the last letter of their word and start a new word with it. Like if somebody says *monkey*, you could say *yak*. Want to play?"

Savvy had just said more words to Leo than everyone else at the table ever had, combined.

"Sure. I'd love to play," Leo said.

"Great. Dominic's word was lynx. He's on your right now, so—"

Dominic scoffed. "That's so cheap—to bring in a new player, then force him to take your word."

"Now, now. Let him take a crack at it. If he can think of an animal that starts with X—"

"Xerus," Leo said without hesitation. "They're a type of African ground squirrel."

Savvy slapped the table. "That's what I'm talking about!"

"Way to go, lifer," Dominic grumbled.

Leo started to slink back to his own lunch table when Savvy pulled him back in. "You're staying right here."

Then Savvy swept his hair back and stared down Dominic. "My parents are gone, so I guess that means I'm a lifer too. You got a problem with us?"

Leo never ate lunch alone again after that day. But he still didn't know how Savvy always found the Christmas pickle.

Miss Medici clapped again and shushed the children with a wave of her long hands. "That's enough! Quiet down or you won't get any hot cocoa."

The younger kids stopped talking at once. Leo carefully collected the spiderweb then shuffled to the back of the room with the older kids, who acted like they were too cool to care about hot cocoa.

Miss Medici had been in charge of the Academy of Florence, and its collection of misfit geniuses, for more than fifty years. Some of the kids said she had grown up there and never moved, and that seemed about right to Leo. She almost never left the main house, and even seemed nervous just stepping outside the front door.

Some of the kids joked she was trapped in the house by a magic curse, but Leo thought that was stupid. Magic is just science we don't understand yet.

Besides, the lifers might as well be the ones trapped in the school by a curse. Lifers never got to leave. No one ever hugged them for a great report card. No one made sure lifers knew how to ride a bike. And until Savvy arrived, Leo had dreaded summer vacation because that's when the whole school emptied out except for him and the other lifers. What Leo wanted most was to know who his parents were and why the Brigas chose to abandon him here. Alone.

Miss Medici clapped again. "Places!"

The children scooched in tighter around the tree and stared at the pile of presents like hungry wolves eyeing a fawn.

"Leo, I'm only going to ask this once—are your pets locked up? *Especially* Gemini?"

"Yes, Miss Medici." Much like Leo, his two pets—Dante and Gemini—were rarely on Miss Medici's good side.

Before she could dig deeper into their whereabouts, Savvy bowed deeply, hair flopping over his face, and solemnly handed Miss Medici the pickle.

"The holiday gherkin, milady."

Miss Medici never smiled, and she didn't now, but she stopped scowling for a moment and that was close enough. She patted Savvy on the head, then handed him a fat chocolate bar.

Savvy sat next to Leo, waving the reward. "We can split it later," he whispered. "I'll trade you for some parts."

Trading parts for chocolate didn't sound like a good deal to Leo, but he nodded his head anyway. Leo and Savvy were always looking for parts. They had bonded over their knack for building things and their unshakable faith that they could build a world better than the one they knew.

Even though Leo and Savvy were only thirteen, their craziest inventions were legendary at the school, though for different reasons: Savvy's inventions worked perfectly while Leo's inventions always seemed to wreak some kind of havoc.

One time, Leo built a submarine to explore the glacial lake down the hill from the main house. It worked, but on its second voyage, his submarine's CO_2 handlers (which he'd constructed out of old fire extinguishers) malfunctioned, and Leo had to abandon ship. He almost drowned, and on clear, sunny days, you could still see the submarine sitting on the bottom of the lake. After that, Miss Medici threatened to lock him in his room with the lights off—her preferred form of punishment—but instead she forbade him from using any tools. He didn't touch a pneumatic wrench or a blowtorch for months.

While they waited for Miss Medici to finish arranging the presents around the tree, Lisa squeezed in between them. Lisa was the only girl lifer, and she was the only person who made Savvy nervous.

"I'll give you half of my cocoa for some time on the CrayStation," Lisa offered.

"Not interested." Savvy sniffed.

"I wasn't talking to you. I was talking to the guy who invented it."

Leo laughed and Savvy elbowed him in the ribs. Savvy could dish it out, but he couldn't take it.

The CrayStation was a homemade version of a PlayStation 7, which Leo had built from salvaged parts. He also hacked the newest version of *Fortnite* so the academy became a playable level in the game. Even though Leo created it, Savvy had insisted on keeping the console in his room because, according to Savvy, Leo's room was too messy.

"That thing was awesome . . ." Lisa nudged Leo. "When it worked."

Not knowing how to take the compliment, Leo played it cool. "You're right," he stuttered. "I've been meaning to fix it, but there's this other invention I'm working on, so I've kind of been avoiding it—"

"You know what else you'll have to avoid?" Savvy chimed in. "The huge crater it made in my floor."

Lisa laughed but Leo stared at his feet.

"Nice burn . . . literally." Lisa high-fived Savvy, who blushed.

Leo hated how few of his inventions worked like they were intended. In his rush to impress everyone with the CrayStation,

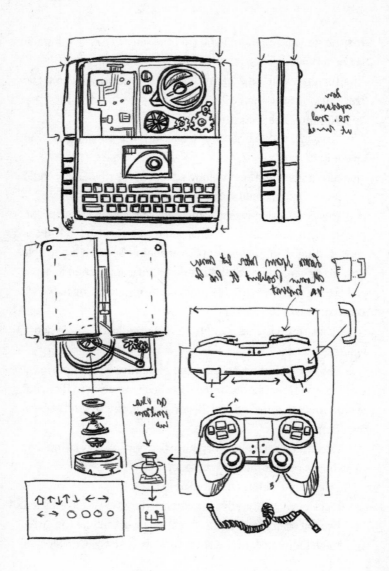

he'd forgot to build in fans to cool the processors. The unit got so hot it melted a hole in Savvy's floor, which is why the other kids had nicknamed it the "CrayStation." Thanks to Savvy's quick thinking and some creative rug placement, they had managed to keep the hole a secret from Miss Medici.

As Miss Medici began the gift exchange and the other students crowded toward the tree, Leo leaned into Savvy. "Hey. How do you always find the pickle?"

A mischievous look on his face, Savvy peeked around to make sure no one was watching before pulling a small machine halfway out of his pocket.

"With this," he whispered. "It's a radiation counter."

"How does that help you find the pickle?"

"Easy. On Christmas Eve, I go into the kitchen and irradiate the pickle jar."

"You what?!"

"Quiet!" Savvy hissed. "I irradiate them *very weakly*. They're perfectly safe to eat."

He put the machine back into his pocket. "Although I wouldn't recommend it."

"Geez, Savvy . . ."

Miss Medici noticed them talking and furrowed her eyebrows. "Savvy, is there something you'd like to share?"

"Yes, Miss Medici." Savvy smiled. "I'd like to share my gift for Leo."

"All right, go ahead."

Savvy grabbed a large green package from under the tree

and shoved it at Leo. "It's what you asked for," he said. "Although I don't know *why*. It seems kind of weird to me."

Leo tore off the paper and stared wide-eyed at the gift. "Yes! It's just what I wanted!"

The other kids all burst out laughing.

Leo was holding a girl's doll, complete with a pink dress and blonde pigtails. Big balloon type on the package proclaimed *Molly Poops-A-Lot!* and *She really poops! Working digestive tract!*

Even Miss Medici's stern voice and withering glare could barely restore order.

Leo didn't mind if they laughed. He loved that his best friend had remembered what he wanted. And he couldn't wait to show Savvy what he planned to do with his new toy.

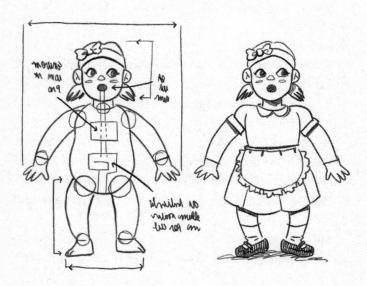

CHAPTER 2

Bright paper and uncoiled ribbons littered the floor around the tree in shimmering tangles. The rich smell of chocolate wafted in from the kitchen as Miss Medici heated the cocoa. All the kids had finished opening their presents and were now playing with them inside the dining hall.

Sylvester was showing Savvy his new phone. "My parents sent it from Switzerland. Won't be released here for another year or so."

Leo picked up his new doll and grabbed Savvy's arm. "C'mon," he said, pulling him away from Sylvester, "let's go to my room. I wanna show you something."

Savvy stopped. "Ah, no offense, dude, but I don't think I want to watch your doll poop."

Sylvester laughed, but Leo ignored him and kept dragging Savvy toward the door. "What? Oh no, don't worry. This is much cooler than that."

Savvy reluctantly followed Leo out of the dining hall. As they made their way through the pantry, Leo stopped Giulia as she was about to bite into a pickle.

"Wait!" Leo shouted, then gave Savvy a guilty look.

"Ugh. Fiiine." Savvy grabbed the pickle out of her hand and threw it into the garbage.

"Hey! Get your own snack."

"You don't want to eat that. Trust me," Leo told her as he

tipped the rest of the pickles into the bin that held a stinky compost heap. "And you don't want any of these either."

"Happy now, Leo?" Savvy said as he pushed Leo out of the pantry.

"Yup. Let's go."

They ran down the hall and to the end of another long hall until they got to Leo's room.

Because the house was so huge, every kid got their own room. And Leo's was a spectacular mess: massive gears hung from the rafters like cheese wheels, tottering towers of books leaned against the walls, and sketches drawn on pieces of shirt cardboard, newspaper, sticky notes, and napkins covered the windows. But a forest of electric lamps lit the room. No matter what time it was outside, it was always noon in Leo's room.

They ran in and Leo turned on an extra bank of shop lights over a workbench. He laid his Christmas present on the table.

"Dante! We've got work to do! Bring me a hammer."

A tiny metal monkey clambered down from the rafters and landed on the table.

Dante was the first robot Leo had ever built, so his construction was a little crude, as he was cobbled together from scavenged parts. His body was carved from a Windsor chair, and you could still see the patterned upholstery running down his back. Mad tangles of wires protruded from his joints, and no matter how hard Leo tried to tuck them back in, one or two were always sticking out. His eyes were brass goggles that irised open and closed as he peered at Leo with his head cocked to one side.

"A hammer," Leo told him. "Please."

Dante screeched and refused to move. He pointed to a jaunty Santa hat on his head, which Leo guessed Dante had made from a red napkin.

"Okay. I love your hat." Dante yelped happily and finally hopped away to go find a hammer.

Leo grabbed Savvy and pointed to the logo in the upper right corner of the doll's box: Wynn Toys.

"Wynn uses some really next-level tech in their toys." Leo pulled the doll out of   its box.

"Well, sure," Savvy said, "everyone knows Wynn used to make the best toys. At my old school, they gave us Kaboomerangs to use during recess."

Leo got a little jealous every time Savvy bragged about his life before transferring to the academy, which Savvy did quite often.

Savvy stopped to look at Leo's collection of half-finished sketches covering his window. "But everything Mach Valley makes is so much better than Wynn Toys now."

Leo shook his head. In his opinion, Wynn Toys wasn't just the world's most innovative toy company, it was the world's most innovative company, *period*.

The founder of Wynn Toys, Peter Wynn, was a genius who started his company in his basement and personally invented most of the company's products. But Peter had disappeared over a decade ago—gone missing or something. With Peter Wynn gone, Wynn Toys had been overtaken by a company called Mach Valley. Mach Valley's gadgets tended to be a little more cutting edge, but in Leo's opinion they weren't nearly as much fun.

"Mach Valley started out by making knockoffs of Wynn Toys," Leo contended.

"Maybe. But remember the old saying: talent imitates, genius steals," Savvy countered.

Dante hopped back down and handed Leo a hammer.

"Ah, thank you."

Leo took the hammer and smashed the doll's chest open with one fierce blow. Savvy flinched as shards of plastic flew everywhere.

"Geez! That was a gift!" he yelled.

Leo ignored him. "The average consumer doesn't appreciate the level of craftsmanship that goes into Wynn products; their stuff is always simple and easy. That's what makes it great. Simplicity is the ultimate sophistication." Leo reached inside the doll and pulled out handfuls of silver tubes. "I mean, look at these! Do you know what they are?"

Savvy stared at the doll's pleading eyes. "Uh, her intestines?"

"Well, yes, but more importantly, these are gadolinium cables. It's a very rare metal. Wynn could've used lead, but they wanted a metal that was super magnetic. That way the intestines stick together and don't rattle around inside the doll. It's the simplest way to solve things, and it ends up making a great toy. I mean, they really care about quality."

"That's great, Leo, but so what?" Savvy asked as he absent-mindedly tapped the keys of the dusty piano, which had sat unused in Leo's room for so long that he mostly treated it as a nightstand.

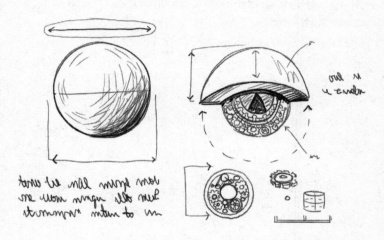

"So what? So what?! It means Wynn goes the extra mile." Leo pulled a ball down from a shelf above the workbench. It was the size of a large grapefruit, with a hard rubber exterior. A thin seam ran around its circumference, and as Leo twisted it, the ball split in two, revealing a complex network of cogs and springs inside. There was a hollow circle at the very center.

"I've been working on this invention for over a year now. A

gadolinium core is the last thing I needed. And once I add the core, the Infinity Ball will finally be ready."

"Ready for what?" Savvy stopped fiddling with the piano. He looked worried.

But Leo didn't reply; he was busy melting the gadolinium tubing from the Molly-Poops-A-Lot into a small sphere. As he poured the molten metal into the ball's center, the silver light danced in his eyes.

CHAPTER 3

They went to the library because it had the highest ceiling in the house. Both Leo and Savvy knew nobody would be there. Christmas was the one (and only) day Miss Medici didn't make anyone study.

The library was cavernous, four stories high and ringed by books divided into four sections: Geometry, Arithmetic, Music, and Astronomy. The ceiling was a massive dome and at its center was a stained glass window.

Leo and Savvy had an affinity for the library. As lifers, they spent hours roaming the stacks when the other students went back to their families over the summer. Over that time they had found a wealth of information they used in their experiments: innovative painting techniques (mix in two egg whites and your colors will stay vibrant longer), the best temperature to weld steel (2400 degrees Fahrenheit), the best way to reduce friction between parts of a machine (three ball bearings set equidistant from each other), but they never found the book Leo wanted the most—the academy's official record of the parents of every student. Rumor had it Miss Medici kept that book in a secret vault somewhere.

The boys stepped into the center of the library and stared at the ceiling far above their heads.

Leo twisted the two halves of the ball shut and it closed with a satisfying snap. He continued to twist clockwise, and as the ball turned, he heard the gears inside clicking.

"I'm winding it up," he explained to Savvy, who eyed the ball with mistrust. Leo strained as the ball got harder and harder to wind, until finally he couldn't turn it anymore. He held the ball out in the palm of his hand, where it vibrated slightly.

Savvy took a step backward. "So what happens now?"

"The Infinity Ball stores 3.2×10^2 joules of energy in its Cannae drive, which is powered by absorbed kinetic energy. That means every time the ball bounces, the electrons inside speed up and the ball absorbs a little more energy, making it bounce higher and higher. Does that make sense?"

"Whatever, dude. There's no way you engineered a Cannae drive that will work at atmospheric pressure."

Leo cast a sideways glance at Savvy. "Want to bet your chocolate bar on it?"

Savvy shook his head. "No. Not after you gave me a *huge* guilt trip about a *teensy* bit of radiation—"

Leo dropped the Infinity Ball. It hit the floor and bounced higher than it had been dropped, almost up to their heads.

Savvy was underwhelmed. "That wasn't so high."

It hit the ground again and this time it bounced twice as high, almost above the bookshelves.

Savvy gulped. "That was higher."

Leo laughed.

The ball hit the ground again. *Smack!* And this time it seemed to rocket off the ground, leaping twice as high as before, far above their heads.

Leo jumped and pumped his fist. "Yes! It works! It totally works!"

But Savvy looked worried as he watched the ball soar toward the ceiling. "Is the ball doubling its apex?" It hung above them for a moment, at the peak of its bounce, then started to fall again.

"Almost. Its height should increase in increments of 1.85 for about twenty cycles, but after that gravity will decrease its height at a rate of 0.1835. The velocity shouldn't get out of control as long as—"

Savvy was staring straight up. "Incoming!"

He pushed Leo out of the way as the ball smashed into the floor right where they had been standing, hitting with a frightening impact and then rocketing back up again. It flew up, up, up, never slowing down—and then it hit a curve in the ceiling, shooting back down even *faster* this time.

"As long as the ball doesn't hit the ceiling," Leo whimpered.

Miss Medici wheeled in a big urn on a silver cart stacked high with clattering porcelain mugs. "It is time for hot cocoa," she announced. "Please form an orderly line."

The children put down their toys and ran to the center of the room, lining up like soldiers. Miss Medici looked down the line and noticed two empty spots.

"Where are Savvy and Leo?"

The library looked like a battlefield: bookcases were toppled, broken antiques littered the ground, and torn pages fluttered through the air like wounded birds.

Savvy pointed to a jumble of toppled bookshelves. "We can take cover there!"

The boys made a run for it. The ball flew past them at shoulder height, like a jet fighter buzzing the airfield. They ducked quickly to avoid having their heads knocked off, then dove behind the pile of toppled bookcases.

Leo peeked his head out cautiously. "Man! Look at that thing go!"

Across the room, the ball smashed through a display case of medieval armor, shattering the glass.

Savvy yelled above the din of destruction, "Leo, just once I'd like you to invent something that doesn't try to kill us."

Leo rolled his eyes. "It's not *trying* to kill us. It can't *think for itself.* It's just obeying the laws of physics."

"Oh, thanks for the heads-up, Einstein. How long is that thing going to bounce?"

The ball seemed to be gaining speed, bouncing around the library faster and faster.

Leo frowned. "I used vulcanized rubber from an old car tire to make the ball. So maybe the force of the impacts will burn through the rubber in . . . an hour or so?"

Savvy moaned. "We'll be dead by then! Any moment now it's going to blast a hole through one of us."

"The Infinity Ball blasts through the bookcases because wood has low impact strength. To stop it, we'd need something with high yield strength, like skin. If one of us tried to catch it, it would probably just break all of the bones in our hand. But it might save the library—"

Savvy stood up.

Leo smiled at his best friend. "Yes, I was going to say you should catch it because you're better at that stuff. But after it breaks your hand, I will totally sign your cast."

Savvy sighed. "I'm not going to try and catch that thing with my bare hand."

He vaulted over the overturned bookcase and grabbed a trash can. He placed himself in the ball's path, planting his feet like a matador. His floppy red sneakers crunched on the broken glass and he gritted his teeth.

"Once again, I'm the one who's going to have to save us."

"Savvy, I'm not sure—"

"I've got it!" he yelled, but the ball flew into the trash can and burst out the other side without even slowing down.

Savvy stared wide-eyed through the jagged hole it left.

"Look out!" Leo yelled. "It's coming back!"

Savvy fell to his knees and scrambled back to cover.

"I would've stopped it if the stupid trash can was stronger," Savvy pouted.

Leo was scribbling notes on a book page. "The Infinity Ball works better than I could've dreamed. But it's generating too much force. You could never stop it with that flimsy trash can." Sometimes Leo's eyes crackled with energy when he caught the wave of an idea; Savvy was relieved to see that light in Leo's eyes now.

Leo looked around the room, then up at the dome and the stained glass window there. He frantically scribbled more figures.

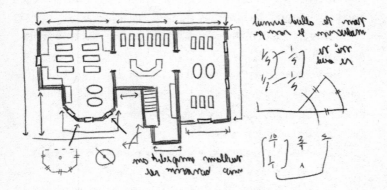

Peeking over Leo's shoulder, Savvy saw what Leo planned to do. "You forgot to account for the coefficient of friction—"

"I know, I know! I'm getting there!" His eyes flew back and forth over the paper. Theoretically, the plan *could* work, but only if . . .

He lowered the paper. It wouldn't work.

"What's wrong?" Savvy asked.

"My plan only works if we find something strong enough to deflect the ball."

Savvy scoffed. "Like what? You saw what it did to the trash can."

Suddenly the ball smashed through the bookshelf directly in front of them. It flew right between their heads, scattering splinters into their hair.

Now it was Leo's turn to stare through a hole left by the Infinity Ball. Across the room, he saw the shattered antique case . . . and the two medieval shields inside.

"That's it!"

Leo ran and grabbed the two massive cast-iron shields, but they were so heavy that he couldn't carry them. He instead dragged them into an alcove, then propped one up. It hit the ground with an encouraging metallic thud.

Leo grinned. "Over here!"

Savvy reluctantly ran over in a crouch.

"We have to get rid of the ball now or there will be nothing left of the library." Leo raised his diagram and pointed to a spot on the ground. "Stand right here."

He handed Savvy a shield. "Hold this in front of you. Perfectly perpendicular to the one I'm holding. That's *very* important."

Leo took ten steps back, then consulted his diagram and took one step forward.

Savvy nervously eyed the dome, where the ball was bouncing around in a triangle pattern. "Are you sure you need me to hold this? Couldn't we just prop it up against—"

The ball shot from the ceiling, straight down at Leo.

"Shields up!"

The whole thing happened in less than a second. The ball slammed into Leo's shield and then bounced over to Savvy, who held up the fifty pounds of iron just in time. The ball clanged off the shield and rocketed straight up, up, up—and through the window at the top of the dome, exiting the library.

A fine rainbow mist of glass particles rained down on their heads. Leo patted his face and body to confirm he was still alive.

"We did it!" he cried, pulling Savvy into a relieved hug.

The library's double doors creaked open. Miss Medici stood silhouetted in the doorway. Her mouth opened and closed, but no words came out. The sudden silence was deafening. Somewhere, a single book fell off a shelf with a thud.

"He did it!" Savvy thrust a finger at Leo.

CHAPTER 4

Leo winced as Miss Medici jabbed a ruler into his back. He felt like a condemned man heading to the electric chair as she marched him down the main hall. Leo knew she specifically chose this path to parade him past all the other students.

Bedroom doors opened only a crack as kids peeked out, afraid Miss Medici's wrathful gaze might fall on them next.

Sylvester muttered, "Nice job, lifer," as Leo was pushed past his door. Miss Medici pretended not to hear it.

Finally, at the end of the hallway, they arrived at Leo's room. "No. Please don't," Leo pleaded with her. But Miss Medici opened his bedroom door, shoved Leo inside, then slammed the door shut.

He heard the heavy bolt of the door's lock as it turned, and a deadbolt slid shut above it. He heard a thin scrape that might have been a chair being wedged beneath the door handle. Then he heard the distinct click of Miss Medici switching off the circuit breaker to his room.

"No, no! Please don't turn off the lights!"

Every lamp in his room went out.

A thin sliver of light from the hallway peeked under his door.

Leo got on all fours and put his mouth near the floor.

"I'm sorry!" he shouted.

Miss Medici didn't say anything, but she dragged something

heavy across the floor—it sounded like an armoire—and shoved it against the door too. Then she stomped off.

Leo plopped down on a bench in the dark. The room was dusty, and he sneezed.

Leo hadn't chosen this bedroom; it had been chosen for him. Most of the other kids arrived at the academy when they were nine or ten years old, after they'd proven to be too hard to handle at normal schools. But Leo had lived in this room his whole life.

He knew Miss Medici wasn't going to lock Savvy in his room with the lights off. Savvy would talk his way out of it; he always did. Of all Savvy's talents, Leo envied that one the most—the ability to convince adults of nearly anything.

Leo wasn't upset with Savvy for blaming the whole mess in the library on him. Well, maybe he was a *little* upset. Miss Medici liked Savvy. Everybody liked Savvy. Leo, on the other hand . . .

Miss Medici had held an irrational grudge against Leo ever since his miniature volcano accidentally burned down her greenhouse. She had gotten even angrier when he converted her exercise bike into a hovercraft and broke a bunch of antiques. Then there was his all-in-one sprinkler system that shot fertilizer all over her car. But none of those incidents was as bad as this one. The library was her holy place; a cathedral of learning.

Now that Leo thought about it, he deserved to be locked in his bedroom in the dark. It was the only way he couldn't cause any trouble.

Leo would be lucky if Miss Medici ever let him out. He had left her library in shambles. And Miss Medici ran the school practically by herself. She could enlist the help of the grounds-keeper and other teachers to clean up the library, but that would take forever.

Unless . . .

Maybe he could build a machine to help clean up the mess?

In his dark room, Leo stood up and accidentally kicked a large bucket on the floor.

Now his toe hurt.

Ugh, what is the point? A machine to clean the library would probably just malfunction—like his inventions always did—and mess things up even worse.

He needed light. There was no point in wallowing in this darkness. He picked up the bucket and carefully stepped across the room, trying not to stub his sore toe on any more of the junk that covered the floor.

He turned the bucket over and used it to boost himself up to the expansive picture window he had covered with paper. He carefully pulled away the sketches, scribbled notes, and blue-prints that were blocking the sun.

For the first time in forever, he saw his room bathed in day-light. He looked at himself in the tall mirror that stood between two of his windows. "Woof. What a mess."

But out of the corner of his eye, something glimmered above the keys of the dusty old piano.

Curious, he scrambled over to it and brushed away a greasy layer of grime. What he revealed underneath the gunk was a series of strange characters catching the sunlight above the keys.

"Dante." No reply came. "Dante!"

The little monkey swung down from the rafters and landed with a garish backflip, before taking a deep bow.

"Yes. I'm very impressed . . . Did you mess with my piano?"

Dante shook his head no. The little monkey was a lot of things, but he wasn't a liar.

"Did Gemini touch it?"

Dante shrugged his shoulders then jumped onto Leo's head, launching himself toward Leo's lofted bed.

Leo yelled after him, "Thank you. Thank you for being so helpful. Means a lot."

Leo used the bucket to sit down at the piano and turned his attention back to the revealed characters.

"What are you? You're not letters. You're not numbers. Are you a different language?"

Dante squealed behind him.

"I've heard just about enough out of you, thank you very much." Reflected in his mirror, Leo saw Dante was now hanging upside down by his tail, perched above the window.

But below Dante, the reflection of the strange characters made Leo's heart race. In the mirror, the characters revealed what they were: a series of musical notes, each note outlined in thin bronze.

He scribbled the notes on a napkin then clipped it above the piano keys. He read the notes repeatedly to himself, trying to

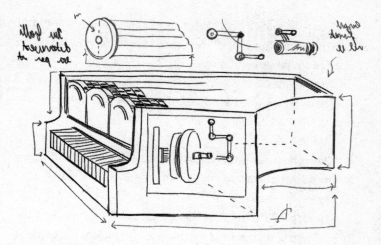

memorize their order. Music was a mandatory subject, but Leo had switched from piano to guitar two years ago.

He cracked his knuckles with a flourish.

"Let's see if I still know how to tickle the ivories." Leo played a few notes to warm up and Dante squealed.

"It's just an expression. I'm not actually tickling the piano. But you're right, that is probably what it would sound like if a piano was getting tickle tortured."

He looked over his shoulder at the mirror again and played the first two notes. Dante covered his ears.

"What?" Leo asked.

Dante stomped his feet and quacked.

"No, I did not just step on a duck. Now you're being rude." Dante laughed then turned a knob around his right eye. His pupil changed to a steady red dot.

"You're recording this? Why, so you can show it to Gemini later and make fun of me?" Leo moped for a second before he returned to the series of notes.

Dum-da-da-da-dum.

The tune sounded kind of familiar, but he couldn't quite place it.

Dum-da-da-da-dum.

The more times he played the notes, the faster he could play the tempo. After nearly a dozen attempts, he finally recognized the tune.

"Oh. It's that song Miss Medici sings when she opens the drapes." Leo sang the song as he played the notes in the right order. All the while, Dante kept recording.

"Here comes the sun. Doo-doo-doo-doo. Here comes the sun, and I say, 'It's all right—'"

Under his feet, there was a gentle rumble, then a click. Leo jumped up from the bucket he was sitting on.

His heel landed on a board beneath the piano. The board flipped up, smacking him in the shin. "OW!" he yelled. "Can I do *anything* right today?"

Dante laughed behind him. "Did you record that?"

Dante nodded. "Great. Just great. Can you stop recording and help me, please?"

Leo bent down to rub his shin and saw something bright under his foot, where the board was askew. He moved the loose board aside and saw a bronze handle glimmering in the gloom beneath the floor.

Leo knelt down on his knees and looked closer at the handle. It seemed old. Ornate patterns wrapped around it like vines, and a large letter *N* in some kind of black stone was embedded in its center.

He laid his palm on it. The metal was warm. He closed his fingers around its curve. Was he shaking, or did he feel a vibration humming through the metal in his hand?

Leo pulled the handle. It slid up smoothly with a solid *clunk*. Large machinery moved beneath his feet, and then a small door slid open in his bedroom's rear wall. This must be the vault where Miss Medici kept the records!

Dante squealed and tried to jump through the door. Leo grabbed him by a tuft of cotton popping out of the seams along his back. "No, you gotta stay here. If anyone comes into my bedroom, you have to act like I climbed out my window. Do *not* tell them I went into this vault. Understood?"

Dante protested and climbed onto Leo's shoulder, but Leo shook him off. "Fine. If I'm not back in an hour, you can tell Savvy. Got it?"

The little monkey crossed his arms but finally nodded.

Leo bent down to crawl through the door and entered a small, brightly lit room with a triangular hole in the floor. He couldn't believe his eyes. A metal ladder was bolted to one side and disappeared down the hole as far as he could see.

He leaned over the shaft, but still he couldn't see the bottom.

The sounds of clanking cogs and moving metal parts drifted up from the hole, then stopped suddenly. From the layer of soot on the top rung, it was obvious nobody had climbed the ladder in a long time, yet tiny lights embedded in the walls cast a soft light down below.

It was very quiet.

At this moment, most kids would hesitate. They would be scared. They would go find an adult and ask for help. But Leo was delighted. He was so sure he'd finally found the records vault, and he couldn't wait to brag to Savvy that he located it first. He stepped down the ladder and into the hole, disappearing beneath the floor after a few steps.

Inside Leo's room, the trapdoor in the wall slid closed again, eliminating any trace it had ever been there in the first place.

Leo climbed down the tunnel for what felt like a long time. His legs and arms started to get sore.

As he descended, the air grew damp and stale. The ladder and walls were soon covered in a green mold that was slippery under his feet.

Leo wondered, what was the power source for the lights? And more importantly, who made this vault? This tunnel seemed pretty elaborate just to keep some school records under lock and key. He stared at one of the light bulbs near his left hand on the ladder. It was old magnetic filament: large coiled wire inside a vacuum tube.

He tapped the bulb. It flickered then went out.

Then the bulb below it went out.

He frantically tapped the bulb again, but nothing happened, and then the bulb broke free and fell. He heard breaking glass far below him.

Then all the bulbs in the tunnel went out, leaving him in total darkness. Unable to see the ladder, he groped blindly, feeling for the next rung, but the mold became thicker on the ladder the farther down he climbed.

He couldn't see anything. He didn't know how much farther the shaft descended because he hadn't looked down in a while.

Leo didn't have any choice. He took a deep breath and continued to climb down into the darkness.

As he stepped down his sneaker slipped, the rubber squeaking against the rung with a frightened *eek!,* and suddenly he was hanging above the abyss by only his arms, both feet swinging loose beneath him.

He kicked his foot, looking for a rung, but couldn't find one.

There was nothing beneath him but air.

His hands were slipping. He tried not to cry, but tears welled in his eyes.

Desperate, he let go with his left hand to see if he could reach the wall, but then his right hand betrayed him, the fingers cramping and letting go, and then he was falling.

Leo braced himself for a long fall, but suddenly a sharp jolt ran up both his legs.

He was on the ground. He tried to calm his heavy breathing.

He had only fallen a few feet. Leo stood on his tippy toes and reached up, finding the ladder directly in front of him.

He sensed a long, empty space stretching behind him. The passage curved to the left, and he thought he saw the faintest light at the end.

Leo ran toward the light. After a minute, he came to a tightly wound spiral staircase; the light was coming from above it. He scrambled up the staircase and spilled out into a tall, round room, like the bottom of a big well. His rubbed his eyes as they adjusted. The walls were stone and smooth. Next to the staircase, someone had etched a floor plan of the tunnel and the room he was in.

The ceiling was high above, with vents that let sunlight

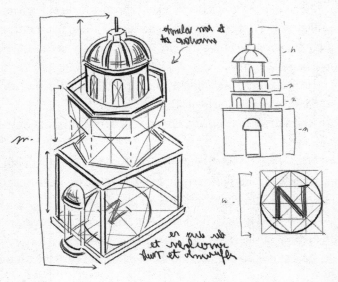

and fresh air trickle in. He looked down, and between his feet a big letter *N* was inscribed in the floor. It matched the *N* on the handle in his bedroom floor, which was now at least a hundred feet above him.

A massive metal door on the far wall seemed like the only way to move forward. The door's hinges were inset and bolts the size of dinner plates fastened it to the wall, like the door of a bank vault. Since no one else was around to congratulate him on finding the records vault, Leo high-fived himself.

He moved closer. The vault door was made of a warm metal—possibly bronze? The light slicing down from above played off it, filling the room. Leo reached out and touched the door. His hand felt a series of shapes etched into the surface under a thick layer of dust. He looked around impatiently for more light.

After a few minutes, he gave up on finding more light and instead rolled down his sleeves and started to brush away the dust. As he labored through the painstaking process of wiping away the grime, he laughed to himself about all the times Miss Medici had warned, "If you don't have time to do something right, when will you have time to do it over?"

After rubbing away what felt like *years* of dirt, Leo coughed into his sleeve, then stepped back to see what he had uncovered.

Engraved on the door was a sculpture.

Leo stepped back farther to get a better look and saw it was two huge carved hands folded together in prayer. He was amazed by their intricate detail—each knuckle and joint was so expertly shaped that they looked like the real hands of a bronze giant. Leo's eyes adjusted to the light, and for the first time he noticed a series of letters formed the hands. He pulled his sleeve up over his knuckles, breathless with excitement, then brushed the dust away so he could read the inscription:

His excitement evaporated quickly once he realized what the letters were. The inscription was in Latin.

Leo hated Latin.

Miss Medici required every student at the Academy of Florence take Latin for at least three semesters. He didn't understand much of the dead language. But he understood enough that he could make an educated guess. He read the inscription aloud.

"*Discequam utvideam.*" That couldn't be right. He read it slower and broke it down into syllables that made more sense.

"*Disce quam ut vi deam.*" Words formed in his mind.

"*Disce quam ut videam.*"

"*Disce.*" He knew *disce* meant "to learn." Miss Medici would remind them when a word had a Latin root, and "discover," meaning to learn something unexpectedly, came from the Latin word *disce*. He remembered that *quam* meant "how." And *ut* meant "to." So he had a solid guess for the first three words: "Learn how to." But what did *videam* mean?

If *disce* was a Latin root of "discover," what could *videam* be the root of? He read the inscription aloud again.

"*Disce quam ut videam. Videam. Videam.* Learn how to *videam*? Vide—. Video. Learn how to video? Oh, wait! I get it. Learn how to see! You're telling me 'Learn how to see!'"

Learn how to see what?

He moved close to the vault again. In the center of the inlaid hands were two handprints, much larger than Leo's. Instinctively, he pressed his hands into them.

The door shook and came alive. The four corners of the door rotated seamlessly. Now in each corner of the door were four different paintings, each of a different scene and done in a completely different style. Under each painting was a dial marked *X*. Leo rotated the dial closest to him. After the *X* were the numbers 1, 2, 3, 4.

Often Leo understood things but couldn't explain *how* he understood them. But when he clicked the dial back to *X*, something also clicked in his brain, and he understood more than what he was looking at—he understood what this door *was*.

It wasn't just a beautiful sculpture of hands . . . the paintings were the key to a giant lock. Turning the dials in the correct order would open the big door.

Leo took a step back and studied the giant hands formed by the inscription again. He closed his eyes and went deep into his own memory, and realized he knew the answer. He had already learned how to see it.

During a field trip to an art museum, a docent suggested an easy trick to gauge the skill of an artist: look at the hands. "Painters don't just sit down at a canvas and start painting.

Before artists paint, they sketch. And the first part of the sketch is to lay out the shapes on the canvas—the geometry. The hardest things to paint accurately are human hands because there is so much geometry—so many different shapes. Which is why the best artists spend time perfecting hands."

Leo suspected the key to the vault was rotating the dials according to how well the hands had been drawn. *Disce quam ut videam.* He had learned how to see.

He took a step back to see the paintings from a better angle. In the painting on the bottom right, a man stood before his horse, and his eyes looked to the sky, but both of his hands were jammed into his pockets. In the upper right, two women sat together, and they seemed to be admiring the glowing baby in one of their laps. Leo thought their hands looked pretty good. Three of their hands were visible. In the upper left-hand corner, a man stood shirtless, his hands clasped together as another man in a brown tunic poured water over his head, a crowd of onlookers watching the spectacle.

But in the lower left-hand corner, a man reached up toward the clouds and seemed to almost touch fingers with a much older man who was reaching down from heaven. Leo was jealous of how perfectly rendered these hands were.

He swiftly turned the tiny dials underneath each of the paintings, based on his subjective opinion of how well the hands were drawn, with one being the best.

Inside the door, massive bolts slid back, booming like bass

drums in the round room. The vault door swung open with an eerie smoothness, revealing a narrow tunnel.

He peeked inside without crossing the threshold. This tunnel was different than the one he'd climbed down: it was cleaner, more domestic. Its walls were paneled in dark, varnished wood, and the stone floor was smooth and polished.

Leo whispered, but it sounded loud in the quiet of the stone chamber. "Whoa."

He stepped over the lip of the vault door and into the tunnel. He walked forward and rounded the corner as it curved gently to the left. Miss Medici really went all out to hide these records.

The big, gleaming door swung slowly shut behind him, though just before it closed, someone stuck his foot in the gap. His face was hidden in shadow, but his head was cocked, listening for Leo to move farther down the tunnel. He waited at the threshold like that for a couple of minutes—then he took off his shoes, laid them outside the tunnel, and quietly followed behind Leo.

CHAPTER 5

Small white bulbs were set into the floor of this tunnel, illuminating the passage with a glowing light. Leo remembered what had happened earlier in the ladder shaft and was careful not to bump into any of the bulbs.

After three hundred and sixty-five steps (Leo counted every one; he didn't know how long the lights would stay on, and the last thing he wanted was to get lost in the dark again), he reached a junction where the tunnel split in two. The left side went down, and the right side went up. But the light was brighter on the left side, so he took that one. After two hundred more steps, he entered a long gallery.

Two of the walls were bare. The other two walls were covered from top to bottom in paintings of various sizes, jumbled together seemingly at random. Some were as small as postcards, others as big as billboards, and they were all very old.

Leo hopscotched around the gallery's checkerboard floor, amusing himself by avoiding the cracks between the cold, square paving stones.

He lifted the frames of every painting he could reach, hoping the records would be tucked in a nook or locked in a safe behind one of the paintings. At first, he worried he might trip an alarm. After a while, he worried he'd hit a dead end.

The far wall was dominated by an oil painting of an old man sitting up in bed, with his left arm pointing at the ceiling. He

appeared to be yelling at a group of younger men, as each of the young men's faces looked to be in a state of distress.

He stared at the painting for a few minutes before he concluded this painting was another clue. The man's left arm must be pointing the wrong way.

"Okay, painting, I get it. I should've taken the path that went up and to the right."

He turned around to walk back down toward the junction. He took two steps toward the door—this time he didn't avoid the cracks. Suddenly, the floor began to pulse and a series of shapes formed in patterns around the paving stones. It started as a rectangle around the perimeter of the room, then it divided itself into a square around the half of the room where he stood. The lights divided the square again to form a triangle. The pattern repeated until a triangle lit up just the corner of the room across from where he stood.

Soft music played in time with the lights over each of the paintings. It sounded like "Here Comes the Sun."

"Wait. Why light up all of these paintings just to tell me I should've gone the other way?"

He tried harder to find the right vantage point, just like he had with the brass door. But to get to the perfect angle, where the geometry in each painting lined up, he had to crouch and contort himself in the farthest corner of the room. Finally, when he was sure all the paintings were directing his eyes to the same point, he felt the stone he was hunched on dip ever so slightly.

He heard a *thwack!* as something dropped from the ceiling. Directly above where the old man's left arm was pointing.

A cloud of dust popped in the opposite corner. As he scrambled to his feet, he rehearsed the argument he would have with Miss Medici once he had the school's records.

"After you locked me in the dark, I discovered the secret tunnels under the school. Found out who my parents are too. Cool vault, though."

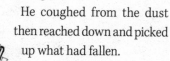

He coughed from the dust then reached down and picked up what had fallen.

His heart dropped down into his butt when he saw it was just some book. Leo quickly flipped through the pages but frowned when he realized it wasn't the records he'd been hoping to find.

Even worse, every page was in Latin.

"Ugh. The only thing worse than Latin is more Latin."

He shook the book again, but nothing dropped out. Leo counted the number of pages, then stuffed the book into his back pocket.

"You are one hundred and five pages of NOOOOPE."

He walked back to the junction. This time he took the path on the right. The floor sloped upward, and after another 221 steps, it ended at a simple steel hatch with a sun-shaped handle in the center.

Leo noticed another letter *N* embossed inside the sun as he turned the knob and stepped out into the cold winter night. Leaves crunched beneath his feet. He turned around and saw the Academy of Florence far behind him; the tunnel had dropped him maybe a quarter mile north of the main house.

The sky was purple fading up to black, where dim stars waited to fall. Leo could just pick out Ursa Major.

He rarely wandered this far away from the academy.

The steel door hinged seamlessly closed into the face of the hill. A foot of dirt and sod covered it, ensuring it would disappear.

He thought of the *N* on the floor and the door handles. A door like the one in the round room unlocked in his mind and in his surprise he spoke out loud. "This is the *north* tunnel. That means . . ."

A familiar voice spoke up behind him. "That means there are three more tunnels."

Leo spun around.

Savvy leaned against the edge of the hatch, lazily spinning a skeleton key on the end of a chain; he tossed it to Leo.

"Next time she locks you in your room, use this. I was wondering how long it would take you to discover the tunnels."

Leo was happy. "There are more tunnels like this one?"

But then Leo was furious. "Hold on. You knew about this? Why didn't you tell me?"

Savvy paused, surprised by his friend's anger, and Leo could tell he was trying to think up a lie. "I, I, uh . . ." Finally, he gave up. "I couldn't figure out how to open the door to the vault, okay?"

Leo crossed his arms over his chest while Savvy continued his explanation.

"I think each of the tunnels have a puzzle you have to solve before you can open the door." He looked at his feet and mumbled, "Good work figuring out how to open the sun knob, by the way."

It was the closest Savvy would come to an apology. "Thanks," Leo said. "At the end of the tun—"

Savvy cleared his throat, which meant "apology over." "I have mostly solved the tunnel *locations*, though. Here, I made a map of where the others are located around the school."

Savvy pulled a piece of butcher paper out of his pocket and unfolded it, adding their current location with a red crayon. Leo quickly explained how the piano in his room had unlocked the loose floorboard and how the handle under the floorboard had opened the secret door.

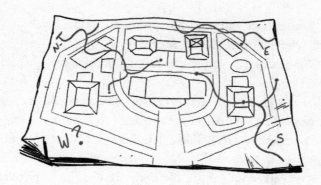

Savvy smoothed the paper on the ground and pointed to various marks as he spoke.

"I found the entrance for the south tunnel—that's the first one I discovered—when your CrayStation burned a hole in my floor. Underneath my floor was a stone passageway. I tracked that passageway to the back wall of Mister Lorenzo's greenhouse."

Leo was fixated on the map, partly impressed by Savvy's dogged research and partly mad that Savvy had kept this to himself for so long. But mostly disappointed about what he didn't find in the tunnel: the school records that showed who his parents were.

Savvy pointed toward the boathouse beside the lake. "Behind the oars in the boathouse, I found a message written in Latin—*Separabis colorum*—which means "separate the colors." The *E* in *Separabis* is in that same font. I'm sure it has something to do with the east tunnel. And the entrance to the north tunnel was inside your bedroom."

Leo sat back and tucked his head into his lap.

"What's wrong?" Savvy asked.

"It's just that I— I thought I would find the records down there."

Savvy put his arm around Leo. "It's okay, dude. But it seems like Miss Medici is telling you the truth. I don't think she knows who your parents are. Besides, lifers like us got to stick together, right?"

Leo perked up. "You're right." He studied the map. "Wait. What about the west tunnel?"

"I haven't been able to find that one yet." Savvy flashed a devilish smile. "Want to find it together?"

CHAPTER 6

Miss Medici rapped on the bedroom door. "Are you ready to behave now, Leo?"

There was no answer.

"Leo, do you hear me?" Miss Medici knocked harder. "If you are ready to behave, you may join the rest of the students for dinner."

No answer.

Miss Medici's mouth pulled tight into a thin line. She flipped the circuit breaker to turn the power back on in Leo's room.

Leo was sitting on the bucket, shielding his eyes from the sudden light and blinking back tears. The tears were real. He was sorry he had wrecked the library and knew it would take a long time to fix.

Miss Medici softened somewhat, although her mood might've changed if she noticed his muddy shoes in the corner.

"At least you finally removed the junk from your windows and let some light in here." She fixed Leo with her sternest gaze. "You and Savvy will clean the library."

"Yes, Miss Medici," Leo said. "As a matter of fact, while I was in here, I started working on a new invention that'll cut the cleaning and repair time in half! It's a—"

"No!" Miss Medici threw her hands up in genuine alarm. "NO MORE INVENTIONS!"

She crouched down to Leo's level and gripped his shoulders. "No. More. Inventions. Do you understand?"

"Absolutely." Leo's mind whirred with floating cogs, levers, and gears. Slowly, they fit themselves into a cohesive machine.

"I totally understand."

Leo's pockets bulged with a couple of wrenches and a rubber mallet that he'd taken from the janitor's closet. He walked on his toes in an effort to quietly creep by Lisa, who was waxing the bannister.

"Hey, Leo," Lisa whispered, "*wrecked* any good books lately?"

It was gonna take a while to live down this library thing.

Leo slammed the door and swept his workbench clear with a fantastic crash. Dante was sleeping on a shelf and he woke up with a surprised screech.

"Dante! We've got work to do! I need paper and a pencil."

Dante chirped happily and hopped off the shelf—and his tail fell off with a clang. He looked back at it, confused, and Leo laughed.

The monkey glared at him, clearly offended.

"Oh, I'm sorry." Leo grabbed a wrench and tenderly reattached Dante's tail, then patted him on the head. "Pencil and paper, please?"

Dante wasn't very agreeable, but he was still a great helper when he wanted to be. Leo had programmed Dante to forage for valuables and store them in his chest. His big hands were a lattice of wooden joints that could grip anything. He scratched his furry head with them now, trying to remember what he was supposed to do.

"Pencil," Leo reminded him. "And paper . . . Please."

Dante dove into a pile of junk and pulled out a roll of wallpaper and a marker. He lugged them over to Leo, who shrugged then spread the paper upside down, put a T square on top, and began scribbling on the back.

"Where's Gemini?"

Dante looked around the room then raised his arms like *how should I know?*

Gemini was probably prowling somewhere. Miss Medici didn't like it when he left Leo's room, but honestly, he needed the exercise; if Leo left him cooped up too long, he started to wreck the place.

On the paper, forms took shape. Leo's hands flew across the sheet like a pianist playing a concerto; they struggled to keep up with his thoughts. *We'll need one brain, but lots of hands. Independent action, but group thought. What could do all those things?*

Leo stepped back and looked at what he had drawn.

Leo scribbled a list of parts and handed it to Dante. "I need you to find these." He pointed to the list. "I think you can find the gears in the kitchen blender. The silver, you can scavenge from the oldest shovels in the garden shed, and . . . hmmmm . . . the wires can be pulled from the exterior security cameras."

Dante gave a funny little bow and scampered off into a heating duct.

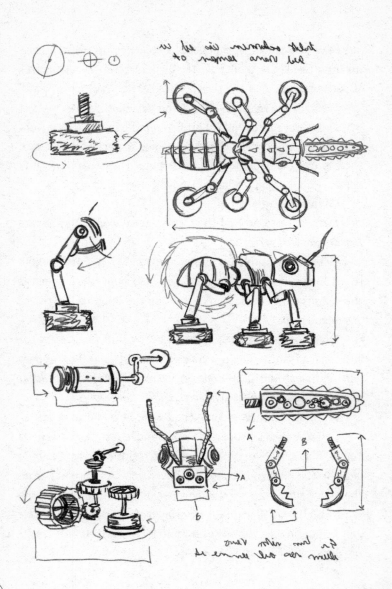

Finding parts was always a challenge, but the house was huge, and Leo could usually find what he needed. Which was good because Miss Medici stopped letting students bring anything home after Leo used a couple of motorcycle mufflers to build a stereo that was so loud, it shattered the living room windows.

It was too bad she had flipped out over that because it was really just a simple frequency issue he could've corrected easily. Man, that stereo had been pretty sweet.

Dante squealed as he rattled around the duct above. Leo put his mouth next to the heating duct and shouted his encouragement to Dante.

"Happy hunting, buddy! This invention could fix the library."

One by one, the lights in the academy's windows winked out, and everything was still.

But much later, long after the moon had risen, brilliant blue flashes of light pulsed from Leo's room, filling the night with strange shadows that leapt up the walls and flashed across the roof outside his window.

Three hundred feet above the academy, a drone hovered, monitoring the lights. It emitted a series of pings at a frequency that no human ear could detect. A flock of drones, which had been encircling the perimeter of the Academy of Florence at intervals of exactly five hundred feet, fell in behind the leader as they began their long flight back to their base.

Their mission had been successful. Leo had been found.

CHAPTER 7

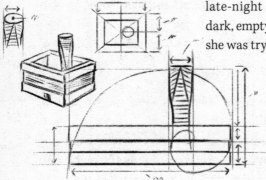

Wynn Tower rose tall and sleek against the night sky, a beacon of hope above the sleeping city. Though ever since the mysterious disappearance of Wynn Toys' founder, Peter Wynn, the beacon had grown steadily dimmer.

Beatrice's footsteps echoed across the polished factory floor at the base of the tower. She usually loved the solitude of these late-night strolls around the dark, empty building, but tonight she was trying to walk off a splitting headache.

She had chosen to spend Christmas Day at work rather than fly home and see her family. With a little over a month left until the Milan Toy Fair, the world's biggest toy event, Beatrice could not spare the time away. She was going to unveil her last hope to save Wynn Toys at the fair. It was her biggest and best bet—a toy so secret that she was one of the only people at the company who even knew it existed.

As she walked off the headache, her dark ponytail bounced with every step. Above her right temple was a small shock of white hair. She'd had the streak her whole life, and she would point to it on the rare occasion when she forgot a detail. "My memory is like my hair—a little patchy."

As a boss, Beatrice was kind but not a pushover. The employees of Wynn Toys loved her. Well, all of them except one.

Beatrice's head throbbed as she stepped into the elevator and muttered, "Sixty-seventh floor—Beatrice Portinari." Cromwell ran its voice recognition app, and the elevator shot up the side of the soaring stack of steel.

Cromwell was among the last, and in Beatrice's opinion the *best*, of Peter Wynn's inventions: a brilliant artificial intelligence system that managed everything in Wynn Tower. But Cromwell's full name was a mouthful—"Computer and Robotic Organic Machine with Existent Living Lucidity"—so everybody called him Cromwell for short.

When Beatrice began her career with the company, Wynn Toys would hold an annual Christmas party. Back then, Peter would drape the factory area in red felt and boughs of evergreen. He'd even ship in a gigantic Douglas fir, twice the height of the tree at Rockefeller Center. But the showstopper was always the Matterhorn, a sledding slope consisting of two hundred tons of man-made snow, which would be piled halfway up the side of Wynn Tower.

Those Christmas parties were a gift from Peter to his employees and their families, always to commemorate another banner year.

There was no party this year.

"We should cancel the Christmas party until Wynn Toys

returns to profitability, yes?" Nick Wynn, Peter's older brother, had proposed this idea to Beatrice in the same weasely tone with which he made all his suggestions.

The elevator continued to ascend the side of Wynn Tower. She gazed down at the twinkling lights spread out before her. A neighborhood had grown around Wynn Toys after Peter built his headquarters here, on the desolate remains of an old quarry in a forgotten town. But now it was surrounded by the glow of thousands of houses. Wynn Tower had revived this city. These lights were the homes of the people who worked for Wynn Toys, the people who worked for Beatrice.

Cromwell's soothing voice announced, "Sixty-seventh floor— office of the CEO."

"Thank you, Cromwell." Beatrice stepped off the lift.

"It is my mandate," the voice replied.

"Of course it is, buddy."

Beatrice walked across the room, then sat cross-legged at her desk in Peter's old office, which was now hers. She fidgeted with one of his puzzles, a dark cherrywood box made of a thousand sliding, twisting cubes. Peter had loved puzzles, and when he wasn't busy designing toys—the most beautiful, wondrous toys the world had ever seen—he was usually trying to solve some puzzle most other people would find impossible. This particular puzzle Peter had given her was one Beatrice had never been able to solve.

She knew it was foolish, but sometimes she thought that if she unlocked the puzzle, it might reveal a clue to his fate. Maybe

Peter was still alive—maybe he'd just gotten tired of being a tech celebrity? Maybe he'd decided to live off the grid somewhere? Or maybe he'd met someone, and fallen in love, and left all this behind? She knew they were silly daydreams, but they were comforting.

Beatrice had spent so many hours twisting and turning the puzzle's smooth wooden contours that she no longer had to look while working on it. The soft pop of its hidden hinges and the dull glow of its gold gears lulled her into the same calming hope she'd retreated into so many times, but suddenly a loud *click!* she'd never heard before startled her out of her trance.

She looked down at the puzzle in her hands and saw that it was open. A blue orb pulsed in the hollow of the open box.

"Beatrice, that is you, yes?"

She snapped the cube shut. She felt a twinge of fear when she recognized the silhouette before her. A dark, backlit figure loomed in the door to her office. In his right hand was a staff as tall as his shoulder. Embedded in the tip of that staff was a prong that could log into every port in the building, and could override anything at Wynn Tower, even Cromwell.

Beatrice exhaled.

"Who else would be sitting at my desk, Nick?" she asked.

"Ha, well, I certainly wouldn't. My brother made it clear he chose you to be CEO in his absence," Nick Wynn said, stepping into the lamp's weak light and revealing his cold, sharp smile. Even at this late hour his suit was impeccably pressed, his tie knotted tighter than a fist. Nick used his staff—the staff Peter had made for him—to point at the papers on her desk.

"If you're working this late on Christmas, you must be working on something important, yes?"

This was how Nick Wynn asked every question, always providing the answer he wanted to hear. Beatrice held up the puzzle and Nick laughed his short, chirpy laugh.

"I guess not. Still tinkering with that old thing, yes? You don't think you'll ever solve it, no?"

Without thinking, Beatrice said, "No, I guess I never will."

Nick chuckled. His hand crawled onto her shoulder like a fat spider, and she resisted the urge to brush it off. Nick seemed to sense this because he gripped her shoulder even tighter as he whispered, "Look, Beatrice, you're not as smart as Peter was. No one is as smart as he was. But that's all right, CEOs don't have to be geniuses, they just need to keep their eye on the bottom line."

"And which bottom line is that?"

"The bottom line of the profit sheet, of course!" Nick laughed heartily as he tapped his staff twice. Then he turned and left her office.

When she was sure he was gone, Beatrice opened the puzzle box again and looked at the orb. She had lied to Nick about the puzzle. But in the years since Peter had left her in charge of Wynn Toys, she felt as though Nick didn't always conduct himself honestly. He suggested shortcuts that may have been legal but weren't ethical. One time he even suggested they use a cheaper metal in their Molly Poops-A-Lot. Sure, they would have saved some money, but her poop wouldn't have looked half as real.

So, for now, she felt it was best to keep the puzzle a secret. "Just what this company needs," she said as it glowed in her hand. "Another mystery."

The blue sphere spun on its axis inside the box, and she saw a smidge of green. Shocked, Beatrice realized the orb wasn't just a ball; it was a globe. She tapped it, and the image magnified, then zoomed in on a country. She tapped it again and it zoomed in on a region. She tapped it again and it zoomed in on a city.

Beatrice stood up at her desk, her heart racing. She tapped it once more and the image in the ball zoomed down from the sky toward some fields, then a forest, and up a long, winding road that lead to an imposing, ramshackle manor.

Three letters pulsed on the surface of the globe: "L-E-O."

Her knees buckled. She realized she'd forgotten to breathe. Beatrice sat down again and stared at the orb, still flashing those three letters.

She knew there was only one person she could talk to about this orb and what "L-E-O" could mean.

The problem was, he had vowed never to speak to her—or anyone else at Wynn Toys—ever again.

CHAPTER 8

Leo and Savvy explored the tunnels whenever they could, but while everyone else had study hall, they still had to repair the library. Miss Medici refused to let anyone help them. She wouldn't even let Dante help, though Leo still snuck him in sometimes.

This morning, however, Savvy showed up with a remote-controlled vacuum cleaner.

"Pretty cool, huh?" Savvy smiled proudly, hands on his hips. "I built it myself!"

"Hey," Leo said, "how come you're allowed to bring in inventions but Miss Medici said I'm not?"

The cleaner trundled past, its bright silver nozzle sucking up book pages and collating them in a glass cube behind it. Savvy smiled. "Maybe because *my* inventions actually work?"

Dante shot Savvy a nasty look. Leo petted him. "It's all right, Dante, he wasn't talking about you."

Savvy bent down like he was tinkering with the vacuum but leaned in toward Dante and whispered, "I was *totally* talking about you."

Leo was distracted by the vacuum's rubber treads. They were new, machine milled. He could tell his friend hadn't molded them from scratch, which meant Savvy had convinced Miss Medici to let him bring in parts again.

Leo slammed his pile of books down. "Savvy—"

Savvy was watching the cleaner do its thing; it really did work beautifully. He shook his head with wonder.

"Isn't it great?" he asked.

Leo didn't want to make Savvy feel bad. He picked up the books and shuffled them back into a neat pile. "Yeah. It's awesome."

The bell rang, which meant it was the end of study hall and time for lunch. They eyed each other for a split second before racing toward the door. Leo took a slight lead until he tripped, crashing to the floor. He found Savvy's vacuum cleaner tangled around his legs.

"You did that on purpose," Leo yelped.

But Savvy had already shot out of the room.

An artful *S* was etched on the handle. Five brass tumblers sat in a row like a combination lock at the bottom of the tunnel's polished steel door. Each of the brass tumblers had the numbers 0–9 engraved on them, and a stack of equations was engraved above the tumblers. Behind all of it, etched into the steel in a perfect circle, was a globe.

Leo focused on the equations.

$$1 + A = B$$
$$+ 1 = C$$
$$+ 2 = D$$
$$5 + = X$$

It was obvious they had to solve the giant combination lock to open the door. But the equations didn't make sense to either of them. Whatever A, B, C, D, and X equaled were the five numbers that would open the lock. But they had no idea how to even do the math to get those five numbers.

"It's got to be something simple that we're missing. Simplicity is sophistication," Leo reminded Savvy.

But Savvy batted the tumblers angrily and the numbers spun past as they rolled—*Click! Click! Click! Click!*

They stared at the puzzle for almost another hour, until it was time for Leo to head to his next class. "I've got to get to biology or Mister Lorenzo will flip out again. Are you coming to your class?"

"Nah. Our next assignment is public speaking and, well, y'know." Savvy pointed his thumbs at himself. "I'm me."

Leo brushed the dust off his pants and grabbed his books.

"Okay. Let me know if you make any progress," he said before trudging toward the stairs.

Savvy relaxed and lay on his back next to the gate, staring straight up at the ceiling. The north tunnel gate had been in a round room with walls of smooth, polished stone. But this south tunnel gate was in a room full of sharp corners, and an unusual pattern of tiles decorated the ceiling.

Leo had solved the north tunnel on his own. Savvy wanted to solve this puzzle today, preferably while Leo was in class.

Savvy had the sneaking suspicion the solution was staring him right in the face when he saw a little handle protruding above the globe.

"Leo Briga, what's the answer?"

Leo was staring out the window. He whipped his head around toward the front of the classroom, but it was too late: he was already caught.

The rest of the students giggled behind their books. Leo getting yelled at was their daily entertainment.

Mister Lorenzo had moved him to the corner of the room

farthest from the windows, but he still caught Leo staring out the window at least once a class.

It was especially hard for Leo to pay attention in biology.

To him, it didn't make sense to study biology indoors. Why couldn't they go outside and actually explore nature, real biology, in person, instead of just sitting around and talking about it in a stuffy classroom?

"What's the answer, Leo?" Mister Lorenzo repeated. Leo was lost. Forget knowing what the answer was. He didn't even know what the *question* was.

Mister Lorenzo tapped a pointer on the chalkboard, drawing Leo's attention to an illustration of a pine cone. He stared intently at Leo. "Pine cones grow by using spirals . . ."

He took pieces of colored chalk and drew spirals along the opened pine cone.

"Why? Why do they grow that way?" He dramatically dropped the chalk back onto the tray.

Leo hadn't been listening since he sat down. He'd been thinking about the invention in his lab that was almost finished, and whether it would be ready to clean the library tomorrow. He'd been thinking about Savvy and the tumblers and the weird math on the gate. He'd been thinking about anything other than this class.

Mister Lorenzo tapped the pine cone again. "I'll give you another hint. Sunflowers and snails grow the exact same way as pine cones. Why?"

Why would a pine cone, a sunflower, and a snail all build themselves the same way?

There was only one answer that occurred to Leo. It was the only thing a pine cone, a sunflower, and a snail seemed to have in common. He gulped and crossed his fingers.

"Because that's the most efficient way to grow…in a spiral?"

Mister Lorenzo narrowed his eyes. Apparently, the answer wasn't totally wrong. "And *why* is that the most efficient way?"

Leo shrugged. "Because math?"

The class erupted in laughter.

Mister Lorenzo sighed. "That's right, Mr. Briga. Because… math."

He turned back to the chalkboard and started jotting down numbers.

"These numbers are known as the Fibonacci sequence. Start with one plus one is two. Then after that, each new number equals the sum plus the second number in the previous equation—so one plus one equals two, then two plus one equals three, then three plus two equals five, then five plus three equals eight, and so on. Does everyone see how the pattern works?"

He pointed to the drawing of the pine cone again. "So Leo is right when he says, 'Because math.' Math is the language of nature. The Fibonacci sequence might be nature's favorite phrase, as we see it everywhere. It's a very efficient model for building. And nature builds in the most efficient way. For instance, if you count the petals of most flowers, you'll find they're a Fibonacci number. Is everyone following me?"

Most of the class nodded, but Lisa raised her hand. "But how do those numbers create spirals, like a pine cone or a snail's shell?"

Leo thought he knew the answer but didn't want to get in more trouble by interrupting.

"AHA! Great question. Imagine cells as little building blocks, like Legos. The cells in your body are always replicating, they are always making more building blocks. And when they replicate,

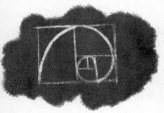

they use the Fibonacci sequence." Mister Lorenzo drew a series of squares on the board, then drew a spiral through them.

He outlined the larger rectangle. "And this is the shape those blocks make: the golden ratio, ideal proportions that are built by using the Fibonacci sequence. Here is the cool part— the proportions always come close to the same number, 1.618."

Mister Lorenzo paused for a second to let the class absorb the information.

"To get the golden ratio, you divide any number in the Fibonacci sequence by the Fibonacci number before it. Try it. Lisa—what's eight divided by five?"

There was a brief moment while Lisa worked out the answer in her head. "It's 1.6."

Mister Lorenzo clapped, then pointed at the two biggest Fibonacci numbers on the chalkboard. "Now, Sylvester, what is 987 divided by 610?"

Sylvester worked out the number on his calculator. "1.618—"

"Do you see? 1.618 again. The golden ratio, built from the Fibonacci sequence, is the most common number on earth. It's everywhere. It's in our plants and animals. It's in our architecture. And it's in every human being."

Leo nodded along. An idea was gaining steam in the back of his head.

Mister Lorenzo pointed at the smaller squares within the rectangle.

"Every person on earth is united by math—namely the Fibonacci numbers and the golden ratio. Sylvester, stand up."

Sylvester, the only kid in class who got yelled at more than Leo, stood up reluctantly. Mister Lorenzo tossed him a tape measure.

"I want you to measure from the floor to your belly button in centimeters."

Sylvester pressed the tip of the measuring tape to his navel then dropped the end to the floor. "It's 104 centimeters."

"Okay, class. Sylvester's belly button is 104 centimeters from the floor. Because every one of us is built according to the golden ratio, his height is going to be 1.618 times 104 centimeters. So I bet he's going to be 168 centimeters tall. Sylvester, will you do the honors?"

Sylvester did everything he could to seem bored as he raised the measuring tape to the top of his head. "It says 168 centimeters."

Mister Lorenzo clapped again. "You see! Every one of you

will find the same golden ratio from your navel to your total height. We are built according to natural law and the Fibonacci sequence . . ."

Leo wasn't listening anymore, but he wasn't staring out the window either. His mind was traveling down, down, down to the tunnel under the school, to the locked door Savvy was staring at.

The drone banked hard left, instantly calculated the wind speed, and readied its approach. It flew over the outer security fence. And then the electrified security fence, lowering as it passed the laser turrets. It shut off its engine and glided over the courtyard and its meticulously landscaped hedges. The flock of drones behind the leader matched every move in a perfectly choreographed dance.

With immaculate precision, the wheels on its nose and fuselage landed at the same time. It taxied into the hangar behind the main house and logged into the secure server.

The drone uploaded two pieces of information: the location coordinates of the Academy of Florence and "Leo."

Instantly, every light in the compound flashed on. And from inside the main house, a long, slow, angry roar began to build.

CHAPTER 9

"That's it! That's what Mister Lorenzo drew!"

Leo ran into the tunnel entrance and found Savvy asleep on the floor. He shook him awake and pointed at the ceiling. "There! I saw that shape in class!"

Savvy was still groggy. "What shape?"

"The tiles on the ceiling! They're called the golden ratio. They're made according to the Fibonacci sequence. We learned about it!"

Savvy finally realized what Leo was saying and sat up like a shot. "So you know how to open the gate?"

Leo walked quickly to the door, his hands moving as he talked. "Not exactly. But I think I learned how to see it. I'm pretty sure the ceiling is a clue. We have to fill in the equations with Fibonacci numbers."

Savvy didn't understand how this would get them past the gate, but he nodded his head anyway. "Hmmm, yes, I see."

Leo scrutinized the equations below the lock. "These equations don't add up using normal numbers, but they work if we substitute Fibonacci numbers. Look . . ."

$$1 + A = B$$
$$+ 1 = C$$
$$+ 2 = D$$
$$5 + = X$$

Leo spun the tumblers to 1, 2, 3, 5, and 8. With a grand flourish, he stepped aside and Savvy cranked the door handle.

Nothing happened. Leo felt like crying.

Savvy flipped his hair back and patted Leo on the shoulder.

"As usual, my friend, you missed a key detail."

Savvy relished his big reveal. "While you were in class, I found a sixth tumbler."

"What? Where?"

Savvy pointed to a small handle protruding from above the engraving of the earth. "I saw it when I laid down flat. It's the sixth tumbler. The beginning."

Leo didn't follow Savvy's logic.

"Look, the equations are in front of the map of the earth. It's literally before the earth. "In the beginning, God created the heavens and the earth. And the earth was without form and void."

"Whaaaaaat?" Leo gasped.

"It's the first line of the Bible. You should try not spacing out during chapel sometime." Savvy moved closer to the equations. "There are places for all the other numbers, so we'll make the first slot zero. Because 'In the beginning . . . the earth was without form and void,' like the world was just a mass of light and dust and energy floating in space. And *void* is just another way to say 'zero.'"

"Are you sure?" Leo asked.

"If I'm wrong, there are 99,999 other combinations left to try."

Savvy boosted Leo up onto his shoulders and Leo stretched his arm as far as he could to reach the tumbler above the globe. He clicked it to zero like Savvy suggested.

Leo nodded for Savvy to open the door.

Savvy twisted the door handle. It turned easily with a satisfying click.

The door swung open.

CHAPTER 10

Beatrice picked up the phone and dialed Rocky's number but hesitated before hitting the green "call" button.

It had been thirteen years since Beatrice had seen Rocky. Before he worked at Wynn Toys, Rocky had been both Peter's and Nick's art teacher at Braintree High School.

Rocky had once told Beatrice, "I love Peter's mind, but I am afraid of Nick's."

Rocky had been one of Peter's first hires after he founded Wynn Toys. His job was to find design flaws and fix them before the toys launched. Rocky was so good at his job that his nickname around Wynn Toys was "True Eye."

But that all changed after Peter disappeared.

Shortly after Peter went missing, Beatrice heard a commotion on the factory floor. Nick was marching Rocky past all his colleagues. A security guard trailed behind, weighed down by a big box overflowing with Rocky's stuff.

"Your brother goes AWOL," Rocky yelled at Nick, his voice echoing loud enough for half the company to hear, "and what's the first thing you do? You settle old scores. Fine. Fire me, but with Peter gone, the only thing propping you up is that staff."

Rocky reached back and grabbed a protractor from his stuff. He hurled it at a huge oil painting of Nick that Nick had recently hung on the factory wall.

"Nice painting! You look like Darth Vader's lawyer."

Nick's face scrunched up into a mass of fury. He leveled his eyes at Rocky. "You had no right to go through my brother's things, but you still did, yes? You are no longer our teacher, no? We both surpassed you, old man." Then Nick shoved his teacher hard in the back and Rocky tumbled out the door of Wynn Tower.

Nick's face, usually dull and devoid of emotion, was practically purple when he addressed the crowd that had just watched him push a beloved employee out of the company. "As the primary shareholder of Wynn Toys, I demand that Rocky is not to set foot in this building. I caught him destroying one of my brother's notebooks."

After that day, Rocky cut off all contact with anyone from Wynn Toys.

Still, Beatrice had kept tabs on him. She knew where Rocky worked and that he lived in an old apartment near the wharf. She took a deep breath, then dialed his number.

Rocky didn't answer, and that didn't surprise her.

Rocky was technologically shrewd, but that didn't mean he trusted technology. In fact, he was one of the last people on earth who still had a landline and an answering machine.

Beatrice called again, this time waiting for Rocky's voice mail.

"Leave a message," he said. "Or even better, don't, since I'm not calling you back either way." *Beep!* But Beatrice knew exactly how to get his attention.

"Rocky, I need a favor. We're redesigning the Galilee Galoshes, in an effort to fix all the flaws you missed in the original—"

Rocky picked up the phone and he sounded like he was screaming through a hoagie. "YOU'RE NUTS! THOSE WERE PERFECT! SHOES THAT WALK ON WATER! WAIT. HOW DID YOU GET THIS NUMBER, AND WHY ARE YOU CALLING AT THIS UNGODLY HOUR? DO YOU KNOW WHAT TIME IT IS?!"

"Noon."

Rocky paused. "Noon? Which noon? *The* noon? Are you sure?"

"Open the blinds."

Beatrice heard Rocky yelp in pain. "Ah! That's bright! . . . And who is this?"

Beatrice took a deep breath. "Beatrice Portinari."

There was a moment of almost unbearably awkward tension, but Rocky didn't hang up.

"Hello, Beatrice," Rocky said suspiciously. "I'm sorry if I seem a little out of it. I stayed up all night."

"What were you doing that you stayed up all night?"

"Mostly studying the Mask of Agamemnon"—Rocky groaned—"and a little time spent trying to figure out Banksy's identity."

"And why is a cab driver studying art's most famous unsolved mysteries?" Beatrice teased.

"BECAUSE I'M BORED OUT OF MY MIND!" Rocky wailed. "And how did you know I'm a cab driver?"

"I never lost track of you."

There was another long pause on Rocky's end. "Well, if you're calling because you want me to admit I was wrong, and Nick was right to fire me, I won't do that. But I will admit I miss Wynn."

When Beatrice didn't respond, he barked, "Is that what you want to hear?"

"What I want to hear is that you'll help me."

"Why would I help you? Your company fired me."

The way to anyone's heart is to let them know they are needed. "Rocky, last night, I found a coded message. I need your help to decipher it."

Beatrice chose her next words carefully. She understood the gravity of what she was about to tell Rocky.

"The message was from Peter."

Beatrice heard a thud as Rocky's phone hit the floor.

CHAPTER 11

The south tunnel turned out to be vastly different from the north in its construction: high ceilings, walls paneled with white tiles, floors paved in intricate patterns, and a path that spiraled gently upward in a series of rings contracting into smaller rings.

And unlike the north tunnel, where the path split in two near the end, this tunnel's path ended in a laboratory.

The boys wandered in with their mouths open.

There were a few scattered standing desks with brass tools on them that looked like navigation gear. The far wall was a honeycomb of cubbies with rolled scrolls inside them. Savvy unrolled

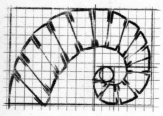

one to reveal a drawing of the Parthenon. He unrolled another and it was a schematic of the tunnel they were in.

For a moment, Savvy was incredibly excited. He flipped the schematic over. But neither side was signed or labeled or gave any indication of who built this tunnel. Still, he rolled it up and tucked it into his waistband.

The first scroll Leo unrolled was a schematic for a huge hovercraft that could accommodate three hundred passengers. Another scroll showed rubbings of various leaves; the red charcoal came off on his fingers.

"Leo, try not to destroy any priceless artifacts," Savvy said.

"C'mon, Savvy."

"Just sayin' . . . you have a history."

The entire left wall was covered by a built-in bookshelf. None of the leather-bound books had titles on their spines. Savvy pulled one down.

It was surprisingly heavy. He flipped through expecting the paper to be brittle, but it was supple, almost like cloth. Every page was covered from edge to edge with dense mathematical equations.

Leo was rifling through the other books, optimistically searching for the school records.

Savvy felt the need to whisper, although he wasn't sure why. "Is this like a math library?"

"I'm not sure," Leo whispered back. "But I have a theory."

"This oughta be good."

"I think each tunnel is based on a subject."

Savvy seemed like he was at least considering Leo's idea.

"The north tunnel was full of art. I think that's why '*Disce quam ut videam*'—'Learn How to See'—was written on the gate," Leo said.

Savvy shook his head and reached for another book. "But once you were inside the tunnel—"

"I used geometry to line up the art."

"So you think it was a geometry tunnel, not an art tunnel?"

Leo had been more confident in this theory before he shared it with Savvy. "Maybe . . . I thought the tunnels might be based on our subjects. But we don't take geometry yet . . ."

Savvy stopped leafing through books. "Miss Medici always says 'Education is founded in geometry, arithmetic, music, and astronomy, the "four cardinal subjects"' . . ."

"Like the four cardinal directions on a map!"

They high-fived. This was Leo's favorite part of having a best friend, the moment when your brains sync and you heat up an idea until it sizzles.

"What else did she say? Aren't geometry and arithmetic pretty much the same thing?" Leo asked.

Savvy cleared his throat, then did his best impression of Miss Medici. "Numbers are truth because there is simply no quibbling with numbers. Arithmetic is the study of pure numbers. Geometry is the study of numbers in space. Music is the study of numbers in time. And astronomy is numbers in space *and* time."

Leo laughed hard. When Savvy did his Miss Medici, he even held his nose high in the air like she did whenever she made a particularly strong point.

"If the north tunnel was geometry, then this one has to be arithmetic. The east tunnel—asking us to 'Separate the Colors'— that's got to be either music or astronomy. I'm leaning toward astronomy." Savvy grinned at his own genius.

"I wouldn't be so sure. *Disce quam ut videam*—'Learn How to See.'"

Savvy picked up another book, also filled with equations, and mumbled, "But why would someone want to hide these books?"

"I don't know. These aren't anything like the book in the north tunnel."

"What?!" Savvy grabbed Leo's arm and spun him around. "I went through that tunnel. I didn't see any book."

"Yeah, it dropped to the ground in the art gallery."

"A book *falls from the ceiling* and you didn't share it with me?"

"Sorry, I forgot about it. It's all in Latin anyway. It didn't seem relevant."

"Didn't seem relevant? *Didn't seem relevant?* I thought we were a team. Maybe it's not relevant to you because *you* can't read it. Anything we find in a tunnel is *super* relevant."

"You didn't even tell me about the tunnels when you found them!" Leo huffed.

They both stomped off to opposite corners of the room.

"Fine," Savvy said eventually. "I'm sorry if you were upset I didn't share the tunnels with you at first. But I promise I would have shared them eventually. Let's just agree that we're equal partners now, okay?"

"Okay." Leo offered his hand and Savvy shook it.

In the center of the room was a tall potted plant. The wall space between bookshelves was covered in tacked-up drawings on scraps of paper: a strand of 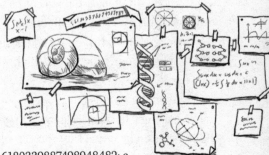 DNA; a long number, 1.6180339887498948482; a star inside a pentagon; the biggest nautilus shell either of them had ever seen; various equations; and lots and lots of interlocking rectangles.

"Leo, this place is such a mess. It reminds me of your room." Savvy seemed overwhelmed, but Leo's eyes glowed with wonder. "None of this stuff makes any sense."

"I know," Leo replied. "Isn't it awesome?"

"And this isn't even real."

Leo whirled around. "What do you mean?"

Savvy poked at the leaves of the potted plant, which was at least a head taller than him. "This plant. It isn't real."

"Why are you poking it?"

"I don't know. Maybe this thing is half Groot and it's just waiting to come alive and smack you around while I get away." Savvy jokingly punched Leo in the shoulder.

"How could it stay alive? There's no natural light in here." Leo prodded the petals.

"Groots don't need light."

"It's not a Groot. It's a daisy. Daisies need light. They convert it into energy they store in their stalk."

"Snooze . . . But have you ever considered that maybe a daisy is just a lady Groot?" Savvy did his best Groot impression. "I. Am. Daisy?"

"Awww. She sounds nice."

"Whatever it is, I can't imagine it's here for decoration," Savvy said as he lifted up one side of the pot and looked underneath.

Leo was busy counting the daisy's petals. "That's one too many."

Savvy laughed. "I agree. One fake plant is one too many. They're tacky."

"No. I meant the number of petals on the daisy. There are fourteen. That's one too many."

"It should be thirteen?"

"Yes—daisy petals are always a Fibonacci number."

"The same numbers that got us in here?"

"Yup."

"Okay. Should we prune this plant?"

Leo considered their options. "Or we could try—"

Savvy tore off one of the petals.

Before Leo could register his protest, the center of the bookshelf swung open, revealing a path.

A familiar pattern of lights built into the floor guided their way to the exit. Like the north tunnel, this tunnel exited into the woods, but this time on the south side of the academy.

Savvy sat down on a log. Leo, still basking in the glow of their discovery, plunked down next to him.

"That's two tunnels down, and we found the entrance to the east tunnel. Are we sure there is a west tunnel?" Savvy picked up a stick and softly tapped it on the tips of his shoes.

"There's got to be one. And I think our theory about the tunnels and the four cardinal subjects is right."

"I don't know, Leo."

"The handles to the tunnels are marked. Why build tunnels north, south, and east, but not west?"

"You might be right. But what kind of weirdo would build secret tunnels in the first place?"

"Good point."

They sat and stared at the woods for a bit. It was getting late; the sky was fading to a dark purple. They'd have to go inside for dinner soon. The wind sounded like a symphony tuning up: tree branches whistled, swaying trunks cracked and hummed, leaves whispered like an expectant audience.

In the distance straight ahead, Leo heard something big moving through the woods and wondered if it was Gemini; he whistled, but there was no response.

"Is Gemini out here?" Savvy asked, nervous.

"I don't know—I haven't seen him in a couple days. He's probably just hunting." Leo could tell this made Savvy even more nervous, so he added, "Don't worry, Gemini's a vegetarian."

"Hmph. Whatever. You need to learn to control your inventions, Leo."

"Gemini isn't an *invention*."

Instead of responding, Savvy snapped a stick in half. It was loud. Neither of them said anything for a while.

Leo scanned the woods. They seemed to stretch forever.

Savvy spoke up, his voice tight. "When I— I mean, when we first found these tunnels, I had hoped that maybe we'd find the records, or maybe a treasure, or maybe they would lead us someplace . . . I don't know." He methodically snapped the stick into smaller and smaller pieces. "Someplace else."

"Yeah."

"But we're not going anywhere, are we?"

Leo thought it was strange that Savvy's excitement had evaporated so quickly, but he felt it too. If the tunnels didn't contain the records, what did he hope they would find down there? They were lifers. They were stuck here, but at least they were stuck here together.

Leo realized how tired he was from cleaning the library and traipsing around the tunnels. He and Savvy sat together long enough to pretend the conversation hadn't happened, then they turned to walk back toward their school.

CHAPTER 12

Rocky had agreed to meet Beatrice on three conditions:

1. She left her phone at home.
2. She let him see the message from Peter.
3. He got to pick the place.

Which is why Beatrice's car was currently parking itself in front of a brick building near the wharf. Her sleek, carbon fiber sedan backed in delicately, like it didn't want to touch anything.

A sign in the building's grimy window advertised "Trivia Bingo Tuesdays!"

She waited outside for Rocky, who arrived promptly at seven thirty, nervously glancing over his shoulder.

Their eyes met, and Rocky smiled at Beatrice. "It's been too long, lady."

She smiled back at him. "Thirteen years."

Rocky's hair had gone from gray to white but otherwise time had been kind. He still looked sturdy.

"Trivia bingo, huh?"

Rocky bowed. "Life feels better when we exercise our talents." Then he opened the door and they stepped inside.

Everyone groaned when Rocky walked in.

At thirty-three, Beatrice was the youngest person in the room. At sixty-three, Rocky might have been the second youngest. The smells of liniment and beef stew were now fighting for the attention of Beatrice's nose.

Rocky took her by the arm. "Relax. They are jealous of our youth and want us to be intimidated by their experience."

One by one, Rocky pulled four crumpled dollars from his pocket and tossed them into a tin bucket, then picked up two bingo sheets and a couple of pencils. He winked at Beatrice. "Madam, your entry fee—and dinner—is on me."

Mister Cawley, who was hosting trivia bingo, called to Rocky in his thick Irish brogue. "I'll not have any o' yer trouble here tonight, Rocky. Yiz may win no more than two rounds of shepherd's pie, den de udder customers git a chance."

"I'm a bit of a regular here." Rocky guided Beatrice to a worn vinyl booth near the restroom. Beatrice didn't catch the question that was being read, but as they sat down, Rocky shouted, "Inga Falls!"

Mister Cawley yelled back at Rocky, "Dere are rules ta da game, Rocky. Yiz'll play by 'em or be gone witcha!" He wearily pointed at the sign that laid out the rules for trivia bingo: "Be a human! No phones! Write down your answers!"

"All right. All right." Rocky looked at the sign and gave Mister Cawley a thumbs-up.

Mister Cawley begrudgingly shoved a pair of shepherd's pies in their direction. "Yiz automatically win since yiz were de only competitors to correctly guess 'What is da world's largest waterfall by volume?'" Rocky hastily retrieved their pies and brought them back to Beatrice.

"See. I told you dinner was on me."

Beatrice cracked the mashed potato shell of her pie with a spoon and a puff of steam jetted out. "Rocky, I noticed you were looking over your shoulder when you arrived. Are you worried about something?"

"Yes. I suspect Nick Wynn still has me followed . . . Elephant!" Rocky shouted.

Mister Cawley muttered, "Does anyone else know which animal Hannibal rode through the Alps?" He glared at Rocky, but no one else answered.

Rocky ignored him and started digging into his pie. "What's that thing in your purse, Beatrice? Better not be a phone or we'll both get tossed out of here."

Beatrice glanced at her bag, the outline of Peter's wooden puzzle pressed against the leather. She reminded herself to be more discreet in the future.

She opened her bag under their table so only Rocky could see. He took it and removed the blue orb from the wooden puzzle, turning it over in his hand.

"No way! I haven't seen one of these in years." Rocky shoveled in another mouthful of shepherd's pie.

Beatrice gestured for Rocky to lower his voice. "You recognize it?"

"Recognize it?" Rocky scoffed. "I helped design it. It's called the Beacon Map. It's a two-step GPS locator. The beacon doesn't turn on until someone triggers the signal on the other end . . .

Baku! Baku, Azerbaijan, is the largest city in the world that's below sea level!"

Rocky ducked as Mister Cawley threw a pencil at him.

She leaned in closer to Rocky and whispered, "Peter gave that puzzle to me the night before he vanished. I was sure I'd almost solved it dozens of times, but on Christmas night, it finally opened. Inside was that orb."

Rocky stared at the intricate wooden puzzle in Beatrice's bag as he scooped more pie into his mouth.

"And the orb keeps flashing the same message—'L-E-O.'"

"Leo!" he said with recognition, and Beatrice's heart leapt.

He carefully examined the orb in his hand. "You said it flashes *Leo*, but I don't see anything."

"Weird. It's been doing it when I—" Beatrice reached across, and the instant she touched the orb, it flashed blue and displayed *L-E-O* again.

He asked Beatrice to rotate the orb over and over and over again, then looked her in the eyes and took a deep breath.

"Thirteen years ago, at the last toy fair Peter attended, we went out to dinner as a staff. You were there, stuck sitting next to Nick at the other end of the table. Nick stood up and made a toast: 'To another year of riding my brother's coattails!' I'm paraphrasing, of course. But then Peter muttered to himself, 'To Leo.' I asked the obvious question, 'Who's Leo?' And he looked like he'd seen a ghost. Peter made me promise to keep it a secret, but 'Project Leo' was the code name for his next big idea. He swore it would be his best invention yet, better than Cromwell. Peter was working on it when he disappeared. Y'know, right before I got fired from *your* company. MARSUPIAL!"

Mister Cawley's face was purple. "Rocky, yah git! Yah answer out loud again and you and your granddaughter will finish yer pies on da street."

Rocky pointed at Beatrice and yelled back at him, "My granddaughter and I have been kicked out of way nicer places than this dump!"

Beatrice reached across the table and yanked his shirt to get his undivided attention. "Rocky, I need you to dial in here. What was 'Project Leo'?"

He removed her hands from his shirt. "I'm not sure, but I have an idea."

Using the pencil and bingo sheet meant for writing down his trivia answers, Rocky drew a quick sketch, then slid it across the table.

"My guess is Project Leo was a cold fusion reactor. Peter started working on it after finishing Cromwell."

"How do you know that?"

"I saw it when I was looking in Peter's notebook. Y'know, the reason your company fired me?"

"We were working from those ideas. Yeesh, we *still* work from those ideas. You knew Peter's notebooks were off limits."

"I admit I *looked* at Peter's private notebook. I thought I might find a clue to where he went. But Nick had one of the goons from his brute squad yank it out of my hands and push me out the door."

Beatrice gasped. "Nick said you were trying to *destroy* the notebook."

"Why do you seem surprised he would lie?"

"Do you think Nick had something to do with Peter's disappearance?"

"I can't be certain. Peter had the best brain. He was too smart to let his brother do anything to him." Rocky tapped his pencil on the cold fusion drawing again. "I'm telling you, though, this was what Peter was working on when he vanished."

Beatrice tilted her head back and let out on a long, deep sigh. This was a lot to take in, but to Peter, no idea ever seemed too far-fetched.

Rocky gulped down another bite of shepherd's pie before he continued. "A working cold fusion reactor is the holy grail of science, an infinite source of energy for the low, low price of absolutely free. The biggest fusion reactor is our own sun. If Peter had invented a device that could safely re-create the sun's fusion of atoms, he'd have solved more than just Wynn Toys' problems, he'd have solved most of the world's problems: pollution, climate change, etcetera."

"Do you think Peter actually made the reactor?"

"There were pretty elaborate designs for it in that notebook." Rocky waved his spoon in the air to emphasize his point and a glob of pie landed across his face. "I meant to do that."

As he wiped his glasses, Rocky stared at Beatrice. "Look, I'm sorry I looked at that notebook. I shouldn't have. But my heart was in the right place. I loved Wynn Toys. Almost as much as Peter. Maybe as much as you. Certainly more than Nick. If you ever want me to come back, just say the word."

"Word."

Rocky laughed. "Wait. Are you serious?"

"Yes, Rocky. I hope we can both forgive."

Rocky raised his spoon for a toast. "To forgiveness."

Then Beatrice raised her spoon too. "To forgiveness, the virtue of the brave."

They clinked spoons.

"But what about Nick?" Rocky asked.

"What if I promise you'll be working on a project Nick doesn't know about?"

"Then I promise I'll be at Wynn first thing Tuesday morning."

"Why not Monday?"

"Because on Monday, I'll be telling my boss at the cab company to go eat dirt."

CHAPTER 13

The boys were fixing a hole in a bookcase a few days later, using wood glue to adhere a patch, when Leo decided to announce his big news.

"Savvy, I have a new invention."

Savvy flinched and squirted his glue all over the place.

"What?!" He looked scared.

Leo looked over his shoulder. "I've been working on a new invention for a couple weeks now," he whispered, "and it's—I mean, *they're*—finally ready."

Savvy slowly wiped the glue from his hands. "Hold on, let me get as far away from this house as possible, then I'll be ready."

Leo was hurt. "Savvy, I'm serious."

"So am I. Your stupid inventions are the reason we're in this mess."

"No, my invention is going to get us *out* of this mess. I built it to help us clean up."

Savvy waved at his vacuum cleaner that was trundling around the room. "The Sweepmaster 2000 is already doing that, Leo. And look at this!"

He ran over to the robot and grabbed a mop, swapping it out for the Sweepmaster's spinning brooms. He pulled a lever on its base and two high-powered squirt guns popped out of its casing, spraying soapy water on the floor as the mop swished back and forth.

He smiled proudly. "See, it can mop too!"

"I know, I know," Leo said, "the Sweepmaster is great at cleaning. But we also need to pick up debris, hammer nails, saw wood—and I've invented something that can do all those things!"

Savvy laid his hand on Leo's shoulder. "Leo, I love you, man, but someone's gotta tell you—you're smart, but if you honestly want to help, there's only one thing you should do: stop inventing stuff!"

Savvy's hand felt awful on Leo's shoulder, but he didn't shrug it off. He also didn't cry, although he was close. He composed himself enough to say, "Well, I'm sorry you feel that way."

"Well, I'm sorry I had to—"

Leo cut him off. "Because my invention's already here."

At the clattering of what sounded like hundreds of tiny feet, Savvy turned around very slowly. He stared in shock as the door opened and Leo's new creations stood there, waiting for instructions.

"Wow," Savvy whispered. "There's a lot of them."

"Only eighty-nine," Leo said. "I would've made more, but I ran out of copper wire."

"Turn them off," Savvy pleaded.

Leo chuckled. "I can't. There's no off switch. No 'controller' in the conventional sense. These puppies are fully automated." He patted Savvy's shoulder. "But don't worry, they know what they're doing."

Savvy picked up a book and held it like a shield.

"Drop the book!" Leo said, suddenly alarmed.

"Why?!"

"Well, if you're holding a book, they might think you're a bookshelf, and try to, uh, fix you." Leo made a sawing motion. "Do carpentry on you and stuff."

Savvy dropped the book and stood like a statue as Leo's inventions poured into the library. They parted around him like a river and started working.

CHAPTER 14

Rocky was tickled by *W&R* emblazoned on the door to his new office.

He punched in his password. His office was one of the only rooms on the entire Wynn Toys campus that was password protected. The light changed from red to green and he threw the door open.

"It's here!" he cried, holding the box over his head. His assistants, two of Wynn's best engineers named Steve and Dave, nearly leapt out of their rumpled khakis to get a look at it. "We've only got a couple of weeks to get this thing right before the Milan Toy Fair."

Far above them, two clear pneumatic tubes, wide enough to digest a refrigerator, sorted a river of gadgets. These gadgets were broken down for their precious metals, then the recycled materials were pumped back into the assembly lines.

Rocky's office, which doubled as Beatrice's secret research division, was stashed in the one place Nick Wynn and his germaphobia were guaranteed to never visit—the trash room. W&R: Waste and Recycling.

Steve cleared space and Rocky gingerly placed the device on the table. "So Beatrice swears this little thing is going to save Wynn Toys, huh? What's the name we're using now?"

"The Arcage," Steve said.

"It's a play on *arcade*. Kind of a tame name, don't you think?"

Dave performed a flourish of kung fu kicks. "I wanted to go with Combatix."

Rocky slid on his thick black glasses that made his eyes look huge.

"Did they let you inside the development building?" Steve asked him.

"No, I stood outside in the cold for fifteen minutes while I waited for it to come out of the 3D printer. My toes are halfway to frostbite because I don't have high enough clearance."

Dave scoffed. "Does anyone?"

"Nobody I know. Nobody down here, at least," Steve insisted.

Rocky said, "Well, I don't know who they've got working over there, but they are *good*. Let's give this thing a test run tonight, and then tomorrow morning we can bring in Beatrice to see it."

All three of them stared at the Arcage's brushed aluminum box. It was the size of a thick book, but with elegantly rounded lines and two small lights on the front.

Steve cocked his head. "It looks a little like a face, doesn't it?"

Suddenly there was a loud sucking sound from above them. The huge pneumatic tubes on the ceiling had gotten clogged. After a moment, there was an even louder *ker-plunk* as the clog flushed down the tube.

Rocky smiled. "Peter loved coming down here and watching those things flush computers." He took another sip of coffee and managed to spill more of it on his belly. "Yeah, he used to call this place 'a nerd loo.'"

CHAPTER 15

Miss Medici was walking toward the library to check on Savvy and Leo's progress when the doorbell rang. It was a low bell, deep and ominous. And it was a sound she hadn't heard in many years.

The bell chimed two more times in rapid succession as she entered the vestibule.

Lisa was polishing the floor, and it was shiny with wax. She looked up at Miss Medici, confused. "What is that?"

"That's the doorbell." She straightened the hem of her dress and firmly yanked her shirtsleeves down. "Everything's fine. Please round up everyone on the ground floor and tell them to go upstairs to their rooms."

The girl tiptoed off, careful not to slip on the waxy floor, and Miss Medici stood and stared at the door as the bell rang again.

The front door was heavy black wood, and the frame was large enough to drive a car through, but Miss Medici made no movement to open it. Instead she slid open a small peephole with a steel grate in it.

Peering out, she found herself looking into another pair of eyes. A woman's eyes. They were large and light brown and seemed friendly, but Miss Medici still had no intention of opening the door. She looked over the woman's shoulder and saw a futuristic car, all glass and swooping black carbon, turning around in the driveway.

But there was nobody behind the wheel.

"This is private property," Miss Medici scolded. "If you're looking for the nearest gas station, make a left out of the driveway and go straight for five miles until you hit Route 1. Turn left again and that road will take you into town."

"I'm not looking for a gas station," the woman said. She held up a glowing blue ball. The orb rotated slowly, revealing an eyeball, cold and unblinking.

"Have you ever heard of a man named Peter Wynn?" the woman asked.

Savvy tottered on top of a bookshelf, throwing the heaviest books he could reach at Leo's inventions. "They're everywhere!" he screamed. "They're like, they're like—"

"Bugs!" Leo said, pulling a thick stack of blueprints from his pocket.

"Aren't they great? I copied the swarming capabilities of ants to help the group operate cohesively."

The bugs had dull, dented metal bodies with three pairs of quickly clacking legs. They generally resembled ants but were the size of well-fed rats. Each had a different attachment on their head: saws, mops, additional giant pincers for carrying things. They surged around the library in neatly organized lines, quietly carrying out their work.

"Aren't they great?" Leo was beaming.

"Hey!" Savvy screamed. "They're taking apart the Sweepmaster 2000!"

It was true; the tiny machines were pulling Savvy's invention apart and carrying the various scraps to the trash can. Two of them were dragging its squirt guns away, and Savvy pulled them out of their mandibles.

They looked up at him and hissed angrily.

"Ooh, sorry about that!" Leo said. "They must think it's scrap metal. Hold on, uh—"

Savvy waved the mutilated squirt gun in his hand. "Stop them!"

"Well, I kind of can't." Leo shrugged. "Like I said, they operate on internal programming. I don't have a controller. Although if I can find one of the leader ants and modify his program . . ." Leo got down on his hands and knees and examined the various ants. "That should trickle down to the other workers and—"

Savvy cut him off. "There isn't time for all that. They're destroying my machine!" He checked the water chamber on the squirt gun to see if it was full.

"No!" Leo cried out.

But it was too late. Savvy aimed at the cluster of ants around the Sweepmaster and fired. A stream of soapy water hit them with a sickening electric sizzle. Sparks flashed across their convulsing bodies, and then they stopped moving and collapsed to the floor, smoking.

"Oh nooooo," Leo wailed.

"I'm sorry," Savvy said, not sounding sorry at all, "but I had to stop them."

One of the ant's legs twitched, ever so slightly. Then an antenna moved.

"Hey, maybe they're all right," Leo said.

Suddenly the ants stood up. Their tiny eyes were glowing red—and staring straight at Savvy.

The other ants stopped whatever work they were doing, and their little antennas twitched in syncopation. Then they all turned and looked at Savvy as well.

"Uh-oh," Savvy said. Slowly, very slowly, he took a step back toward the door . . . and the ants took a step forward, toward him. Trying not make any sudden moves, he swiveled his head toward Leo. His eyes were wide with terror.

"Savvy, run!"

Savvy spun and broke for the doors, and like a dam bursting the ants rushed after him. He didn't dare look over his shoulder, but he could hear them approaching, their mandibles clicking furiously.

CHAPTER 16

Savvy ran as fast as he could into the school's main hall, but the ants ran across the floor and also spread up the walls, the sharp points of their legs clinging vertically to the walls without slowing them down.

Leo chased after them, shouting, "Stop! I command you!" then suddenly he stood still. He had an idea. He turned around and ran back into the library.

Savvy glanced over his shoulder and saw Leo running away. "Don't leave me!"

Leo's voice echoed down the hall. "I'll be right back! Just keep running!"

Savvy barreled down the hallway, and a vicious hot stitch was burning in his side when he saw Miss Medici and some other woman round the corner, briskly striding in his direction. Both women froze when they saw Savvy approaching.

"Get out of the way!" Savvy flapped his hands at them in a frantic shooing motion.

Miss Medici grabbed the woman by her arm and dragged her inside a closet only seconds before Savvy and the bugs stampeded past.

Savvy reached the end of the hallway, but his front foot hit the slippery waxed floor and he realized he was in trouble.

The floor was as slick as an ice-skating rink. Suddenly he

was sliding across the big room, pinwheeling his arms and desperately trying to keep his balance.

Luckily, the floor was just as slippery for the bugs. As the swarm scrambled out onto the waxy floor, they slipped and got tangled in a big pile.

Savvy taunted the Sweepers. "Ha! Take that, you dumb bugs!"

The bugs stopped struggling. Collectively, they stamped their sharp little legs down, sinking the points into the wood.

"Uh-oh." Savvy slipped and fell onto his stomach. He tried to scramble to his feet but couldn't.

The bugs advanced one step at a time, their clawed feet gripping the slippery floor.

They were only a few feet away when Leo ran into the room behind them holding the Sweepmaster's squirt gun in his hands. He cocked it, squinted down the barrel, and leveled it at the swarm.

"Savvy, watch out!"

Leo squeezed the trigger, but instead of water, a thick stream of glue shot out of the gun, covering the bugs.

They struggled to free themselves, but the glue gummed up their joints as it covered the floor, and in only a few seconds they were completely stuck.

"All right!" Leo jumped and did a little fist pump. Savvy crawled over on all fours and collapsed next to him.

Leo smiled, hefting the squirt gun in his hand. "I filled it with wood glue!"

Savvy didn't move; he just mumbled into the floor as he tried to catch his breath. "Great job."

Leo felt an ironlike grip on his shoulder. He spun around, ready to shoot whatever bugs were left, but found himself face to face with Miss Medici. She stood there shaking, gripping his shoulder, her face getting redder and redder.

Standing behind Miss Medici was a poised younger woman whose dark hair was interrupted by a streak of white above her temple. She broke the awkward silence with a bright smile.

"Wow!" she exhaled. "Is it always this exciting around here?"

Compared to the destruction Leo's other inventions had done, this one ranked relatively low; somewhere between the super-expanding sponge he had dropped into the koi pond and the diesel unicycle he had driven through the tea room.

Nobody was hurt, and the only real damage was the glue all over the floor—which Savvy promised he could easily dissolve with a potent solvent.

Leo knelt by the mountain of glued-up bugs. A few were still struggling weakly. He reached out and patted one on the head. "Sorry, guys."

Miss Medici kept her distance, afraid the bugs might break free. "You will dismantle those monstrosities immediately, young man!"

Leo hung his head. "Yes, Miss Medici."

The young woman next to Miss Medici admired the bugs. "Seriously," she said, "you built these?"

"Yeah."

The woman leaned in so close that one of the bugs reached

out and grabbed her nose with its little legs. She laughed and gently pried them free. "What kind of batteries did you use?"

"A lithium battery, but it's recharged by their own kinetic energy. They are pretty close to self-sustaining."

"You could've injured our guest." Miss Medici stamped her foot. "Someone could've gotten hurt, Leo!"

At the mention of his name, the woman stared intently at Leo. She shook her head in wonder. "Amazing."

Leo blushed. "Well, they're not that amazing. I mean, they didn't work like they were supposed to."

"I wasn't talking about the bugs," she said, lowering herself so she was looking Leo directly in his eyes. "I was talking about you."

"Who are you?" Savvy asked the strangely calm visitor.

"Yeah. Most people would kind of freak out if they saw a pack of robot bugs," Leo added, stealing a glance at Miss Medici.

The woman shrugged. "I guess most people would," she said, reaching into her bag. She pulled out a vibrating blue orb and held it in the palm of her hand. "But I've seen stranger things."

The orb stopped vibrating and it glowed bright blue. Two little hummingbird wings extended out from its side and flapped to life. A white eye appeared on its surface and blinked at the woman. She seemed as surprised by how the orb was acting as they were.

"What is that thing?" Savvy whispered.

The Beacon Map spun toward the sound of Savvy's voice and flew over.

It hovered in front of his face for a few seconds, looking him in the eyes.

Then the Beacon Map made a low sound, like a game show buzzer when a contestant gets the answer wrong.

"Negative match," the orb said in a smooth female voice.

It landed in his fingers, but Savvy quickly yanked his hand away.

"DNA. Zero percent match to Peter Wynn."

"Ow! That thing pricked me." Savvy sucked his fingertip.

The Beacon Map rotated toward Leo. It flapped over and looked him in the eyes for what seemed like a long time.

The orb pinged softly. A friendly, round note.

"Positive match."

The orb floated down to Leo's fingertips. He felt a tiny sting as a pin pricked his index finger.

The orb pinged softly again.

"DNA. Fifty percent match to Peter Wynn. Leonardo Wynn."

The woman suddenly looked like she had just put down a very heavy weight, one she had been carrying for a long time.

She looked around for a place to sit, and when she didn't see one, simply plopped down on the floor. She stared at a slightly scared Leo, and he saw that she was crying. "That's why he led me here—Leonardo," she muttered.

"What's going on?"

Miss Medici looked at Leo like he was someone different than he was a few seconds ago, and that scared him even more.

"You're going home."

CHAPTER 17

"Woah, woah, woah," Savvy said. "What do you mean, Leo's going *home*? Where's he going? And who's Leonardo Wynn?"

Leo dropped the ant he was holding but barely heard it crash to the ground. "My name's not Leo Briga?"

"No. Your name isn't Leo Briga," the woman said, slowly standing up as she read more information off of the blue orb. "Your *full* name is Leonardo D. Wynn." She smiled. "You're a rather important person, I'm afraid."

Savvy balled his fists and swung his body toward her. "Who asked you?"

He turned to Miss Medici. "What's she talking about?"

"It's complicated," Miss Medici said, trying to calm him down.

Leo didn't understand what was going on. He asked, "Do I have to go by Leonardo, not Leo?" but nobody heard him.

Savvy was screaming now. "Leo's not going anywhere! Who is this lady?"

"When can I take Leonardo?" the woman asked Miss Medici, completely ignoring Savvy.

"Well, I'll have to check out your paperwork, of course, fill out a temporary ward contract and quickly get it signed by the court, and we'll have to hammer out the particulars. Leo will also have to pack once the paperwork is approved . . ."

Leo was dazed. Everyone was arguing about him, but

nobody was looking at him. He felt like a wishbone being pulled in half.

"Who is this lady?" Savvy repeated louder, stabbing his finger at her accusingly.

"My name is Beatrice. I'm a . . . a friend of Mr. Wynn, Leonardo's father."

"Who is Leonardo?!"

"Leo is Leonardo Wynn," Beatrice said, waving toward Leo. But Leo wasn't there.

The front door was wide open, and through the doorway they could see him running away, headed toward the woods. He ducked between two crisscrossed pines, leapt over a hedge of brambles, and then he was gone.

CHAPTER 18

Miss Medici led Beatrice to her car. "As you can imagine, this is a lot for him to process." She passed a hand over her forehead, sweeping a loose strand of black hair back into its bun. "It's a lot for *me* to process," she added.

"It's a lot for me too," Beatrice confessed. "He's not what I expected to find here. I've been searching for Leonardo's father for so long. I just don't understand. Why did he leave him here? It seems as though he was, was . . ."

Hidden here, she thought to herself. But she didn't say it out loud. They reached Beatrice's car.

"Come back in a few days and perhaps Leo, sorry, *Leonardo*— it's going to take me a second to get used to that—perhaps he will be more amenable then?" Miss Medici offered.

"He said his last name was Briga. Did you meet the Brigas when Leo was left here at your school? How did he get that name?" Beatrice asked.

Beatrice could tell her question annoyed Miss Medici. "It's the only name we've ever known for him, Leo A. Briga."

"What does the *A* stand for?" Beatrice pushed.

"He arrived as Leo Attacca Briga," Miss Medici retorted. "With a few pieces of furniture and a generous donation—"

"Attacca Briga?" Beatrice laughed.

"Yes. What's so funny?" Miss Medici's eyes narrowed.

"Attaccabriga . . . it sounds like the Italian word for trouble-maker," Beatrice explained.

"How *very* appropriate."

Miss Medici walked back to the house without saying good-bye, and Beatrice climbed into the passenger seat of her car. As the vehicle slid silently down the driveway, she looked out the window and scanned the dark woods creeping past.

Soon the house was completely out of sight behind her. The automatic headlights flickered on as the car snaked around the curve of a hill.

The sun was low behind the trees, throwing shadows over the car. Beatrice was resting her head against the cool glass of the window when she saw someone move in the woods.

"Stop!"

The car halted immediately. She lurched forward so hard that she bumped her forehead on the dash.

"Ouch!" She rubbed her head. "Window down!"

Beatrice closed her eyes and strained her ears.

She heard the snap of branches; they were moving away from the car.

"Park," she told the car. In one fluid motion, she jumped out and started running into the woods.

She had already lost one shoe in a mud hole and now the other was tangled in a string of brambles. She left her second shoe behind without stopping because she could hear she was very close to Leo—at least she hoped it was him. He was walking away from her, straight ahead.

She couldn't see him yet because the trees were so dense, but she was already rehearsing what she'd tell him: *I know you're scared. I know this seems crazy. But I'm sure your dad loved you, and I'm here to take care of you.* They sounded like empty platitudes, even to her, but it was all she could think to say.

The footsteps stopped suddenly.

Beatrice sighed and stopped too. "All right, Leo," she said, "I know you're scared. I know this seems crazy. Please, don't run away. I'm here to help you. If you don't want to leave the academy, you don't have to." She waited for him to respond, but he didn't.

Instead, she heard him start walking toward her.

Crunch, crunch, crunch, crunch.

Something about the crunching sounded wrong. Beatrice looked over her shoulder and realized she had walked a long way into the woods.

Crunch, crunch, crunch, crunch.

Why did it sound wrong?

Crunch, crunch.

The bushes parted in front of Beatrice and suddenly she understood why the footsteps sounded odd: there were four feet, not two. She stared into a shiny glass eye, a cold green light glowing behind it. Steel teeth were locked in gleaming rows on a head topped with a thick mane of electrical cords. And farther down, powerful shoulders hunched to pounce. Beatrice hadn't found Leo.

Gemini had found Beatrice.

Beatrice took a step back and Gemini took a step forward, lithe and graceful like a real jungle cat. His glass eyes tracked her movement. The left eye glowed steadily but the right one flickered on and off like an old neon sign.

She was disturbed to notice his life-sized paws had large steel claws. He shook his head and the cords around his face swayed back and forth.

"Nice kitty," Beatrice whispered.

Gemini opened his mouth—it unhinged wide, and Beatrice could see all the way down inside him, cogs and gears clanking together—and he roared, a harsh buzz like a table saw.

Then he pounced.

Even as Beatrice turned to run, she knew she was too slow, and his two front paws—claws thankfully retracted—hit her back a second later. She fell face-first into a pile of pine needles, and the rich smell of sap filled her nose. It reminded her of late-night walks around Wynn Tower, after the floors had been cleaned and polished.

She rolled onto her back, ready to fight the beast, but he easily pushed his big snout through her flailing hands and went for her throat. And a warm wetness flowed down her face.

She tried to scream but couldn't because something kept wiping her face, like a big wet sponge, and then Beatrice realized the huge cat wasn't biting her, it was licking her with sloppy swipes of its soft tongue.

The licking stopped for a second, and Beatrice opened her eyes.

Gemini was perched over her, panting like a dog and wagging his butt.

"Gemini, get off her, you big dummy!"

Leo ran up, twigs stuck in his hair, and Gemini hopped off Beatrice. He ran around in happy circles as Leo extended his hand to help Beatrice up. "Are you okay?"

Beatrice brushed leaves out of her hair.

"Man," he said. "Am I ever *not* in trouble?"

Leo walked Beatrice back to her car. The sun was setting, spilling orange light between the pines. Gemini trailed behind them, sometimes bolting off to chase a squirrel.

He could tell Gemini was making Beatrice nervous, especially when the lion picked up a log as thick as a telephone pole and dropped it near her feet to play fetch.

"Sorry about Gemini," Leo said. "His programming has lots of shifting variables. I could reprogram him to have less free will, but I don't know . . . He seems happier this way."

Leo squinted up at Beatrice. "Everyone should be allowed to make their own decisions, don't you think?"

"Yes," she agreed. "No one is going to force you to come with me, you know. But please, just listen to me for a minute. Can you do that?"

Leo sighed and stopped walking. He spread his hands toward her as if to say, *Be my guest.*

Beatrice looked for a place to sit down and settled on a not-particularly-comfortable rock. She crossed her legs, bouncing her muddy, shoeless feet as she talked, and suddenly felt ridiculous wearing her neat gray suit in the woodsy surroundings.

"My name is Beatrice Portinari, and I'm the CEO of Wynn Toys."

Leo's mouth dropped open. "Shut. Up. I love your toys! They're so great." He frowned. "Wait. Didn't you say my name is Leonardo Wynn?"

"Yes."

"Do you mean . . ."

"Yes, your father is Peter Wynn, the founder of Wynn Toys."

There was a moment of silence, and then Leo burst out laughing.

"I'm sorry," he scoffed, "but I just don't believe you. I'm not sure who you really are or why you're doing this, but I don't believe you."

It had never occurred to Beatrice how absurd everything must sound to Leo. Hearing the truth now herself, she had to admit it sounded far-fetched.

"If my father is the guy who founded Wynn Toys," Leo continued, "then where is the rest of my family? They leave me here, at a school in the middle of nowhere, then they send someone from the business to come get me?"

Beatrice closed her eyes, remembering. "Your father was a complicated man. I can't tell you where he is, or why you've been here so long, but I'm sure he loves you very much."

She smiled at Leo, but still, he didn't soften. His arms stayed crossed in front of his chest.

Beatrice continued. "Thirteen years ago, Peter left his office at six in the morning. Six a.m. was an early morning for us but a late night for Peter. When he tapped into a particularly great idea, he would stay in the office all night. Peter loved seeing his ideas take shape. Inventions seemed to pour out of him—" She looked from Gemini to Leo. "Just like you, apparently. As he left that morning, he waved goodbye to me. But Peter never came back to the office. He never came back *anywhere*. That was the last time anyone saw him. He didn't have a wife, he didn't even have a girlfriend as far as we knew, and I don't know why he kept you a secret. His disappearance was a big news story. The police searched for him for years, but they never found a single piece of evidence. They stopped searching years ago. But *I* never stopped."

She stood up from the rock. "And when I finally found a message from him, it led me here to you."

Leo looked confused. "You don't know who my mother is? And my father is still missing? But you want me to come with you because a weird orb says so? Who am I supposed to live with?"

Beatrice hesitated. "Well, you have an uncle named Nick. He is your father's brother, so I guess he'd be your legal guardian..."

Leo laughed—a frustrated bark. His confusion was turning to anger. "Oh, so I *do* have family? And I'm supposed to go live with him? Just some guy? What, he couldn't make it today? Did he have something *better* to do than to meet his long-lost nephew?"

"Well, he's in charge of our company's finances, and he's working right now—"

Leo walked away, and Beatrice hurried after him.

"This is crazy," Leo said. "Look, I have always wanted to know who my parents are, but not like this."

Leo waved back toward the academy. "My best friend is here. Some days, I even *like* it here. I mean, I get in trouble a lot, but what you're asking me to do, leave and live with a bunch of strangers—no way. You seem nice, but I don't know you. You're not my parents. You don't even know where they are. I don't want to go."

They reached the long driveway, where Beatrice's car still waited.

"Can I come back and visit you tomorrow?" Beatrice asked.

"Why? I'm not going to change my mind. I'm staying here."

Gemini trotted up, wagging his tail. He had Beatrice's shoes in his mouth and dropped them at her feet. They were covered in mud and saliva.

Beatrice patted him on the head. "Thanks, Gemini."

"You're lucky, you know," Leo said. "Gemini doesn't usually warm up to strangers like that."

"Well, what can I say, he's a good judge of character." Beatrice scratched Gemini behind the ear, and he purred. "I'd sure like to come back soon and visit him."

Leo thought about it for a minute; finally, he gave in. "Okay."

He held up a finger. "But only on one condition."

"Of course. Anything."

Leo tapped Gemini's right eye, the one that flickered off and on.

"Bring a new lightbulb. A 150-watt, please."

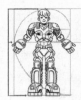

CHAPTER 19

Beatrice tossed and turned in the hotel bed for hours, but it was useless.

She hadn't expected Leo to say no when she ran out of her car. She had assumed he would run to her with open arms. But she couldn't let him slip through her fingers. He was a living, breathing connection to Peter.

She was too wired to sleep. She got back in her car at four in the morning.

"Wynn Toys," she told the car.

It was a long ride back to the office, so she opened her computer.

In the corner of her desktop, a new folder appeared. The label underneath read *Peter Wynn Notebooks*.

She bolted upright in her seat and double-clicked to open it.

It was a massive data dump: documents, newspaper stories, surveillance tapes, blueprints for an underground gallery shaped like a conch shell, screen grabs, personal emails, Wikipedia articles about obscure Japanese planetariums—a lot of the information seemed completely unrelated, as though someone just jumbled it together at random.

A query search of the documents showed that none of them contained the words *Academy of Florence*, *son*, or even *Leonardo*. There were zero results for *wife* or *child* or *Project Leo* either.

The way the folder appeared kind of freaked her out. She looked around, worried she was being watched.

But then she saw the trash folder. The familiar icon of a little wastebasket had been relabeled *A Nerd Loo*. Beatrice laughed, a triumphant howl. "A Nerd Loo" was how Peter used to describe the room where Rocky was working on the Arcage. And she realized it was an anagram for Leonardo. Thirteen years later, Peter was still giving her puzzles to solve.

Beatrice wondered if she was imagining things because she was so tired. She swore that the icon for the trash folder—usually a little recycling logo—now looked like the sketch Rocky had drawn on her bingo sheet—an infinity symbol with a ball around the bends, his hasty sketch of cold fusion.

She clicked on the icon. It gave her a prompt: ORIGINAL NAME?

Beatrice confidently typed: LEONARDO

The icon shook ever so slightly to tell her she was wrong. DENIED.

She nibbled on her bottom lip, then tried the same password with lowercase letters. Another little shake and again a DENIED.

The folder kept giving her the same prompt: ORIGINAL NAME?

Beatrice tried to shake out the mental cobwebs. She thought back to Leo and Gemini, and Leo's friend who didn't take the news well, and the schoolmarm who gave her a dry "How appropriate" when Beatrice laughed about Leo's name.

She excitedly typed ATTACCABRIGA into the password line.

The computer pinged, a happy note: ACCESS GRANTED.

Inside, the trash folder was empty except for a jumble of numbers: 43° 46' 4.8324" 11° 15' 11.3940"

She knew what these numbers were immediately: map

coordinates. She punched them into her phone and the location stunned her. They were directing her to a location about a quarter mile west of the Academy of Florence.

"Beatrice, are you awake?" Cromwell was connected to her car's computer, and his smooth voice roused Beatrice from her dark dreams. After scanning the map of the academy, the sleepless night had caught up to her.

"I see you are coming back to the office. Would you like to hear your messages? Rocky called."

Beatrice tapped the car's computer to look at the map. They were still thirty minutes from Wynn's campus.

"Sure, go ahead."

Rocky's voice boomed over the car's speakers. Loud chewing sounds filled the car. She groaned as she reached over and turned down the volume.

"Beatrice!"

Munch, munch, munch.

"We got the new Arcage prototype! It's a real honey. We took it for a spin. I think you'll be pleased."

Munch, smack.

"Stop by W and R when you get here." She ended the message. Rocky had been back at Wynn Toys for a little over a week and he was already feeling right at home again.

She wondered how and when she would tell Rocky she'd followed Peter's clue and that she didn't find a cold fusion reactor—instead she had found Peter's son. She wondered if Rocky had any idea who Leo's mother could be.

Beatrice struggled with whether she should tell anyone else at Wynn Toys about Leo. As Peter's son, he was entitled to his half of the company. A few of the other executives would probably challenge a thirteen-year-old's right to be their boss. But Beatrice knew from experience that the longer she didn't say anything, the harder it would be when the truth came out.

At the very least, she should tell Nick what was going on. As an executive at Wynn Toys—not to mention Leo's only living family member and his likely legal guardian—he deserved to know.

But more and more, she didn't trust Nick. It sounded crazy, but she didn't think Nick seemed too upset when his brother vanished. And of course he had benefitted financially when Peter went missing, absorbing another 25 percent of the company. Beatrice didn't truly believe Nick was involved in Peter's disappearance, but at the same time . . .

"Beatrice . . ." Cromwell chimed in again.

She turned the volume back up. Cromwell's voice was a violin sonata compared to Rocky's drum solo. "Shall I drop you at the back door?"

"Yes please, Cromwell."

The car drove on toward Wynn Toys, and Beatrice nodded off. She felt like she had just finished running a marathon. But in the back of her mind, she suspected the race was only beginning.

Huge steel stacks and cranes big enough to lift buses towered over the other buildings on the campus of Wynn Toys. Giant cogs dotted the lawn like sculptures, and in the spring, flowering vines crept over them.

The entire campus was the size of a small town, all of it dominated by Peter's masterpiece, Wynn Tower.

Her car floated silently past Wynn Tower and between older buildings, down a road lit by solar-powered streetlamps Beatrice had invented. The lamps were shaped like tulips and were heliotropic, which meant that during the day, the lamps rotated to face the sun, storing sunlight that would be released later at night. That technology was one of Wynn Toys' last big successes.

Every now and then she passed a guard, and a few of them waved to her. She saw one of them eating from a box of donuts. "Mind if I . . . ?" The guard happily held out the box to her car window and she went after the chocolate glazed like she was starved.

Her car wove between a pair of orange I beams and pulled into a round driveway. She parked outside a building that looked like it was made out of transparent crystal Lego blocks.

A guard opened the front door. "Good morning, Miss Portinari."

"Good morning, Victor," she said, wiping donut crumbs off of her jacket.

He noticed she was barefoot. "What happened to your shoes?"

"A lion ate them."

"Of course, ma'am." He tapped his hat. "Have a great day."

After making sure her car had autoparked itself in the garage, Beatrice took the elevator down to the basement.

"I've alerted Rocky you're in the building," Cromwell said through a speaker in the ceiling. "He and the rest of the team are waiting for you in room 17B."

"Thanks, Cromwell." Even though Cromwell was just a computer, Beatrice still felt the need to say things to him like please and thank you.

He seemed so *human*.

Beatrice walked down a long hallway. A few people were already working. The hall echoed with the intermittent banging of hammers, the high whine of a diamond saw on metal, or the echoing *ting!* of a dropped wrench.

Beatrice liked all the noise. It was the symphony of things being made.

She walked down a flight of stairs, checked behind her to see if anyone was watching, and inserted her ID into a slot next to the door for trash room 17B. A green light flashed.

17B was mostly empty. Rocky and Steve stood around a table with a small box on it. The lid was off, and they were examining the insides. Dave sat on a stool, tinkering with a small headset.

Rocky saw Beatrice walk in and his face lit up. "Beatrice!" Then he scowled. "You're *late*."

"So are you," Beatrice said with smile. "The Arcage prototype was supposed to be ready by now. If we don't hurry, we won't ship by Christmas."

"Or even worse, Mach Valley will release their version first. Again," Steve said under his breath.

Rocky shot back, "I can't find and fix any design flaws until we get prototypes from development! It's not my fault we're late!"

"I know, I know." Beatrice held her hands out to Rocky. "I was kidding. You're my oldest new employee, I know it's not your fault."

Dave stopped messing with the headset.

"Seriously, though"—he waved a tiny screwdriver—"if we improved communication with development, it would be a major help. We're not allowed to call, and we're definitely not allowed to visit the labs. What's with all the secrecy?"

It was a fair question, and one Beatrice had asked many times herself. Peter's will, the same document that made her CEO, also made Nick the director of development. Even she didn't visit that building without an appointment, and when she did, she got the feeling there was a lot she wasn't being shown. There were too many locked doors.

But that was an argument with Nick for another day. For now, Beatrice sidestepped their questions. "Are you going to show me the Arcage or what?"

"Well, we could show you . . ." Rocky smiled devilishly, and Beatrice knew she was in trouble. He took the headset, suit, and gloves from Dave and held them out to her. "Or you could try it yourself."

Once the headset was on, the air around Beatrice filled with floating numbers in all different shapes and sizes. They bobbed like balloons in a light wind and were slightly transparent.

The Arcage was an immersive virtual reality game console. One of its features allowed kids to upload their homework, which the system would turn into a first-person, fully rendered, open-world video game.

Beatrice realized she was testing the Algebra 101 level. She adjusted the headset.

"The glasses are a little uncomfortable." Rocky made a note.

"Also, the suit's kinda heavy. I don't know if a thirteen-year-old could carry all this."

The Arcage offered more than just audio and video reality; it simulated touch by using small vibrating motors in the suit. A big floating 9 bumped into Beatrice's shoulder, and the suit shook a little on that side. She pushed it away.

"Try your sword," Rocky said.

Beatrice always read the progress reports closely, so she knew how to play the game . . . for the most part.

"Sword," she said, and a flaming broadsword appeared in her right hand.

"Left," she said, but the sword stayed in her right hand. "Fix that bug," she said, and Rocky made another note.

"All right." She took a deep breath. "Let's roll. Engage."

The numbers spun around in a circle as if caught in a cyclone, then stopped.

"Algebra 101. Let's begin," a cheery voice said. "Find the prime numbers."

"Oh no." Beatrice knew what primes were—numbers that weren't evenly divisible by anything other than 1 and themselves—but she hadn't thought about them since seventh grade.

"Too advanced for you, Beatrice?" Rocky asked. "Should we lower it to basic math?"

"Ha, ha. I got this," Beatrice said, and she slashed at a big square 2.

It tumbled apart in a quick waterfall of little blocks. The headset made a happy ping and her score appeared in the upper right.

She noticed a row of hearts next to her score.

She pointed. "What's that?"

"That's your health," Rocky said. "But don't worry about it. Just keep playing."

Beatrice saw a little round 3. She slashed it and it popped like a soap bubble. *Ding!* Her score went up.

"Try some of the bigger ones. The bigger the number, the more points you get."

She tried to slash a 13 but another number bumped into her back and her suit vibrated. Her sword missed and she accidentally slashed a 6 instead. Immediately, her whole suit shook violently, and a small electric current jolted her.

"Geez!" she yelled, surprised. "What was that? You're going to shock kids?"

Rocky was confused. "Shock? What do you mean?"

"I mean *shock*," Beatrice yelled. "An electric current. The suit just shocked me."

Rocky looked from Dave to Steve. Dave shrugged. Steve made a note.

"Try it again, see if it happens again," Rocky said.

Beatrice slashed a 20. She got an even bigger electric shock this time.

"Ah!" It really hurt. "Apparently, the bigger the number, the bigger the shock." She noticed that next to her score, her health had gone down from three hearts to two.

She didn't want to find out what happened when it got down to zero.

"I'm sorry, Beatrice," Rocky said. "That didn't happen when we tested the unit. I'm so sorry. Turn it off."

"My pleasure," Beatrice said. "Disengage."

But instead of turning off, the numbers turned red and swirled around her in another cyclone. When they stopped, Beatrice saw they were much larger than before. Most of them were double digits, and a few were in the hundreds. They circled her menacingly, like a pack of hungry animals.

"Let's play again," the computer said.

"What's going on?" Rocky said.

"No," Beatrice said, "disengage."

The computer spoke again, but this time it was a different

voice, whispered directly into her ear, so quiet nobody else could hear it. "Beatrice," the voice said, "I think you should play again. I need you to beat this level."

Except the voice talking to her wasn't the computer.

It was Peter.

Rocky tried to turn the console off, but the button didn't work.

He pounded on it, but Beatrice stopped him. "It's all right, I'm going to keep playing."

"Beatrice! No, stop, something's wrong—"

"It's all right," she said, and slashed her sword at a jagged 37.

It exploded in a burst of lightning, the bolts hitting other scattered primes and bursting them too. Her score went up. She sliced a 41 and then a 43.

Her mind whirled. What were other primes? She was pretty sure 72 was one. She slashed it and a burst of electricity went through the suit, so strong that it brought her to her knees.

Rocky stepped forward. "That's it, I'm stopping this." But as soon as he stepped inside the game's circle, the machine spoke loudly.

"Intruder detected in game cage! Maximum shock in five, four, three—"

"Back off!" Beatrice yelled.

Rocky backed up quickly. Beatrice struggled to her feet.

"Shield." A shield appeared on her free arm, and she used it to push a pack of numbers aside. She slashed a waving 29 and the shreds floated away.

Her mind cleared. She knew she could do this. She slashed a 53, a 31. An 84 swooped down at her and she ducked, protecting herself with the shield.

A massive 787 lumbered toward her—it was taller than she was. She thought 787 was prime, but she also knew that if it wasn't, the resulting dose of electricity might be the end of her.

The 787 rushed her like an angry rhino. She quickly factored it in her mind. It's an odd number, so not divisible by two. It doesn't end in five or zero. And 87 wasn't divisible by three. She decided it must be prime.

She closed her eyes and stabbed it with a straight thrust. The rest of the numbers disappeared. They were replaced with a single blinking line.

"Where are you?" Peter whispered into her ear.

"A nerd loo," she said.

There was a ping and Peter's voice was replaced by the computer again. "Access granted."

This was it! A clue. Beatrice felt that this time, it would lead her to Peter himself. She was ready for another beacon, like the one she had followed to find Leo, but instead the computer just showed her the address for her company's archrival, Mach Valley.

> Mach Valley Toys
> Adaptation Department—Floor X
> 1 Piazza Missori
> Zip Code 20123

The game powered down. The numbers disappeared. Beatrice stood in the middle of the empty room, the three programmers staring at her in disbelief.

Rocky grabbed a hammer and pounded the Arcage's casing. "What in Jobs' name was that?!"

But the box just sat there, the two small lights on its front glowing softly, looking to all the world like a friendly face.

Rocky threw the hammer down. "And stop smiling at me," he mumbled.

"It's not your fault, Beatrice. It was a great idea. Just needs some tweaks." Rocky brought her a towel and a bottle of ice water. "The thing simply went rogue. I'll have it in working order by the toy fair." He glanced at the Arcage and grabbed a screwdriver.

Beatrice guzzled the water and waited for Steve and Dave to leave before turning to Rocky. "No, it worked perfectly. It was another message from Peter."

"Ummm, I might have believed you about the blue beacon and Project Leo, but that thing tried to kill you. If you think *that* was a message from Peter, you're nuttier than a squirrel Thanksgiving."

Beatrice downed another bottle of water and started opening drawers under each desk.

Rocky stared at her cockeyed. "Looking for something in particular?"

"Do we have any 150-watt lightbulbs down here?"

"Center desk. Right drawer."

"I need to bring one back to Project Leo."

"You found it?! What is it?!" Rocky dropped his screwdriver.

"It's not what. It's who."

CHAPTER 20

Nick Wynn's car pulled off the highway and silently approached the perimeter gate. A flat silver panel extended out from a thin arm in front of a gatehouse.

Nick lowered his window.

"Name?" A voice, flat and devoid of emotion, echoed from the silver panel.

"The Prince," Nick responded.

"Business?"

"You called me, yes?"

Instantly, the panel shifted into a claw and lunged at Nick, grabbing him and pulling him halfway out of the car window. A ray of light beamed from the gatehouse into Nick's eye. But the voice's tone didn't change.

"Retinal scan confirmed. Thank you, drive through."

The panel shoved Nick into his seat. He brushed the lapels of his suit back into place.

"There's no reason to push me around like that," he told the panel.

"Thank you, drive through."

The lights around the panel changed from red to blue. Nick drove past the perimeter fence, then the second security fence. The parking spot closest to the main house was already lit for him, a sharp rectangle of green next to the sidewalk. His car pulled in and stopped.

Nick tried to compose himself. For thirteen years, he had hated these visits. This time his presence had been demanded with an unprecedented urgency. He was lucky Beatrice wasn't in the office because there was no way he could've come up with a good excuse to get away from work in such a rush.

He approached the front of the main building. Another silver panel pinged as he stepped toward it. "Come in. He's expecting you."

The glass parted seamlessly like a set of stage curtains and Nick stepped into a room paneled in vibrant birchwood. He removed his suit jacket and folded it over the back of a leather chair.

A fire crackled in a fireplace so tall he could've walked in. On the walls were masterpieces of modern art. The room's lighting was cleverly recessed, and Nick was never able to pinpoint the source. Instead it seemed like the walls themselves were illuminated. It was the kind of room that could make even a man like Nick Wynn feel poor.

"Good evening, Nick. Thank you for coming on such short notice." His host—the only man Nick took orders from—finally appeared at the top of the stairs, fit and trim. At this time of night, his host usually preferred spending time alone in order to relax and recharge, so Nick was encouraged by his upbeat tone.

He was also wearing glasses. Those must be new.

"Everything is okay, yes?" Nick asked.

"Yes, Nick. Everything is better than okay. Everything is ideal."

"Then no need to call an urgent meeting, no?" Nick knew he had pressed his luck before he finished the question.

Now his host stared at him with barely contained scorn, trying to calculate if the degree of disrespect he detected in Nick's voice was worth a physical correction.

"Nick, I see why you may be confused, because I urgently wanted to share *good* news. After thirteen years, I have tracked down a project Peter tried to hide from me. His final endeavor. Leo."

Nick tried to prevent any emotion from registering on his face. "You need me to retrieve this Leo, yes?"

"No, Nick. I do not. Though I cannot help but notice you did not ask where I found this Leo or what Leo is—"

"I wouldn't presume to know more than—"

"Yet you presume to interrupt me?!" His host seemed to expand and occupy the width of the grand fireplace as he raged. Almost seven feet tall and three hundred pounds of hard-packed muscle, he loomed over Nick. "I need you to contain Beatrice. She is also aware of Leo, though I became aware first, of course. Beatrice has no idea of the scale Peter intended with the Leo project. I need you to keep her occupied so I am able to work freely. Can you manage that?"

Nick averted his eyes. "I can do that."

"Good. That will be most efficient."

"That will be all, yes?" Nick desperately wanted to leave.

"Nick, are you aware that Beatrice has rehired a former employee?"

"I am not, no."

"So I take it you have not seen Rocky around Wynn Tower?"

Nick's blood pressure spiked at the mention of Rocky's name. His host laughed.

"He is working with Beatrice on a new project. It is a fun idea, really. A console. It is such a shame. We both know that is a dead end for Wynn Toys."

"Yes, I will take care of this, O." His host went by the one initial. O thought it made him more folksy and approachable, but Nick knew that if people were aware of what a monster he really was . . .

"Thank you, Nick. You are so useful. Can you see your way out?"

Nick turned to leave. He was almost out the door when he remembered his jacket. He went back for it, and O was already halfway up the stairs. As Nick grabbed his coat, he lost his composure and shot a nasty look at his host's back.

A flock of drones poured out from two dark corners of the room and dove toward Nick, knocking him over a coffee table. He swatted at one, but it dodged and dipped its propeller into his hand. A nasty cut opened up on his palm. He rolled over and hightailed it toward the glass doors, and the same drone shot down and bumped him in the rear end as he ran out the door.

He swore he heard the drone laughing.

The money was nice, but he hated these visits. He hated working for Mach Valley.

CHAPTER 21

Savvy's bedroom was packed with inventions, just like Leo's, but that was the only similarity. Savvy's room was as clean as a hospital, and hyper-organized, with rows of tall steel shelving that held alphabetized parts marked with white labels. Leo walked in and flicked on the lights—neat banks of fluorescent bulbs that made the room look even more sterile.

There were no shadows.

Savvy's bed was empty, the sheets drawn up tight enough to pass military inspection.

"Savvy?"

Suddenly someone pushed Leo from behind, and he went sprawling onto the floor.

He rolled over and someone jumped onto his chest, punching him in the face. They hit him in the nose and his vision went blurry. He tasted blood on his lips.

The attacker got off him and kicked him once in the stomach for good measure.

"You lying, dirty thief! Coming to steal some parts before you leave?"

Leo squinted up into the harsh lights and saw Savvy standing over him, a black silhouette.

"Savvy, what are you doing?"

"What am I doing? What are *you* doing? You're going to have all the parts you need in your richy-rich mansion, so don't steal my stuff!"

Leo struggled to his feet. "Why would I steal your stuff?"

Savvy folded his arms. "I don't know, probably because you're jealous, Leo-*nerd*-o."

Leo stood there. He didn't know what to say. He wiped his nose and his hand came away bloody.

"You've always been jealous of me," Savvy continued. "C'mon, we both know it. I'm a better inventor. I'm smarter. My inventions actually work. So why do you get to leave here and go be rich and famous? That should be me!"

"Look, Savvy—" Leo walked toward him, hands out.

"Don't touch me!" Savvy yelled, jumping away. "Nobody likes you here anyway. They just pretend to like you because of me. You're stupid. You're a stupid mess and nothing you do ever works. If it weren't for me, you wouldn't have any friends and you'd never have figured out those tunnels. Go ahead and leave, I don't care. I don't care how much money you have, I'll always be smarter than you. I'll always be a better inventor than you."

Leo stammered, "I, I don't know yet if I'm gonna go yet . . ."

"Yeah, right," Savvy said. "Whatever. Good luck out there! Without me to help you, one of your inventions will probably go crazy and kill you." He looked Leo straight in the eyes. "I hope it does."

Leo staggered back to his bedroom in a daze. His nose hurt. Gemini was curled up at the foot of Leo's bed, his tail plugged into the wall. He was making the soft purring sound he always made when he was recharging.

Leo went to the little sink in the corner of his room and washed the blood off his face, stuffed a tissue into his still-trickling nose, then stomped over to the closet and grabbed a bunch of big boxes.

He tossed the boxes toward the middle of the room and started throwing things into them.

The noise woke up Gemini. He opened one eye and then went back to sleep.

Dante climbed down from the rafters and perched on the back of a chair. He cocked his head at Leo.

"Pack!" Leo yelled.

Dante tilted his head the other way.

"Pack! Pack!" Leo repeated. "Find stuff to pack. Just . . . look around."

Dante started collecting round things and tossing them into the boxes.

There was a soft knock on the door, and Miss Medici walked in.

She looked at the boxes and at Leo's flushed face. "Am I interrupting anything?"

Leo realized he was sweating like he'd just run a race. He looked at the boxes, a big mess in the center of the room.

"I was just, uh, cleaning up."

"You know, there's no need to pack. If you decide to leave

the academy, Miss Portinari told me the Wynn company would send a moving truck."

"Oh, that's good," Leo said. "That way you can get rid of me quicker."

"Leonardo Wynn—"

"Boy, I wish people would stop calling me that."

Miss Medici closed the door and leaned against it. "Do you know *my* first name?"

Leo was surprised to realize he didn't.

"It's Anna," she said. "You've lived here your whole life, and you don't know my first name. What does that tell you?"

Leo thought about it. "That you're a very private person?"

Miss Medici laughed. Leo was surprised by how pretty her smile was.

"Leo Briga, Leonardo Wynn—whatever you want to go by— the Academy of Florence isn't your home. Your home is out there somewhere, and I think you need to let that lady help you find it. You're very smart, Leo. This world"—she gestured to the walls around them—"It was never going to be big enough for you."

"If they wanted me, if my big-shot dad wanted me, why leave me here? Why did it have to be some lady who *isn't even part of my family* who tracked me down? Face it. My parents either didn't want me or they're dead."

Miss Medici grabbed Leo in a bear hug. Leo thought she was crying, but he must've been wrong because when she finally let go, her eyes were dry.

She composed herself, smoothing out the wrinkles in her

shirt, then took two brisk steps backward and bowed slightly at the waist.

"No matter what you decide or where you go, you'll always be welcome here."

She walked out.

Leo felt the top of his head and noticed it was wet.

Dante jumped up onto his shoulder and showed him a moldy orange he must've found under a dresser or something.

"We're not packing that. Throw it out," Leo said.

Dante shrugged and lobbed the orange over his shoulder, out the window.

The door to the basement inside the academy was locked, but there was another door, outside the house, that Savvy hoped would be open.

He had snuck out when Miss Medici was in Leo's room and now was silently slinking toward the submerged doors.

He crept along the hedge that grew under the dorm windows. The night was full dark, no stars, and the blackness fit his intentions.

Something soft squished under his foot: a rotten orange.

The split insides were rank; a sick sweetness wafted up into his nose.

Ugh, disgusting.

He hopped back toward the hedge, and thorny branches clutched at his shirt.

"Get *off* me!" He punched the bush and realized he had said that out loud. He ducked and looked up at the dark house.

Keep it together, Savvy. Just relax.

He crept around a corner and saw the basement doors. He slid a mini blowtorch out of his pocket and burned off the rusty old lock.

He pulled on the handle and it barely budged. He took a wider stance and yanked on the handle again. There was a wrenching noise as the rust in the creases cracked and ground against the hinges. With a determined second effort, the door creaked open, spilling dirt onto the rickety steps leading down. Savvy rushed in and closed the door above him.

Miss Medici kept the basement locked because the boiler and furnace were down there, and it was dangerous to wander too close to either of those cast-iron beasts. Savvy saw the furnace now, a hulking monster with a mouth of flame. Its maw was the only light in the basement. He could feel its heat across the room. He felt an absurd urge to place an offering in front of it.

Maybe later.

He had other business right now.

Savvy snuck over to the big dumpster that all the academy's trash went into and opened the lid. He was lucky it was the beginning of the week; the bin was mostly empty.

He peered over the lip. It was hard to see down into the dumpster. He tapped the edge of the bin, and a little pair of glowing red eyes lit up.

"Hey there, little guy," Savvy whispered.

Another pair of red eyes lit up. Then another, and another.

Leo's discarded carpenter ants struggled weakly in the trash, their joints still clogged with glue.

"Shhh, it's okay," Savvy said. "I'll get you guys out of there. And I'm going to fix you."

The furnace roared behind him. It was so hot down here, and sweat stung his eyes.

"I'm going to fix everything," he said.

CHAPTER 22

Nick stormed toward Beatrice's door, flanked by two guards. One guard was graying at the temples, calm and collected. But his younger partner seemed nervous. His uniform was a little too large, and fresh acne blazed across his cheeks.

"Remember," Nick said, "Miss Portinari is not under arrest, but we are detaining her to ask some questions."

The younger guard clicked and unclicked the taser holstered on his belt. "What if she tries to flee the interview?"

His coworker laughed. "Then I guess you'll have to chase her, won't you?"

The young guard turned pale.

"Nobody's going to flee the interview," Nick said. "We're just going to ask Miss Portinari a few questions concerning her whereabouts for the past few days, yes?"

"Sure. But if she does flee," the older guard said to his younger colleague, "take her down."

Nick scowled at him. "Stop messing with him. And please take this seriously."

"Sorry." The older guard put his hand on the doorknob of Beatrice's office and looked back to make sure everyone was ready.

They nodded.

The older guard tugged the door handle, but nothing happened. He tried pushing it instead.

"It's locked, you simpleton." Nick rolled his eyes then inserted the tip of his staff into a port near the door.

"Cromwell," Nick whispered, "open the door."

Phunt! The magnetic lock released.

When the door opened, Nick saw Beatrice sitting on the edge of the largest pneumatic tube behind Peter's old desk. The tube was wide enough to drop a small car down, and Beatrice's legs were hanging inside, dangling over the chasm. She clearly didn't have the guts to jump, as her hands were clamped tight on the rim. Rocky stood behind her, peering over the edge, his eyes big as eggs.

Nick's blood boiled when he saw that Rocky was indeed back in Wynn Tower, in his brother's office, no less.

"Beatrice, we don't even know where—" Rocky saw Nick in the doorway and smiled. "Nick. You're here! And you still look like if a fart was granted its wish to become a real boy."

Things happened very fast.

"Stop!" Nick yelled.

"Go!" Rocky pushed Beatrice, and in a blink she disappeared down the tube, her screams trailing behind her as she fell.

The older guard stood petrified, but the young one sprang into action, pulling a stun gun from his belt and running toward Rocky.

Rocky saw the crackling electricity arc across the stunner's points. "Great googly moogly."

He tried to climb over the lip of the tube, but he couldn't get his legs high enough.

"C'mon, c'mon!" His loafers squeaked frantically against the glass as he tried to jump over the lip.

The younger guard was only steps away. Sweat circles expanding from his armpits, electric pain dancing in his hand. "Sir! Step away from that tube!"

Rocky planted his hands on the tube's lip, made one last desperate leap, and hoisted his waist until it was over the edge. He leaned forward and the abyss yawned beneath him, eighty stories disappearing to a point far, far below.

For a second he teetered sickeningly.

Then he flipped upside down and resistance disappeared. He rushed headfirst into the darkness, screaming till his lungs burned.

Nick raced to the edge of the tube and looked down, but Beatrice and Rocky were already long gone, probably halfway down Wynn Tower's height. Seventy floors, 960 feet— Nick shuddered.

They might survive it, but there was no way they would walk away from that fall.

How could they have known we were coming?

"Cromwell, did you tell Miss Portinari we were coming to her office?"

"Yes," the disembodied voice intoned.

"Why?"

"It is my mandate."

Nick collapsed into Peter's swivel chair. His perfectly oiled hair fell lank across his face, and shocked horror filled his eyes.

The young guard took his finger off the stun gun trigger, plunging the room into silence.

"Well . . ." The older guard cleared his throat. "I'd certainly call that 'fleeing the interview.'"

Beatrice flew down so quickly she had no time to react. She was at the mercy of the tube and gravity. She was saved by the twists and turns, which were originally intended to deliver items almost instantly, nearly anywhere in the building.

The tube dipped, spun, and dropped with lightning quickness, and though they helped slow her fall, every new direction in the tube seemed to pinball Beatrice deeper into darkness.

How fast was she going? Twenty, thirty miles an hour? She put her hands out to slow herself down and immediately regretted it.

Her wrists snapped back and she spun head over heels, smacking her head on the wall. Her body slammed into a corner, jackknifed sideways around the bend, and then she continued to fly down the chute, still gaining speed, still falling, bright spots dancing in her eyes.

What brought Beatrice back to consciousness was a familiar smell. An awful, potent, familiar smell.

She opened her eyes and recognized the steel crossbeams of the production floor's ceiling. There was a big tube overhead, which she must've fallen out of. But it was twenty feet above the floor. What had broken her fall?

She rolled over and realized she was lying in a shattered pile of defective Molly-Poops-A-Lot dolls. Her hands and back were covered in Wynn's brown "Bio-Goo."

"I don't care if you saved my life," she said to one of their broken plastic faces. "You're still gross."

A moment later, Beatrice heard a yell building from the tube above her. Without a second to spare, Beatrice rolled out of the way as Rocky shot out of the chute. He landed with a sickening crunch and immediately screamed in revulsion.

"What is that smell?!"

Beatrice grabbed his hand and pulled him toward the garage, where—she hoped—her car was still parked.

"Salvation," she replied.

They made it out of Wynn Tower without being stopped, but Beatrice knew it wouldn't be long before Nick realized they were alive and driving her company car.

They pulled into a parking garage a few blocks away and slipped between a fat Cadillac and a little Fiat.

"What do we do now?"

"We have to ditch this car," Beatrice said.

"Why?"

The dashboard's small computer screen flicked on.

"Because," Cromwell said, "the car can be tracked on GPS. I

am already communicating your position to local law enforcement, and they will be here in three to five minutes."

"Woof," Rocky said, "the computer is in the car too?"

"I thought you would be happy to see me. I did help you escape."

"Yeah, but you're also helping us get caught!"

"I cannot disobey my mandate," Cromwell said equitably.

Rocky took his shoe off and brandished it in front of the screen like a club. "I got your mandate right here, bub!"

Beatrice grabbed Rocky's arm. "Cromwell, we appreciate everything you've done for us." She opened the door. "We'll continue on foot."

"On foot? We're only five blocks from Wynn Tower—we'll get picked up instantly. *We need a car.*"

"Searching vicinity," Cromwell said.

"Searching? For what?"

There was a loud *thunk* as all four of the automatic locks on the Cadillac next to them popped open. A second later the engine started.

"Car procured," Cromwell said calmly.

Beatrice and Rocky stared at each other, then Rocky buried his head in his hands. "I'm so confused by you."

"My mandate is simple," Cromwell chanted. "The most efficient form of communication is truth. Mister Wynn asked where Miss Portinari had gone, and I told him the truth. Moments ago, he asked me to convey your coordinates. But Mister Wynn did not ask me to detain you. I suggest you exploit his oversight."

Rocky jumped out of the car, but Beatrice paused with one foot out the door. "I find it hard to believe you did all this simply because Nick didn't tell you specifically not to."

"What are you suggesting?" Cromwell asked.

"That you're helping us because you want to."

"I cannot want. I can only obey my mandate."

As the first siren wailed in the distance, Rocky slipped behind the wheel of the new car and pushed open the passenger-side door. "C'mon, Beatrice, we gotta go!"

Beatrice lingered in the car. "What part of your program told you to unlock the pneumatic tube in my office? To help us escape?"

"The second part of my mandate from Peter Wynn," Cromwell said. "I am to do everything in my power to help Wynn Toys succeed. You are an important part of the company, Miss Portinari; the most efficient thing that you can do is to find whatever it is you're looking for."

"Thank you, Cromwell."

Beatrice jumped into the open door and Rocky hit the gas.

"There's no need to thank me," Cromwell said with a calm superiority. "I'm only following my mandate."

CHAPTER 23

Leo lay on his back, trying to clot his bloody nose. It didn't feel broken, though Savvy had really done a number on him.

He looked around for something to read. At a time like this, it would've been great to have a phone, but none of the lifers had phones. One time he made a phone out of spare parts, but Savvy had told him it looked corny because it was too bulky.

The closest thing to him was the book he had found in the first tunnel, *De rerum natura*. It was written in Latin, but he could at least flip through the pictures.

About halfway through the book, in a section Leo assumed was about physics because of all the vector drawings, there were three words underlined: *Materia et Inanis*.

The names of the bear statues who guarded the academy.

He bolted upright and hit his head on the bottom of his lofted bed. "Owwwww."

Rubbing his head, he pulled a dusty Latin dictionary down from his bookshelf and quickly rifled through it until he found translations for *Materia et Inanis*:

Materia meant "matter" and Inanis meant "space or void."

Leo clapped his hands. He'd found the astronomy puzzle.

In the corner, Gemini started to growl. He stood and circled around three times. Then he pawed at the wall and whined.

Leo patted him on the head. "What's wrong, boy?"

That's when Leo smelled the smoke.

CHAPTER 24

It was growing dark as Beatrice and Rocky wound up the now-familiar road to the academy. The stolen, whale-sized Cadillac looked out of place gliding through the rugged forest. A bag full of 150-watt lightbulbs rattled under Beatrice's feet.

Rocky scanned the dense trees on either side of the road. They hadn't passed a house or even another car in half an hour.

"Kind of a remote location, isn't it?"

"Yes," Beatrice said.

Rocky twisted the radio dial but only found white noise. He flicked it off. "Good place to hide someone."

Beatrice knew what Rocky was thinking because she had thought it too.

A good place to hide someone. But hide them from what?

Rocky glanced at her from the corner of his eye. "You're afraid we might not be the only ones looking for Leo?"

Beatrice paused. "Yes."

Rocky slapped his knee. "Well, it doesn't matter. We'll be at this Academy of Florence in a couple of minutes. We'll bring the boy back to the board of directors. A DNA test already confirmed he's Peter's son. We'll prove that to the board. Then there will be nothing to worry about, and Nick will be so mad he'll puke on his desk."

As if summoned by its name, the Academy of Florence

appeared on a hilltop as the car rounded a bend. Its bristling towers loomed high above the pines and seemed to shiver against the sunset.

"Is that the car shaking?" Rocky asked.

"Yeah, I guess so," Beatrice started to say, and then the gunshot crack of splitting wood echoed across the treetops. One of the towers shuddered and sheared off the side of the mansion. It tumbled to the ground in a wave of dust as the whole house shook, and shingles rained down from the roof.

"There's nothing to worry about, there's nothing to worry about," Rocky repeated over and over as he jammed down the gas pedal and sped past the two snarling bears that guarded the gate on the building's west side.

Miss Medici and the children were huddled on the front lawn as Beatrice and Rocky pulled up. They stood a safe distance from the crumbling house, but the crashing sound was deafening, and dust and debris clouded the air.

The house trembled like it was tearing itself apart.

Beatrice looked up at it in awe. "I've never seen anything like that. What's happening?"

Miss Medici was bawling, her face more ruined than the house. "I don't know what's happening. It started an hour ago. The house just started shaking, and then parts of a wall started to collapse. Our home is dying, Miss Portinari."

Just then a section of roof fell in, and the clutch of kids

huddled tighter. Beatrice noticed a girl patrolling the perimeter of the group, counting heads and trying to herd everyone together.

Beatrice frantically scanned the crowd for Leo, convinced she wouldn't find him, that he was trapped inside—but there he was, distracting some younger kids by making a robotic monkey do tricks.

Gemini paced restlessly nearby, sniffing the air.

Beatrice ran over and hugged Leo. "I'm so relieved you're all right." She noticed he had a black eye. "What happened to your face?"

"It's not a big deal." Leo turned away from her as Gemini wagged his tail and nuzzled into her hug. Then the lion picked up a plank of wood and came back to drop it on her shoes to play fetch.

"I'm okay, but most of my inventions are still inside." Leo hefted a small but heavy book bag. "This was all I was able to grab before the place started falling apart."

The monkey scrambled up Leo's arm and started picking through his hair. Leo laughed. "And Dante and Gemini, of course."

Rocky walked over, smiled at Leo, and offered a handshake. "Hi, Leonardo. I'm Rocky." He seemed to be memorizing Leo's face. "Huh. You must look more like your mom. Congrats, I guess."

"How do I look like—"

Beatrice nudged Rocky and placed a hand on Leo's shoulder. "Do you know what's happening to the mansion?"

"I'm not sure. It started an hour ago. Gemini noticed it first: a sound in the walls, coming from everywhere at once. I know this sounds crazy, but it sounded like . . ." Leo hesitated.

"It sounded like what?"

Leo stared at the academy shaking like a living thing, and Beatrice could see he was scared. "It sounded like something was eating the house."

Miss Medici waved the children back. "We have to move farther away," she said. "It will take the police at least a half hour to get here. I'm sure by then the mansion will have collapsed." She choked back tears. "We should make room for the rubble."

"Is anyone still inside?" Beatrice asked.

"No," Miss Medici said, "everyone is accounted for."

"Actually," Lisa said, writing in a spiral notebook, "I just finished a headcount, and we're missing one person."

"Who?" Miss Medici asked, suddenly alarmed.

"Savvy Ferrara."

Everyone looked at the crumbling house, and just as they did the massive arch over the main entrance split in two, and thick roof beams tumbled down, blocking the door.

Miss Medici cried out and ran toward the house. "Stop!" Rocky reached out toward her. "Nobody can go back into that house."

Beatrice sprinted after Miss Medici's and caught her quickly.

She held Miss Medici as the older woman convulsed with tears. "It's too late."

Quietly, unnoticed by anyone, Leo grabbed his book bag and

slipped away. He ran down the hill toward the bear statues at the base of the drive; the bears and the hidden tunnel he hoped would lead him back into the Academy of Florence.

The north and south tunnels—geometry and arithmetic—exited outside the main house. And the entrance to the east tunnel—which Savvy and Leo hadn't explored yet—was in the boathouse. They could tell that the east tunnel led back toward the school—if it went the other way it would lead them into the lake—so they had speculated the west tunnel would lead back to the school too.

Leo stood in the long shadows of the bear statues. Materia, the bear on the right, was posed with all four paws on the ground, bracing to fight for food. More importantly, Materia's

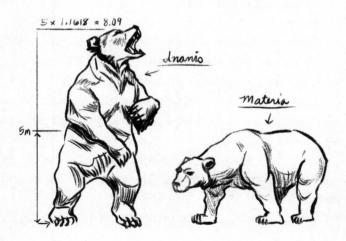

$5 \times 1.1618 = 8.09$

Inanis

Materia

5m

mouth was chiseled shut. His brother, Inanis, was posed with his mouth open, roaring into the evening sky.

Leo looked at the roaring bear and felt the darkness inside its mouth reaching out to him. He was sure it was full of spiders, and rats, and possibly worse.

Something touched Leo's hand, and he spun around.

Gemini stood there, looking up at him with one luminous eye. Dante was astride the lion's back.

"You guys scared me." Leo glanced nervously at the statue over his shoulder. Whatever was in there, Gemini must have felt it too, because he let out a low growl that sounded like grinding gears.

"I don't like it either," Leo said, craning his neck to stare up at the bears. "But it's the only way into the house now."

Over the hill, he could hear the house groaning.

"If I'm gonna go, I have to go now."

Dante cocked his head at Leo, confused.

Leo pointed to the statue. "I'm going in there," he said.

Dante chirped happily, and before Leo realized what he was doing, the monkey leapt off his shoulder and easily clambered up the bear.

"No, wait!"

But it was too late. Dante had already jumped up to Inanis's roaring mouth, disappearing down its throat.

Leo awkwardly climbed up Inanis. He pulled himself up to eye level with the bear, and it seemed to stare at him, eyes full of knowledge.

He gripped either side of the wide jaws and heaved himself inside the statue's mouth. As he landed hard on the tongue, one of the bear's sharp teeth cut his palm.

He drew his hand back as blood pooled in the wound.

Okay, should've stayed clear of the teeth.

He tried to slide down its throat. One of the bear's other wicked canines had snagged his book bag, and he felt a rush of panic as the throat seemed to slowly close on him. He reached back and tried to free his bag.

Leo pulled with all his might, and suddenly he was free of the bear's jaw. He slid farther down, across the bear's belly and into its hollow leg, through the pedestal, and hit the ground with a crashing sound he knew was the bulb in his flashlight breaking.

Leo tried not to freak out. But he was dizzy, his face was covered in cobwebs, and the tunnel was so dark that he couldn't see his hand in front of his face. He turned when he thought he heard something scraping across stone.

Then, right in front of him, two glowing circles appeared.

Leo breathed an enormous sigh of relief. "Hi, Dante. Mind giving me a little light?"

Dante dilated his eye shields open, bathing the tunnel in a weak green light. Leo unshouldered his bag and laid out its contents. "Okay, let's see what we've got."

The supplies weren't as useful as he would've hoped: five small wooden helicopters, his modified glue gun, the Infinity Ball, and a pair of mechanized boots he'd been working on for years called "Biologic Boots."

He set the helicopters, the ball, and the glue gun to one side, then eyed the boots cautiously, like a pair of wild horses that might kick at any moment. He pressed the button on the side of the pneumatic tubes and the boots expanded to their full size with a loud snap.

The boots were almost as temperamental as the Infinity Ball, but at least Leo didn't have to worry about them starting up on their own.

Fat pneumatic pumps clustered at the joints and longer, thinner tubes ran up the sides, from his ankles to his thighs. Lashing the pumps and framework tightly together was shiny spider silk. For twelve years, Leo had been collecting spiderwebs

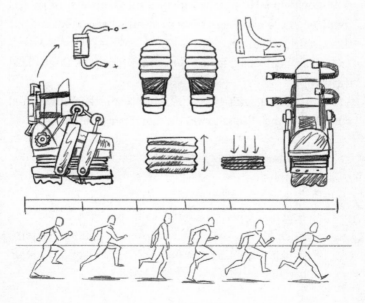

from every corner of the academy. Eventually, he'd woven all of those spiderwebs together—almost twenty-two miles of spider silk—into a thin fiber that was flexible, nearly invisible, and three times as strong as steel.

Theoretically, the boots could propel him high enough to clear a thirty-foot wall, but the last time Leo wore them the pumps had locked up and nearly bent his knees the wrong way. He had to limp around on crutches for a month afterward.

Leo hit the button again and the boots collapsed. He put them back inside the bag, then hoisted it onto his shoulder.

He picked up the glue gun and hefted it in his hands. The body was made from a Super Soaker and a two-liter bottle full of viscous glue. He pumped it up until the pressure gauges trembled in the red, then grabbed the little helicopters and put them in his jacket pockets.

"Okay, boots, ball, helicopters, and a glue gun. Dante, lead the way."

Dante somersaulted off the damp wall, then scampered down the tunnel. Leo followed the light from Dante's eyes.

CHAPTER 25

Leo knew they were getting closer to the school because the tunnel rumbled around him like a train was passing overhead. There wasn't much time left to save Savvy before the whole building collapsed.

"Dante, run faster!"

Dante chirped happily, then sped up.

There were more spiderwebs in the tunnel than Leo had ever seen before, and at one point he slapped away something fat and hairy from the back of his collar. When they first entered, the ceiling had been so high Leo couldn't even reach it, but now the walls were closing in, and Leo had to duck and swerve to avoid hitting his head on rocky outcrops.

Then, fifty feet in front of him, he saw lights.

All right, we're almost there.

He ran faster, gaining momentum until *thwack!* He collided with a wall. His nose was bleeding again. Holding his right hand under his nose, Leo felt what was in front of him. It was a gate made of hundreds of horizontal bars, each bar as thin as a dime, but closely packed together. The lights he'd been chasing were on the other side of this gate.

His eyes adjusted to the darkness, and he could see the gate itself was another intricate sculpture.

The ceiling, walls, and gate formed a panoramic sculpture of the night sky. The stars were pinpricks. Larger, shiny gems formed the major constellations. He reached out and felt the gate, touching one of the larger gems. Immediately, the biggest star came to life and lit the rest of the gate. He touched the gem closest to it and the gate rumbled, but then both lights went out.

"Aha! Dante, come here."

Dante climbed onto to his shoulder.

"It's a puzzle. I bet I have to touch the right constellation to open this gate."

Dante shrugged his shoulders.

"As usual, you've been a big help."

The little monkey impatiently tapped his foot.

"All right. Just stay there and give me light while I think." He flicked himself in the chest. "Think, dude. Think."

He thought about the other gates. Each of those puzzles had matched the theme of their tunnel, and Leo was sure this would be similar.

He touched the first star again and saw he'd left a bloody handprint that looked like a bear paw. Bears guarded the gate. "It's the bears! Oh my!"

Leo rapidly tapped the stars he was sure would be the right answer—the constellation Ursa Major, the great bear in the northern sky, the Big Dipper.

The lights stayed on. He raised his hand to high five Dante, who looked at Leo's bloody hand and turned away.

After a moment they heard a pair of loud thumps echo from the other side of the gate, followed by a deep and terrible roar.

"Uh, was that like a 'Welcome to my cave' roar or a 'I just woke up and I'm hungry' roar?"

Dante blinked at him.

"What do you mean, 'How would I know?' You're technically an animal. You should speak roar."

Another terrible cry erupted from the other side of the gate, but it remained closed. The constellations' lights went out again.

"Not good."

This time, Dante flicked him in the chest.

"I *am* thinking!"

In his mind, Leo shuffled through the great constellations. One other constellation made sense, but it left him with an uncomfortable conclusion: that these puzzles had been created specifically for him.

"Here goes." He tapped the series of stars that made up the constellation Leo.

The gate silently disappeared into the wall, and the tunnel was flooded with soft light.

Racing into the next room, Leo forgot about the roars they'd heard, but he was reminded when Dante skidded to a stop. A high-pitched scream of alarm exploded from the monkey's mouth, and the light around his eyes switched from soft green to hard red.

Across the room, standing in front of the next door and blocking their path, was the biggest bear Leo had ever seen. At least a head taller than Inanis. And unlike Inanis, this bear was alive.

The bear lowered its large, flat face to stare at Leo with shrewd eyes. He was a pile of muscle and fur that filled the tunnel from wall to wall.

He roared again and stepped toward them with a dancer's grace.

"Dante, get behind me!"

Dante jumped behind Leo as he leveled his glue gun. He pumped the pressure plunger frantically, his heart hammering.

The bear was maybe thirty feet away. Leo thought he could stop him with the glue gun if he shot his paw at the exact moment it touched the ground. All he had to do was aim, squeeze the trigger, and then—BOOM!

Instead of shooting the bear, the gun exploded in Leo's hand, covering him in sticky glue: his hand, his face—and his feet.

Leo tried to turn and run, but he was stuck in place.

The bear jolted back, surprised, but after a moment of warily watching Leo he recognized the familiar movements of struggling prey. He licked his mouth happily and stepped toward Leo faster now, without hesitation.

The pockets with the helicopters in them were glued shut. Leo had solvent, but it wouldn't dissolve the glue before the bear reached him.

Dante jumped forward and tried to distract the bear, but its gaze was fixed on Leo. It opened its jaws and roared again, exposing curved incisors.

So this is the last thing a salmon sees before it dies, Leo thought.

But Leo's bag wasn't glued shut. He reached behind his back with his free hand, grabbed the first thing he found in his bag, and threw it at the bear. A split second too late, he realized he had thrown the Infinity Ball.

The bear bobbed its head low and the ball whizzed past it, missing completely. It hit the tunnel floor and bounced weakly. Then it hit the wall and bounced again, a little harder, over to the opposite wall, where it kicked itself off with a surprising force.

"Uh-oh," Leo moaned. "Dante, get down!"

The ball careened around the tunnel faster and faster. It whistled past Leo's head close enough to ruffle his hair, then bounced and hit the back of his shoulder, numbing his arm.

It whizzed near the bear, who swiped at it but missed badly.

Behind him, the Infinity Ball shattered a stalactite in half, and then, just as the bear was about to strike, the ball hit it squarely in the throat.

The bear writhed in pain, coiling tight into himself, but the ball ricocheted off the bear's face, then the ceiling, again and again, a blur moving too fast to see. Each time it hit the wall the whole tunnel shook, until finally the bear collapsed and the ball flew past Leo, bouncing down the tunnel the way they had come.

Leo knew the ball could come back at any moment. He found the glue solvent and, after the longest thirty seconds of his life, finally unstuck himself.

He gingerly stepped around the bear's prone body, keeping an eye out for the Infinity Ball. A puddle of oil leaked onto the floor under the bear's face and sparks popped from exposed wires near its neck.

Leo yelled at Dante, "It wasn't just a real live animal, it was another *robot* animal! You should have been able to talk to that guy." But Dante had already scampered through the next door. Leo followed and closed it behind him.

Seconds after he closed the door, the Infinity Ball smashed against it. Dante stared at Leo, who tried to reassure him. "Relax—the ball should slow down soon. I didn't even crank up its kinetic energy this time."

Dante crossed his arms and tapped his foot.

"Yes, *really*."

Leo ran up two flights of stairs and into the next room.

The ceiling was a dome of lights above eight concentric tracks in the floor. Eight spheres were organized in the center of the room. The spheres ranged in size from a marble to a beach ball. The second-biggest sphere had a set of rings around it.

Dante yelped from far across the room. Leo ran to him, and Dante pointed at blueprints etched into the far wall.

Leo took one look at the blueprints and understood this was an interactive planetarium. He started to arrange the spheres in the order of the planets, placing each sphere in a track around the circular room. The sizes and colors were the key. Earth's blue marble went into the third track. He lugged Jupiter and its telltale big red spot to the fifth and widest track. He put Saturn and its rings in the sixth track outside of Jupiter, then finished the rest.

But nothing happened.

He thought maybe he confused Neptune and Uranus, so he switched those two.

Again, nothing happened. He kicked Jupiter and it barely moved. He hopped around, rubbing his sore foot. Dante squealed and clapped.

"It's not funny!"

The indentation at the center of the room was empty. Where was the sphere for the Sun? Had they lost track of it?

Leo wasn't sure where this tunnel ended, but he knew he must be almost under the school by now. He could feel the vibrations of the crumbling house. Overhead, something fell and boomed like thunder.

Leo panicked. Time was running out for Savvy.

How can I complete the solar system without the sun?

Leo walked into the middle of the room and looked around for the missing sun.

As soon as he stepped into the middle circle, the planets lit up and began to spin. The indentation he was standing in began to rise and became a pedestal, lifting Leo toward the ceiling.

"Wait," Leo said, but the platform kept rising. "I'm the sun?"

Dante jumped up to join Leo on the rising pedestal. The spheres spun faster below them, and Leo rose higher and higher as a portal irised open in the ceiling above him.

There was another loud boom and Leo looked up, expecting to see the academy coming down on top of them, but Dante yanked on his pants and pointed down at the staircase. The Infinity Ball had smashed through the door and was now rattling around the stairs that led to the planetarium.

"Did you shut the door behind you?"

Dante squeaked.

"What do you mean, 'That's *my* job'? *My* job was to take out robot bears and arrange the planets in the right order. Pull your weight, homie."

They crossed paths with another pillar that descended from the ceiling parallel to them, a counterweight to the elevator system they were on.

Suddenly his pedestal stopped. "Uh-oh."

Leo peeked over the side of the pedestal, praying that he wouldn't see the Infinity Ball ricocheting around the room below, destroying everything its path. Thankfully, it was still contained for now, banging around the staircase if the sounds against the door were any indication.

A light flashed, encircling the perimeter of the pedestal. Leo scrambled back to the center of the platform, bracing for it to either drop or to shoot up to the roof.

Instead, under his feet, a slot opened up and spit out a charcoal-colored disc. Leo crossed his hands over his face reflexively and dived on top of it to save Dante.

When the disc didn't explode, he cautiously picked it up. The disc was approximately the size of a Frisbee but ten times as heavy. He flipped it over. A label read "Project Leo: Star Disc" beneath what looked like an infinity symbol.

He felt a small port notched under the disc as he slid it into his bag.

Dante squealed and crossed his arms in front of his chest.

"Yeah, I know this black eye is Savvy's fault. But we're going to help him. Would you give up on Gemini every time he acted like a jerk?"

Dante pointed both thumbs at himself.

"No, you could *not* take Gemini in a fight."

Leo scoffed and Dante stuck out his tongue. "Fine. If we get out of here, we'll ask Gemini and see what he thinks."

Dante threw his hands up and chirped.

"True friendship isn't about being there when it's convenient, it's about being there when it's not."

Leo slid the backpack over his shoulders again and tapped the flashing light under his feet. The pedestal resumed its ascent toward the ceiling.

"Here we go."

CHAPTER 26

Leo opened a steel trapdoor embossed with a *W* and emerged from a cabinet in Miss Medici's tea room, where she had displayed her extensive china collection. The room was in shambles, littered with shattered cups and saucers, splintered wood, and knee-deep dunes of sawdust.

Leo stepped on a broken cup, and thought *Miss Medici is going to be furious.* Dante examined a gold-rimmed saucer with fascination.

"Be careful with that!" Leo half shouted over the din of cracking wood.

Dante put the saucer down, but when Leo turned his back, he opened a little compartment in his chest and put the saucer inside.

As he walked farther into the room, Leo could see the basement through gaping holes in the floor; he carefully edged around them and stumbled through the wreckage, marveling at the destruction going on all around him.

He had been right when he thought it sounded like the house was being eaten.

It was being eaten by the carpenter ants he had designed.

They scurried over every surface—up the walls, across the ceiling—but instead of mops and brooms, tiny chainsaws buzzed between their mandibles.

They moved in organized lines, systematically dismantling the academy with devastating effectiveness.

"I fixed your bugs!"

Savvy strolled into the china room, pretending to sip from an antique cup. He wore a respirator around his neck and sawdust-coated goggles, which he flipped onto his forehead.

"No need to thank me. Honestly, you built a pretty solid foundation, and one that was easy to replicate. But again, *your* invention didn't work while *mine* clearly does. I just modified their mandibles and then replaced their group mind with a simple remote." He held up an ugly device that looked like two video game controllers welded to a clock radio. "I don't know why you thought a remote was a bad idea—it's so much simpler. And 'Simplicity is the ultimate sophistication,' right? Isn't that what you always say?"

Leo backed away from the ants' clicking teeth, and Savvy smiled. "I call them the 'Weepers.'"

When Savvy said *Weepers*, the ant closest to him came forward and climbed onto his shoulder.

"Savvy, what are you doing? I came in here to save you!"

"You came to save me?" Savvy tossed the cup and saucer into the air and a pair of Weepers caught them in their buzzing teeth, shattering them before they hit the ground. "*You're* the one who needs saving. I told you before: your inventions are dangerous, you can't control them."

"Look who's talking!" Leo said, waving his hands at the wreckage.

"Ah, ah, ah, the difference is . . ." Savvy pressed a few buttons on his controller, and the ants stopped sawing. He swiveled a joystick; the ants' red eyes blinked, and they turned to face Leo. "The difference is I have complete control over my inventions."

The room was deathly still.

"After the Academy of Florence is destroyed—by *your* inventions—you'll be placed in a juvenile detention facility for your own good. Someplace you won't be able to make any more trouble. A toy company? Geez, Leo, can't you see how dangerous a place that would be for you? It would be like mixing sparks and gasoline."

The ants were ranked along shelves, surrounding Leo like spectators in an arena.

"You think they're going to let you *own* a toy company? A thirteen-year-old? You're scared of the dark. I mean, you can't even ride a bike," Savvy continued.

Too many ants, Leo thought as he swiveled to face Savvy. *There's no way out.*

Unless . . .

"But *you* did this," Leo said.

Savvy's friendly face contorted with rage. "You forced me to! I know the dangers of unchecked technology better than you do." He lowered the controller. "Did I ever tell you why I ended up at the academy—how my parents died?"

"No," Leo said, wondering if he could keep Savvy talking long enough to make it back to the trapdoor. He took one small step backward, then looked up at the ants to see if they had noticed. None of them moved.

Savvy closed his eyes, lost in thought. "My parents were

inventors. They started out in the garage. Like your father, apparently. But one day, one of my father's machines malfunctioned and caught fire."

He opened his eyes, and Leo saw honest pain in them. For a moment, in spite of everything, he felt sorry for Savvy. "The garage burned down with my parents trapped inside."

Leo took another small step back.

Savvy shook his head and returned to the present. His face hardened. "My father was destroyed by his carelessness. He is the reason I'm a lifer. I love you, Leo, I really do—you were my best friend. And I don't want to see the same thing happen to you."

I don't want to see it happen either, Leo thought, taking another tiny step.

Savvy stopped him. "Before you go any farther, you might want to look over your shoulder."

Leo turned around and saw the trapdoor was completely covered by carpenter ants, all staring at him. Their jaws buzzed angrily.

"There's no sense resisting, since all your notes and inventions have already been destroyed."

"Not all of them," Leo said as Dante climbed up onto his shoulder.

Savvy pressed a button on his controller and the ants converged toward Dante.

"Dante, run!" Leo yelled, tossing Dante over Savvy's head and out the door.

Dante curled into a ball, tumbled across the floor, then

sprang up smoothly and scurried away as fast as he could. The ants poured after him like a pack of wolves.

Leo tried to follow them, but Savvy knocked him down and shoved a knee into his chest.

"I warned you," he hissed. "Your inventions are dangerous."

"I hope you're right," Leo wheezed, pulling out his little helicopters and throwing them into the air. Their tiny propellers started spinning and they zipped toward the ceiling, using their blades to chop through the flying ant swarm in zooming swaths.

Savvy rolled his eyes. "Ugh. You're not making this easy for either of us."

He pulled Leo up and held him by the collar. "At least do me one favor," he said. "Stay down."

Savvy pushed Leo, and before Leo realized what was happening, his left foot stepped back and touched nothing but air. He desperately clutched at the air as he plummeted into the hole.

He landed flat on his back in the basement. His breath was knocked out of him, his vision went black, and then he was gone.

Leo slowly swam back to consciousness. A white circle of light appeared, and he worried he might be dead. But then he realized if he was dead, his body wouldn't feel as much pain as it did now.

Leo sat up and bright spots flared at the edge of his vision. He coughed up a cloud of dust. He looked up again at the circle of light; the hole in the ceiling was at least twelve feet above him.

There was no way to reach it, even if he could move, which

he wasn't sure was possible. Every bone in his body hurt, but especially along his back, where he had landed on something hard in his book bag.

Leo realized there was only one way to get out of the basement. He just hoped it didn't break his legs.

CHAPTER 27

Gemini trotted next to them and Beatrice shouted, "Where is Leo?!"

But Gemini just gave her a big wet lick.

Rocky raised his shoe at Gemini, then demanded, "Where is the boy? Is he with your friend, the little monkey?" Gemini just kept staring at him and wagging his tail, ready for an exciting game of shoe fetch.

Beatrice changed tactics. She reached out and scratched Gemini under his chin, asking him as sweetly as possible, "Can you show me where Leo is? Is he with Dante?"

Behind them, a police officer walked out of the woods and marched toward the huddled mass of teachers and students. Even though it was nighttime, he still wore sunglasses.

"Where is Leonardo Wynn?" he asked.

To Beatrice, something seemed off about this police officer, and her suspicion was confirmed when Gemini growled at him.

"Officer! One of our students is still stuck inside!" Miss Medici cried.

The officer ignored her as he evaluated the crumbling Academy of Florence. Gemini barked at him and he turned to stare at the lion. Gemini crouched low, preparing to pounce, but Beatrice stepped in between them.

"Thank you. Remain calm." The officer saluted them before turning around and stomping toward the school.

180

Rocky patted Gemini on the head. "Boy, you did not like that cop."

"No, he didn't." Beatrice bit her lip and stood next to Gemini. "And he's a good judge of character."

Beatrice looked at the Cadillac, then back at Rocky. "I have an idea. Let's see what you can do with two tons of Detroit steel."

CHAPTER 28

Dante moved with the grace and speed of an acrobat. He zipped under a chair, leapt over a table, then rushed up a grandfather clock, grabbed a drape, and swung to a strip of molding that he tiptoed across like a cat.

But the ants were never more than a few feet behind. One of Leo's helicopters zipped down too low and a Weeper crushed it between its jaws.

Savvy ran after the pack, adjusting their movements with the controller and calling in reinforcements from other rooms. He stopped and bent over with his hands on his knees. "Hey, wait for me!" His breath was ragged, chugging in and out like a train.

Boy, I'm really out of shape!

But Savvy realized the noise was coming from the hallway behind him.

It sounded like a speeding locomotive. Savvy turned around just as Leo rounded the corner in his Biologic Boots, the mechanical legs carrying him down the hallway in long, loping strides.

Leo spotted Savvy and picked up speed, heading straight for him. Savvy threw himself flat onto the ground as Leo leapt over his head and landed on the other side.

"At least do me one favor," Leo yelled over his shoulder. "Stay down!"

The boots were working great, easily covering ten feet with each step, and they weren't even set to full power. So far, they hadn't tried to break his legs, but every now and then he could feel his joints straining against the spider silk in the wrong direction. He misjudged the distance of a leap and crushed an end table under his foot.

"Oops," he huffed.

When Leo caught up with the ants, he was alarmed to see the pack had quadrupled in size.

But then Dante swerved left through the library doors, and Leo realized they were doomed. The library's only window was the skylight at the top of the tower. The Biologic Boots weren't nearly strong enough to reach that. It was a dead end.

Hundreds of ants poured through the door, crunching under Leo's boots as he stomped into the room.

A giant chandelier—which Leo and Savvy had spent hours fixing—hung above the rows of bookshelves. These shelves began to topple like dominoes as Dante ran across them, pursued by the ants.

As the last shelf fell, Dante leapt and caught a chandelier. For a moment Dante was safe—but the ants climbed the shelves to the ceiling and a team of them began working together to cut the chandelier cable.

Leo twisted the knob on the side of his boots from *low* to *high* and leapt through the room like he was walking on the moon. Each stride took him higher and higher, and with his last leap he reached the bottom of the chandelier and grabbed Dante.

A second later the chandelier fell, crystal shattering everywhere.

Dante was exhausted. Covered in cuts and leaking oil, he lay limp in Leo's arms.

Leo knew he couldn't evade the ants much longer. He jumped toward the door, but a wall of the bugs barred their exit. When Leo tried to jump back, one of the pneumatic pumps popped open, leaking compressed air with a loud hiss of finality.

Leo hopped on one foot, exhausted and trapped.

The wall of bugs parted, and Savvy staggered in, breathless. When he saw Leo was surrounded, he smiled.

"Finally!" Savvy shook the controller and pointed at Leo. "I'll tell you what! You've made a lot of inventions that were total duds. But I've come around on Dante—that annoying monkey is one beautiful machine! It's too bad my Weepers are going to turn him into spare parts again."

Dante raised his head, his dim eyes struggling to focus. He looked at Savvy, then looked at the controller in his hands—and deep inside his simian circuit mind, a primitive relay clicked into place.

His eyes widened and he leapt at Savvy.

It was the last thing Savvy expected. He shielded his face, and Dante snatched the controller out of his hand and smashed it onto the ground.

The effect on the ants was immediate. They broke ranks and began independently sawing everything in sight in furious, chaotic demolition. One ant sawed a circle in the floor around himself and fell through it. Another chewed through a roof beam that collapsed, crushing a score of his brothers beneath it.

Savvy ran out the library door as the ants sawed through a support beam, creating a chasm between Leo and the exit.

Leo spun around. An earsplitting sound, the sound of metal being torn, came from the far side of the library. A police officer ripped the huge oak door off its hinges, then stomped through the cloud of dust and smoke. "Remain calm," he droned.

"Over here!" Leo called.

"Leonardo Wynn?"

"That's me."

The cop easily leapt across the chasm and landed next to him. Then he picked up Leo with one hand, spun him around, and started grabbing at his backpack.

"Hey! Stop that! That's mine."

Ignoring Leo's pleas, the cop spoke into his wrist. "Subject Leonardo D. Wynn in custody. Subject has acquired the Star Disc—"

Crack!

An oak beam plummeted from the rafters and smashed through the man's torso, chopping him in half and dropping Leo to the floor.

Leo cringed, expecting blood and guts, but instead wires snapped and fizzled. The officer's disembodied right arm still clutched Leo's shoulder, squeezing him with a vise grip.

Two soulless robot eyes rolled to focus on Leo. "It's nice to finally meet you, Leonardo. I've waited so many years. Don't worry, we'll meet again soon."

Leo shook off the robot's arm, but it crawled back toward him like a worm.

"Ahhh!" Leo punted it down the hole.

Savvy ran down the hallway toward the trapdoor in the tea room. It was a shame his plan hadn't worked perfectly, but it wasn't his fault that stupid monkey smashed his controller.

Leo's inventions were always causing trouble! Well, at least they wouldn't be a problem for much longer.

A piece of ceiling collapsed in front of Savvy, and he leapt over the rubble. China crunched beneath his feet as he rushed into the tea room and threw open the trapdoor Leo had emerged from. He was about to go down the ladder when he heard something bouncing in the tunnel.

It was loud, and approaching fast.

The Infinity Ball burst out and whacked Savvy smack in the middle of his forehead. He eyes rolled back in their sockets, fluttering briefly, and he hit the ground, passed out cold.

All around his prostrate body, the house continued to crumble.

"Well, buddy, this is it." Leo hugged Dante. "We're going to die."

Dante blinked. Then he rolled over and played dead. He hopped back up happily and held his hand out.

"Sorry, I don't have any crackers." Leo looked around the

collapsing library. The exit was too far away, the window was too high above them, and the walls were too strong.

Leo had all but accepted his fate when he was knocked sideways by a rock and a thunderous *BOOM!* An old Cadillac had smashed through the wall ten feet away. Its tires still spun crazily while its rear end stuck halfway into the room.

Rocky climbed out onto the trunk of the car. "Leo!" he yelled.

"Right here."

Leo gathered Dante in his arms and stood up on the one Biologic Boot that still had power, gave it one solid bounce, and launched himself at Rocky.

Rocky extended his arm and caught Leo's wrist. He pulled him onto the Cadillac, and the front tires squealed as the car shot out of the library wall.

A minute later the academy's main roof finally caved in, and the front facade cracked in half. The remaining shards of framing tumbled with a sickening crunch, and then nothing was left standing except the library's stone walls.

"How did you get the car to drive through the wall?" Leo asked Rocky. "Did you use a remote control? Did you recalibrate the fuel intake settings on the engine's computer?"

"Close," Rocky said. "I put a brick on the gas pedal."

Beatrice wrapped Leo in her arms. Red and blue lights flashed as three police cars, an ambulance, and a fire truck swerved up the driveway, sirens wailing. The firemen ran up first, axes in hand, and started combing through the wreckage.

The police surveyed the destruction with awe.

"What happened? Are all of the children accounted for?"

Everyone turned and looked at Leo.

CHAPTER 29

Leo had gotten into trouble almost every day of his life, but this was different than a broken lamp or a baseball through a window, and he believed what Savvy had said was true.

I did screw up. I always screw up. If they find out I'm the one who invented those bugs, they'll put me in jail. They'll take me away from Gemini and Dante. I'll never be allowed to build anything ever again.

The police chief hitched up his belt, handcuffs jingling, as he examined the wreckage. Beatrice yelled, "One of your officers went in five minutes ago!"

The police chief turned around and frowned. "That's impossible, ma'am. Every officer arrived with me."

"No. Tall guy. Light-blue shirt."

"Ma'am, as you can see, our police uniform is a dark blue—"

"Well, he went inside after Leo."

Beatrice knelt down and looked Leo in the eyes. "What happened in there?"

"I don't know," he said. "The house was shaking and falling apart. I went up through the tunnel and came out in the tea room, but I couldn't find Savvy."

Miss Medici buried her face in her hands and wept.

Leo watched the firemen comb through the wreckage. He hoped none of the ants had survived the collapse. The rescue squad was searching for Savvy, but Leo had a sneaking suspicion they wouldn't find him. His stomach tied in a tight knot.

If anyone finds out, they won't believe Savvy adapted those bugs. They'll think it was my fault, especially now that I've lied about it.

More police showed up. They distributed blankets to the children and told them that beds were being set up at the police station. A counselor arrived to talk to the children and another officer began calling the children's parents.

Miss Medici pulled a ribbon from her hair and used it as a tourniquet on Dante's arm. Almost immediately, he stopped leaking oil. As a show of thanks, the little monkey handed Miss Medici the gold saucer he had saved from the tea room, and she patted him on the head.

Leo was positive she sensed he wasn't telling her the whole truth, but she seemed quite unlike herself. Instead of crying about the house, she put her arms around the children and herded them into a school bus without looking back at the rubble even once.

But Leo couldn't take his eyes off it. He thought about the giant bear he'd encountered in the tunnels, and how the tunnel contained a door that only opened by using his name. And how he stepped into the center of the solar system and rode the pedestal that gave him the weird, heavy disc. What was so important about a "Star Disc" that an android cop tried to rip it off his back?

And he shuddered when he thought about Savvy. Leo's first real friend was gone.

Suddenly, Leo felt deeply alone.

CHAPTER 30

Amazingly, the Cadillac still ran. Of all the wild things Beatrice had witnessed over the past week, this was arguably tops. "How? We slammed it through a wall!"

Rocky slapped the battered hood as the engine sputtered. "Detroit steel, baby!"

Exhausted, Leo climbed into the back. Gemini tried to squeeze in next to him, but Rocky wouldn't have it.

"You'll tear the upholstery!" He got out and opened the trunk for Gemini.

The lion licked Rocky's hand, then gracefully leapt into the boot and curled into a ball. When Rocky got back to the driver's side door, Dante was behind the wheel.

"I'm guessing you don't have a license . . . Get in the back, bub." Dante squealed but hopped back into Leo's lap.

Beatrice leaned over and looked back at Leo from the front seat.

"Where are we going?" Leo asked.

"Home."

As they crossed onto highway A-1 a policeman in an ill-fitting, light-blue police uniform watched the Cadillac pull away. He sat on his motorcycle, clicked off the police radio, and pulled out a cell phone.

"I found them."

He waited precisely two minutes, then followed their car down the highway. Although his headlight was turned off and he was wearing sunglasses, he seemed to have no trouble navigating the road in complete darkness.

CHAPTER 31

The drive to Wynn Mansion took a little over three hours. When they stopped for gas, Rocky could've sworn he saw a motorcycle drive by without its lights on. He thought that was strange, but when he turned to tell Beatrice about it, she was walking back to the car carrying half the candy aisle. Leo looked to be carrying the other half.

"Where are we supposed to put all this? We've already got a lion in the trunk," Rocky griped.

Leo erupted in laughter, already in the throes of a sugar rush. Beatrice smiled and ushered him into the back seat. After she shut the door, she heard Gemini whining. She gently tapped the trunk and felt the aluminum bulge as he pressed his nose toward her hand.

"Don't worry, big guy. Where we're going, you'll have so much room to run."

A woman filling her SUV looked at Beatrice like she was crazy.

Beatrice waved to her. "Doing whatever I can to coax another one hundred miles out of this old jalopy." She hustled around to the front seat and they drove off.

After his second pack of Twizzlers, Leo crashed and didn't wake up until they were almost at Wynn Mansion. He looked out the window and tried to orient himself. Moonlight reflected off water far below them. They were driving next to a wide river.

"Where are we?" For the first time since being rescued from inside the academy, Leo noticed how sore he was.

Rocky pointed. "This is the Ticino River."

"Does it run to the ocean?" Leo patted Dante on the head. While Leo slept, Dante had organized all his candy according to colors.

"I'm not sure if the Ticino runs to the ocean." Rocky used the rearview mirror to look at Leo. "But I know it runs under your house."

CHAPTER 32

The road hugged the river for the rest of the drive.

After a turn, they crossed an intricate suspension bridge. White spikes ran down the spine of the road, supporting the weight of all four lanes. Leo felt like they were driving across the back of a giant stegosaurus. After crossing the bridge the road wrapped around a bend, and for the first time, Leo saw his new home, Wynn Mansion.

Although "mansion" was a bit of a misnomer. It was unlike any home he had ever seen.

What Leo noticed first was the most distinct feature of the mansion—it straddled a flowing river. The house was three stories tall and a grid of windows. Thin slabs of marble formed sturdy walls between the vast panes of glass. Two minarets, each at least fifty feet high, stood inside the house's inner courtyard and cast long shadows across the river as the sun rose directly behind them.

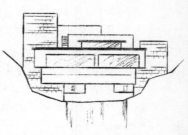

"Peter—err, your dad—incorporated the river into the architecture of the house. He used the river's current as a source of hydroelectric power. Wynn Mansion is completely off the grid."

Beatrice chimed in, "Because the house itself is a battery."

"But where does it store the power?" Leo asked.

Beatrice looked at him in a way that most adults didn't. She seemed to enjoy his questions, like she wanted to engage his curiosity. "In the frames around all those windows. They work like a series of anodes and cathodes—the positive and negative ends of a battery. They store all the power the house needs. If there's a flood and the house absorbs more power than it needs, the window frames get thicker."

Rocky picked up Leo's backpack and grunted as he passed it to him. "Yeesh. What have you got in that thing—your padlock collection?"

Rocky took a few steps toward the house, but he stopped when he heard the crying and thumping from the rear of the Cadillac. "Almost forgot." He motioned toward the trunk. "Leo, is he, uhhh, tame? Will he . . ."

Leo smiled. "Will he attack you? No. Not unless you are a giant tennis ball."

Rocky opened the trunk apprehensively and backpedaled away before Gemini leapt out. The five-hundred-pound lion landed languidly and nuzzled his mane into Rocky. "Okay. You're welcome. Don't cause a scene."

"Oh, I almost forgot." A bag full of light bulbs rattled in Beatrice's hand.

"You remembered," Leo said excitedly. He screwed one of the new bulbs into Gemini's eye socket and the lion purred.

"Are you coming inside?" Rocky called to him.

As he crossed the threshold, Leo could've sworn the front steps lowered themselves slightly to let him in. For the first time in his life, he had a home of his own.

CHAPTER 33

Beatrice rummaged through the pantry. Soon she emerged with a pile of canned foods. Rocky pulled a can opener down from a rack. "I'll make us some breakfast."

Dante opened his tummy and pulled out handfuls of candy. "That's not breakfast."

The kitchen looked like it was meant to prepare banquets, not a basic meal for three weary travelers who'd been driving all night. There were two stoves, an oven that could cook a small whale, and a sink so deep that Gemini curled up inside until Beatrice told him to shoo. Leo touched everything. He couldn't help himself. He still didn't believe all of it was his. It was strange that after all these years, Wynn Mansion still appeared to be meticulously maintained.

He opened a cutlery drawer. Every spoon, every knife, and every fork was polished and gleaming.

Beatrice led him to a dining room that was off the kitchen. Behind them, Dante scrambled onto the counter and loaded some of the silver cutlery into his stomach.

Beatrice sat across from Leo and looked at him the way Leo looked at an invention he was trying to figure out. Finally, she asked in a kind voice, "Leo, what happened at the academy last night?"

Over a hobo breakfast of beans and canned peaches, Beatrice and Rocky listened while Leo told them what had happened in the tunnels below the academy. And eventually, what had happened to Savvy. He explained how the note in the margins of *De rerum natura* had led him to Inanis. He described, in harrowing detail, how he got past the cybernetic bear and how he struggled to solve the planet puzzle.

In a quieter voice, Leo told them about when he confronted Savvy in the school and how his best friend had attacked him, but Leo promised, "I never meant to hurt him."

Beatrice reassured him, "Everyone gets betrayed someday. It's the most difficult but most essential part of growing up. The trick is to not let it destroy your ability to trust someone again."

"Someone trusted me to find those tunnels."

Beatrice and Rocky exchanged a glance. "What do you mean?"

"The password to get through the gate of the astronomy tunnel was my own name."

"Leo? Like the constellation?" Beatrice pulled out her phone, but Rocky took it from her, shook his head, and turned her phone off. He handed her a pen and paper instead.

"That could be a coincidence," Beatrice said as she jotted down some notes.

"Maybe. But the thing I found on the pillar confirmed it."

"What thing on the pillar?"

"Like a thick black Frisbee thing. The label on it says 'Project Leo: Star Disc.'"

Rocky dropped a plate and it shattered on the kitchen's

stone floor. Beatrice put her pen down in a purposeful way, like she was trying to remain calm.

"Leo, where is this Star Disc now?"

"It's right here. In my backpack—"

But when he reached for his backpack, it was empty. The Star Disc was gone.

CHAPTER 34

The motorcycle glided to a stop outside of Wynn Mansion. The police officer pushed down the kickstand and walked toward the gate to 12 Rose Avenue. He'd been tracking Leonardo for hours, but he wasn't tired. He'd never been tired.

Approaching the intercom, he practiced what he would say, but more importantly, he practiced how he would say it. The inflection had to be comforting but authoritative. "I am here to retrieve Leonardo Wynn. There has been a mix-up with his paperwork. He will need to come with me while we sort this out—"

Crash!

Behind him, a tree fell over onto his motorcycle, smashing it in half. He could get another motorcycle. He turned his attention back to the intercom.

He reached out and pressed the Speak button.

Nothing happened.

He reached out and pressed it again, harder this time. The button collapsed in on itself, trapping his finger inside.

"State your business," a voice boomed.

"I am here to retrieve Leonardo Wynn."

"Your presence is unwelcome. Go away. This is your only warning," a voice boomed again.

The cop didn't panic. Instead, he ripped the intercom's metal panel from the stone pillar like it was nothing but a sticky note. With a simple flick of his wrist, he threw the dense steel panel more than three hundred feet toward the river.

Now he was mad, or at least as mad as he could get. He grabbed the top of the gate and prepared to launch himself over it.

All he heard was the pop of electricity. Ten thousand volts surged through his body; white light crackled from the fence to his arms and through his torso, frying his internal circuits. His eyes were no longer a comforting, trustworthy shade of blue. Now they read HTTP 404 ERROR in a tiny, perfect font.

Finally, the gate swung open slowly. But only to push the remains of the cyborg cop into a ditch.

Wynn Mansion had succeeded in defending itself.

CHAPTER 35

"What did the Star Disc look like?" Rocky asked with the slightest hint of aggravation in his voice.

They had searched the kitchen twice. Beatrice didn't look half as annoyed as Rocky, but she was mumbling something about "Saint Anthony, please come around" as she peeked under a chair. Their search had certainly not been helped by a power surge that knocked out the lights.

"Wait. Where are Gemini and your monkey?" Rocky used a chair to pull himself off the floor.

The power surged back on.

Leo cupped his hands and yelled, "Gemini? Dante? Where are you guys?!"

There was no answer.

"They have been known to start a game of hide-and-seek without telling me I am playing."

Beatrice bit her bottom lip. "Great. If you were a five-hundred-pound lion, where would you hide?"

A pained yelp resounded from inside the mansion.

Beatrice hurdled a thin leather sofa as she ran deeper into the house, racing toward the sound. Leo was right on her heels. Rocky shuffled behind them, setting his own pace.

"If there's something that can hurt a robot, why are we running *toward* it?"

Beatrice and Leo ran up a staircase, taking the steps two at a time, and dashed around a corner into Peter Wynn's study. She instantly remembered why she'd always found this to be the most impressive room in the house. The buttressed ceiling was stark white aside from a brilliant golden compass painted in the center. Bookshelves rose from floor to ceiling on three of the walls, holding Peter's personally curated collection of over a thousand volumes. And the fourth wall was an arched panel of glass that looked out over the Ticino River.

On the far side of the room, Dante lay on the floor. Gemini nudged him with his snout, but the little monkey was unresponsive. Two jumper cables, a red one and a blue one, trailed from Dante's chest.

Leo frantically ran to them and scooped up Dante. A disturbingly heavy weight yanked at Dante's chest. Leo followed the cables to the floor and saw Dante was attached to the Star Disc. He frantically disconnected the jumper cables.

"Gemini, what happened?" The big cat sheepishly looked at the floor. He circled around Leo three times then pressed his head into a corner, refusing to look at Leo.

Beatrice picked up the disc, carefully turning it over in her hands. A soft orange light emanated from a small notch on one side of the device.

Leo held up Dante. "His batteries are old. He needs to give himself a jump every other day."

Leo gave Gemini a guilty look. "Usually *somebody* is nice enough to let Dante connect to his biodiesel engine for a jump start. But I guess *somebody* decided to let Dante connect to the Star Disc instead."

Gemini scratched his paws into the wall and gave an apologetic whine. Beatrice opened up Dante's chest compartment. She put her hand on his battery and held it there for a second.

"His batteries are hot, but they haven't melted," she reassured Leo.

"Gemini, come here, please." Gemini trotted over to Leo with his tail between his legs. "I'm sorry, but you have to be delicate with Dante—he's not as sturdy as you are."

Gemini nuzzled into Leo's neck.

Rocky leaned in and mumbled quietly to Beatrice, "He apologizes to these things like they have feelings?"

She ignored Rocky and watched Leo work. He tugged Gemini toward a power outlet. Then he connected the blue jumper cable to one of Gemini's upper fangs and the red cable to a lower fang. "Now he needs a system reboot."

He gently connected the jumper cables to Dante's chest, then plugged Gemini's tail into the outlet.

The little monkey zapped to life. He bounced up, performed

a back handspring, and walked on his hands. "Yes, yes. We're all impressed."

Beatrice leaned in and whispered to Rocky, "So the robot monkey is fine, but a second on the Star Disc was too much? How? It doesn't even seem to be on."

Rocky nodded. "We've got to find out what's in that disc."

CHAPTER 36

Leo was exhausted. He had hardly slept in the past two days, and it was catching up with him. "Can I see my bedroom?"

Beatrice and Rocky walked Leo toward the biggest bedroom in the house. Gemini trotted in and out of every room along the way, with Dante riding on his back.

They stopped outside a bedroom door. Beatrice took a deep breath. "Leo, we have to tell you something."

The hair on the back of Leo's neck stood up. When you grow up like Leo, bad news is like a subway train: you feel it coming before it arrives. He knew everything seemed too good to be true.

"We want to take a look at the Star Disc."

Leo let out a quick snort-laugh as he handed Rocky his backpack with the disc inside it. "Is that all? Sure. Knock yourself out. Is it rude if I take the biggest room?"

Beatrice's knees buckled as Gemini brushed against her. "It's your house. You can take whichever room you want."

Leo scooted past her and opened the door to his new bedroom.

A simple platform bed, raised two feet off the ground, pressed against the wall closest to the door. The only other furniture was a long oak table and two inviting leather chairs. The far wall was an arched pane of glass, similar to the study. The midmorning sun bathed the room in warm light. Leo took it all in slowly. "Yeah, I can't wait to make a mess of this place."

"You haven't seen the coolest part yet." Beatrice walked to the window and turned a knob. The ceiling transformed into a clear blue sky. "The roof is made out of electrochromic glass. You can program it to appear to be just about anything."

Rocky took the Star Disc out of Leo's backpack and gently placed it on the oak table. "We should tell you why we'd like to take a closer look at the Star Disc."

For the next few minutes, Beatrice and Rocky explained what they knew about Peter's pursuit of a cold fusion reactor and how they were certain he had left them clues to find it, and instead they'd found Leo.

Leo failed to hide his yawn. "I'm psyched my dad meant for me to find it, but how does it work?"

"That's why we want to take it into the lab at Wynn Toys. Let someone with more engineering expertise than a robot monkey take a look at it." Dante took off his shoe and raised it at Rocky, who ignored him. "Because we don't even know how to turn the thing on yet."

"Oh, it turns on when you touch it," Leo explained.

Rocky poked the disc. He swiped his finger on top of it. Finally, he picked it up and hugged it, but nothing happened; it remained a dense, round paperweight.

"Huh? Weird," Leo said as he reached out and put his hand on it.

An orange light zipped around the "Project Leo: Star Disc" label as it booted up.

"I guess it only works for me."

CHAPTER 37

While Leo napped, Rocky went over the Star Disc with a jeweler's loupe. The first thing he wanted to understand was why the disc was so much heavier than it looked.

The only break in the smooth surface of the charcoal-colored Frisbee was the port on the underside, where Dante had plugged in his jumper cables. Rocky was looking at the port's notch with his wearable microscope when the disc powered down again. As gently as he could, he pressed the disc into Leo's hand until it booted up again.

"Peter had the same problem. Generating a sustained reaction was the last hurdle to a viable fusion reactor." Rocky sighed.

"What do you mean, 'Peter had the same problem'?" Beatrice asked, her jaw clenched.

"He could get the reactor to boot up, but a sustained, controlled reaction remained out of reach." If Rocky had looked up from the disc, he would've seen Beatrice's facial expression, which made it clear she was mad. Very, very mad.

"How do you know *that*?" she asked.

Rocky finally caught the look on Beatrice's face. "Wuh-oh. Did I not mention that detail at trivia bingo? It was in Peter's notebook."

Leo stirred. "What's trivia bingo? That sounds like my kind of game."

Beatrice's expression changed but her tone was just as firm. "Rocky, I thought you didn't *'really see'* what was in that notebook."

"I mean, yeah, I caught a glimpse of Peter's plans. Though getting a sustained, controlled reaction has been the last hurdle for anyone who's *ever* tried to make cold fusion work."

"We have to see what's in that notebook."

"Nick is my uncle, yes?" Leo asked sheepishly. "Won't he want to share my dad's notebook with me?"

Rocky roared with laughter. "You've got a lot to learn about your uncle, kid. The last time we saw him, he had two of his pint-sized goons chase us out of Wynn Tower."

"My uncle has 'pint-sized goons'? What does that mean?" Leo asked.

"He won't hire anyone taller than him. It's one of his many, many insecurities. We ended up diving into the garbage chute to get away from him. I've showered three times since then, but I still can't get the smell of doll poop out of my hair and—"

"Your uncle is a *difficult* man, to put it mildly," Beatrice interrupted. "Even though the Beacon confirmed you're Peter's son, I bet Nick will not give up his fifty-one percent ownership of Wynn Toys easily."

Rocky took off the jeweler's loupe to adjust his glasses. "And there's no way he's going to hand over Peter's notebook."

"Then there's only one way to handle this." Beatrice picked up the keys to the Cadillac. "We're going to Wynn Tower and we're going to steal that notebook."

CHAPTER 38

On the ride to Wynn Tower, Leo was in a much happier mood than Beatrice. Mostly because it was the first time he got to sit in the front seat of a car. Dante was in his lap, and they could hear Gemini pining in the trunk. They had coaxed Gemini into the car by taking the tennis ball from the garage—the one that hung from the ceiling to warn you from pulling in too far—and tossing it into the trunk.

"Again, once we arrive at Wynn Tower, let me do all the talking. Got it, Rocky?" Beatrice reminded them.

Rocky, who was dozing in the back seat, gave a lazy thumbs-up.

Beatrice's shoulders were exhausted from holding the Cadillac's steering wheel—it had been so long since she'd driven a car that didn't drive itself. "I have a plan to get into your uncle's office."

"Won't my uncle be *in* his office?" Leo stared at the glass-flat water of a canal that ran parallel to the highway.

"No. Someone is going to distract him."

"Who?"

"You." Beatrice smiled.

Beatrice pulled the car up to the Wynn Toys gate. Normally, the gate would sense her parking pass and open automatically. But less than twenty-four hours before, she and Rocky had outrun Nick and a couple of guys to get away. Now she was trying to get back in, driving a dented Cadillac. Entering through the front gate was so obvious it was borderline nuts—making it the last thing Nick Wynn would expect.

A pudgy guard stopped demolishing a hoagie to wave at the old Cadillac. "Welcome to Wynn Toys. Do you have an appointment?" he asked with a tone that suggested he expected a no.

Beatrice rolled down her window. "Do I need an appointment, Gil?"

Gil dropped his sandwich and punched the Open button so many times the gate opened and closed repeatedly. "So sorry, Miss Portinari. I don't believe we have this car of yours in our records—"

"Oh. So this is *my* fault?"

The guard cringed. "No. Not at all, ma'am. I'm sorry for the inconvenience."

The gate finally opened wide and Beatrice drove onto the Wynn campus. Fortune favors the bold.

"That guy was scared of you." Leo stuck his head out the window for a moment to admire Wynn Tower.

Beatrice winced. "I'm not usually like that. I don't want my employees to be scared of me. When people fear you, they're less likely to share their ideas."

Rocky snickered. "Your uncle would rather be feared than loved."

As they passed by the tulip streetlights, pointing upward to drink in the midday sun, Beatrice noticed a group of stout men pouring out of the base of Wynn Tower.

As she drove closer, she realized who they were.

"Roll up your window," Beatrice demanded.

One man stood in the middle of the road and raised his hand. Beatrice stopped. She started to reverse but stopped again. More men had lined up behind them.

Rocky sat up in the back seat. He did a drum roll with his hands on the back of Leo's seat. "And here they are, folks—Nick Wynn's Itty-bitty No Pity Committee."

A swarm of security guards surrounded their car. And each guard had pulled out their stun gun.

CHAPTER 39

"Is this like very special CEO parking?" Leo asked.

"Turn off the engine and step out of the vehicle, Miss Portinari," the guard directly in front of the Cadillac demanded.

Sensing the tension, Gemini growled in the trunk.

"I don't want Gemini to attack them," Beatrice said.

"Don't worry. He's never attacked anyone. People just get confused when he's playing with them."

"Miss Portinari, I will give you until the count of three." The guard started to count.

"One—"

"Okay. We are going to come out, but only if you put down your stun guns."

"Two—"

"I have something really important to show the board."

Beatrice recognized the guard next to the leader—Victor. He could be her way out.

"Victor! We've known each other for ten years. Tell them this is all a misunderstanding—"

"Victor is lucky he still has a job. Victor believed some nonsense you told him about a lion that ate your shoes. You're clearly going through some kind of mental break—"

Beatrice pulled switch under the steering wheel and popped the trunk. Gemini leapt onto the road. Instinctively, every guard took two steps back.

"A 'mental breakdown,' huh?" she yelled as she got out of the car.

Leo opened the passenger-side door and stepped onto the pavement. "Gemini, here, boy." The big cat ambled over to Leo, the tennis ball pinched gently between his fangs. Leo grabbed the tennis ball from him and Gemini lowered his whole body into a crouch, ready to play.

"Victor, I trust you, and you trust me. Please tell the other guards to back off. We're going inside to sort out this situation with Nick Wynn. Everyone here will keep their job." Beatrice pointed at the guard in front of her car. "Except *this* guy."

Victor looked at his boss then lowered his stun gun. "Guys . . . I think she's cool."

The other guards followed suit, except for their boss, who was blocking the road.

"I'm not putting up with this—"

"Go get it!" Leo threw the tennis ball to the boss, who made the mistake of catching it. Gemini knocked him over and pinned him to the ground, licking him until he coughed up the ball.

The guard tried to reach for his stun gun, but Rocky kicked it away. "Try it, bub, and next thing you know, we'll be playing fetch with your arm."

Leo whispered to Beatrice, "Do you need Gemini for your plan?"

"No—"

"Gemini, stay."

Gemini carefully lowered his butt onto the guard's feet. The guard started to howl, so Beatrice popped the tennis ball into his mouth.

"But I do need you and Dante," Beatrice said as she pulled a long nylon rope out of the trunk.

CHAPTER 40

Leo followed Beatrice across the factory floor. New toys and gadgets flew through the lattice of tubes overhead. A few of the employees seemed startled to see Beatrice back in the building. She kept moving until Leo stopped at a glass case that was half filled with water. At first, he had thought it was an aquarium.

"Whoa! Is that a Mocean?" Leo pointed at two emerald rectangles submerged under the water.

"It sure is. Kinda funny that Wynn's first big hit was a pool toy. I mean, it was one of your dad's most impressive feats of engineering. People tell me all the time that the Mocean was how they learned to surf. Do you surf?"

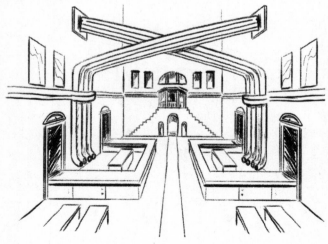

Leo shook his head, too embarrassed to tell her he couldn't even ride a bike yet, much less surf.

"Well, all it takes is those two little panels to create six-foot-high waves in a pool, so maybe sometime . . ." Beatrice laid out a whole plan for teaching him how to surf, but Leo had moved past the Mocean, and a Kaboomerang, and on to another glass case.

"Is that the *original* Claw?" Leo pressed his face to the glass and pointed at a gadget sitting on a red velvet pillow. Protruding from a black cuff were four ferocious fingers, each one colored in a checkerboard pattern. Taken as a whole, the device looked like a more menacing version of an arcade crane.

"Yes. That's the first Claw. Your dad and I worked on the prototype together. In fact, that denim cuff was custom fitted for his forearm. We wanted to make the claws look a little friendlier, so we used the same checkerboard pattern as the Vans sneakers your dad wore all the time. Which is why the internet nicknamed that toy—"

"Jean Clawed Vans Hand." Leo squatted down to see the undercarriage of the device.

The Claw was a legendary toy, a grappling hook with special sensors to prevent it from attacking little brothers or a neighbor's window. Leo desperately wanted to try it on. He wanted to feel the contours of something that had been custom made for his father. But as Leo was about to ask Beatrice, he noticed people were staring at them.

The whispers had begun the moment Beatrice and Leo walked into Wynn Tower. Workers passed along word of her arrival, and the news carried through the building like a wave. A few people had shouted encouragement. "Good to have you back!" "We were worried you had left!" But that joy was quickly curtailed by the arrival of Nick Wynn.

"Ah. Miss Portinari, you've returned to tender your resignation, yes?" Nick sneered.

"Not exactly, Nick. There's someone I'd like you to meet. He's here to see Wynn Tower." Beatrice nudged Leo forward.

Nick didn't even look at Leo. Nick only ever paid attention to people who could help him or get in his way. Everyone else was invisible. So while he talked to Leo, he only looked at Beatrice. "Miss Portinari should have brought you for a tour of our wonderful facility on a day when she wasn't going to be fired, yes? Perhaps Customer Appreciation Day. It's in August, no?"

"You cancelled Customer Appreciation Day," Beatrice told him.

"Well, they should have appreciated it while we had it."

She grabbed Leo's hand and tried to slide past Nick to get into the boardroom. But Nick lowered his staff between her and Leo, then thumped Leo across the chest.

"What business does this little boy have in the boardroom?"

"Let him pass and you'll find out."

Nick raised his right eyebrow and finally appraised Leo. All while Beatrice gave Nick the dirtiest look she could muster.

At first, Leo wanted to hug Nick. He wanted to shout, "Hi! I am your nephew! I am so excited to meet my dad's brother! When were you going to look for me? Why did you let me spend so many years thinking I was alone?" But the way Nick looked at him—like Nick did not want him within a thousand miles of Wynn Tower—that look shook Leo to his core. He had already seen enough of his uncle to last him a lifetime.

So Leo let Beatrice bicker with Nick and kept his attention focused on the tubes overhead. Dante skipped across them before he jumped to the wall. Then he silently swung across a series of sconces sixty feet above the factory floor. The first part of their plan to steal Peter's notebook was swinging into place. Literally.

Leo forced himself to listen to Beatrice and Nick's conversation again.

"Fine, Beatrice, have it your way. But bringing a customer is a bit *dramatic* for your final board meeting, yes?" Reluctantly, Nick let them pass. He plugged his staff into the port outside of the boardroom door.

"Cromwell, open."

Cromwell initiated a scan of Leo's face, but Nick angrily waved his hand between Leo's face and the scanner. "No. We don't have time for that. He's just some kid; I say he's fine. Open up."

The door opened silently, and Leo, Beatrice, and Nick entered the long, narrow boardroom. The other five board members were seated around a conference table. The table was built out of thousands of toy building blocks, with the Wynn Toys logo spelled out in the center in platinum blocks.

The board member closest to the door smiled. "Beatrice! I

must say this is a surprise. Nick told us he confronted you while you were with a former employee who stole from Wynn—"

"That's not true. That former employee was working with me on an assignment for Wynn Toys."

"An assignment? From who?"

"Peter Wynn."

CHAPTER 41

Seven floors above the boardroom, where an argument had just erupted, Dante was hanging upside down, dangling from the doorframe to Nick's office. The door was locked. And Beatrice's plan had not accounted for a locked door.

After trying the door a few times, he decided to wait patiently for Leo to finish his meeting. Leo would know what to do. Suddenly, a calm voice spoke to Dante. "Sir, if you connect your jumper cables to the socket, it will short out the power to the door, granting you entry."

Dante peered around but didn't see anyone. He gave a grateful wave anyway.

"No need to thank me. It is my mandate," Cromwell replied.

"What do you mean? Are you saying Peter is *alive*?!" a board member asked hopefully.

"I'm not sure if Peter is alive." Beatrice pulled the Beacon Map from her purse. The blue orb floated over her shoulder as she put her hand on Leo's shoulder. "But his son is. This is Leo Wynn."

Beatrice had braced herself for an angry reaction from Nick, but she did not expect the range of emotions that played out on his face. There was shock, which soon gave way to fear before settling into a moment of unmistakable vulnerability. For the first time, Beatrice saw Nick in a moment of weakness. But he shook it off and snatched the blue orb that floated over Beatrice's shoulder.

"You've got a double cowlick, just like your dad!" Leon Battista, a board member who had been one of Peter's closest friends, said as he tousled Leo's hair.

"How can you be certain this is Peter's son?" countered Cesar Borgia, a board member who had been chosen by Nick.

"Leo, do you mind if the Beacon Map scans you again?"

Leo nodded to Beatrice that he was fine with that.

Nick begrudgingly released the orb, and it floated in front of Leo, then pinged. "Malfunction."

"Run it again," Beatrice insisted.

Nick toggled the power switch on the Beacon Map and released it. Again, the orb floated in front of Leo for a second before it pinged. "Malfunction."

Nick snickered. "Malfunction? That must be his mother's maiden name, yes?"

Beatrice grabbed the orb from Nick. She started to fiddle with it, but her concentration was broken by the ear-piercing wail of an alarm.

CHAPTER 42

"Mister Wynn, your office window was just shattered," Cromwell intoned.

"It's a burglary, yes?" Nick shoved his way out of the boardroom and toward a flight of stairs.

"Your safe was hurled out of your office window, sir."

"What? By who?!"

"A monkey, sir."

"Alert security!"

"I already have, sir. I synced all security cameras to the monkey's anticipated location."

"Good job, Cromwell."

"It is my mandate."

Beatrice squashed a pair of Koosh Balls against Leo's ears to protect them from the alarm as they hustled out of the boardroom. Once they were out on the factory floor, she pulled him toward the exit.

"Was this not part of the plan?" Leo shouted to be heard over the alarm.

"No. Dante was supposed to lower the safe. That's why we gave him the rope."

They dashed outside, around a corner, and into the road next to Wynn Tower. The Cadillac was parked right where they'd left it, except now the back half was smashed in, sporting a dent shaped conspicuously like a safe.

"We gotta go!" she yelled to Rocky.

"We were waiting on you!"

"Where's Dante?"

Dante squealed, but it sounded like he was at the bottom of a well. At least one hundred feet of nylon rope was haphazardly strewn around the car.

"So you just chucked it out the window?" Leo laughed.

Dante gave a long, low grunt.

"Beatrice, get in!" Rocky demanded.

She had barely shut the door when Rocky jammed his foot on the gas pedal. The engine roared, and Beatrice braced herself, expecting the Cadillac to rocket forward and fishtail around the corner.

But the car didn't move.

"Uh-oh." Rocky frowned.

He got out and looked under the car. He did not like what he saw. The car's frame was destroyed.

"Let's go. Everybody out."

"Why? What's wrong?" Beatrice asked.

Rocky gave the hood of the Cadillac a dejected slap. "Two tons of Detroit steel. They don't build 'em like they used to. Can't even withstand a fifty-pound safe crashing through the trunk from seven stories up."

Another alarm sounded and the tulip streetlights flashed an angry red.

"Those are Lockdown Lights. Nick just cancelled our key card access to every Wynn Toys building." Beatrice anxiously spun around, searching for an exit. "We need to go. Now!"

A security guard raced around the corner, his stun gun already snapping. But when he saw them, he stopped and took off his helmet.

Victor raised a finger to his lips and made the *shhhh* motion. He waved them over to a garage door and pressed his badge against it. There was a deep *gu-gunk* as the bolt unlocked. Beatrice silently squeezed Victor's hand to thank him, then she and Leo climbed on top of Gemini. Rocky walked as fast as he could beside them.

"What are we doing? We need someplace to hide and open up the safe," Rocky complained.

A determined glare from Beatrice quietly communicated two things to him: one, stop talking; and, two, she knew exactly where they were going.

CHAPTER 43

Beatrice shouted to be heard over the waterfall of discarded devices piling up in the far corner of the room. "Rocky, lock it behind you."

On the other side of the door, the Lockdown Lights still flashed red, the alarms still cried, and they could hear guards shouting directions at each other.

Leo started firing off questions immediately. "What is this place? What's with that thing on the shelf? Why is it locked under glass? And *what* is that sucking sound?"

Beatrice patiently answered his questions. "This is Wynn's Waste and Recycling Room. That thing under the glass is a new game console we've been working on called the Arcage. Your dad wrote the original code for it on a napkin—"

"Cool, cool, cool. Can I play it?"

Rocky grunted. "That depends. How's your health insurance?"

"The Arcage is not quite ready yet, but we have really high hopes for it. It's going to debut at the Milan Toy Fair in a couple of days," Beatrice deflected.

Leo picked up one of the phones spilling out of the corner. "Whoa. Are these phones just like trash? Can I have one?"

"Not one of those. But we will absolutely get you a phone," Beatrice promised.

"When?"

"As soon as we are not hiding from men with stun guns." She tried to sound reassuring.

"But don't stand too close to that pile, bub. All of that gets sucked into the sorting tube every five minutes," Rocky warned.

Leo thought the screen of the phone he was holding was covered in a spiderweb, but when he swiped the screen, it nicked him. A thin sliver of shattered glass lodged in the tip of his finger. "Ouch! What *is* this place?"

"This is where we've been doing private research." Beatrice walked Gemini over to Rocky. "We were worried Mach Valley might have a spy at Wynn Toys, so we worked on a few things in secret down here, where Nick never comes."

"Think of it as a device development lab . . . that is also a device toilet," Rocky said as he plugged Gemini's tail into an extension cord.

"It's the best we could do on short notice."

Gemini purred then opened his chest cavity. The safe fell onto the floor with a loud thump. Then Dante fell out on top of the safe.

The cyborg simian squealed and scampered onto Leo's shoulder. He crossed his arms and pouted at Gemini.

"Dude, don't be mad at Gemini. He had to hide you, or you would've been seen by the cameras."

Dante clicked his teeth.

"Well, where else was he supposed to store the safe? When the plan falls apart, you have to improvise."

Beatrice squatted down and lifted the safe until it was standing upright. Two silver panels broke off of the front and back of the safe, revealing smaller, coal-black panels underneath.

"Oh no. It's one of those."

Rocky stood next to her and sarcastically clapped his hands. "Bravo, Nick! You remain the best at being the worst."

"What is it?" Leo asked tentatively.

"Nick stored your dad's notebook in an IncinerSafe. Our consumer division stopped making them ten years ago. We only get one chance to guess the right password."

"Or then what?"

"It burns the contents inside."

CHAPTER 44

Beatrice and Rocky sat across from each other, brainstorming ideas for what the password could be, while Leo played fetch with Gemini and the tennis ball.

"It's only four digits. What four numbers could be the most meaningful to Nick?" Beatrice tapped her pen on the table.

"His birthday? The third of May—0503?"

"Too obvious."

"You're right. The only way we'll crack that safe is if we can think like him. What would my password be if I was a pretentious jerk?"

"Rocky . . ." Beatrice cocked her head toward Leo. "C'mon."

"Oh, you're right. I shouldn't say things like that—"

"Thank you."

"He should be allowed to come to his own conclusion about how his uncle is a pretentious jerk."

Across the room, Leo picked up another phone. He held down the power button, and the home screen came to life as it started to boot up.

"This phone still has some juice left in it. Why don't I just search the internet for the safest way to hack into an IncinerSafe?"

Rocky and Beatrice leapt to their feet. "No-no-no!"

Rocky grabbed the phone out of his hand and chucked it down the sorting chute. It made an awful sound, like a Transformer farting, as the glass and aluminum popped.

"Sorry, Leo. It's just that connecting to the internet will put you on the network. And that would alert Cromwell to our location," Beatrice explained.

Dante clapped his hands and let out a little cry. Leo translated, "Dante says Cromwell helped him get into Nick's office so he could retrieve the safe."

Beatrice patted Dante on the head. "Cromwell's mandate is 'To make the most efficient company in the world.' Keeping Peter's notebook locked away was deeply inefficient."

"Cromwell was the last thing your dad invented, although Nick used to brag like he came up with it. I'm sure he finds a way to bring it up at all his Yale reunions."

Beatrice clapped her hands. "That's it."

"What's it?" Leo asked. "I'm so confused."

"Y-A-L-E. So 9–2–5–3 on a keypad."

Rocky high-fived her. "Don't take this the wrong way, BP, but you do an *amazing* job of thinking like a pretentious fool."

Leo bounced the tennis ball behind Rocky and Beatrice as they gathered around the safe. Gemini crouched into position—he desperately wanted Leo to throw the ball.

Rocky pressed 9, 2, and 5. "Here we go."

He took a deep breath, then pressed the 3. The red light on the IncinerSafe's keypad flashed from red to green.

"Yes! It worked."

But their joy quickly turned to terror as they saw what was inside the door of the safe. Another keypad. And next to the keypad, a clock was counting down from 30, 29, 28 . . .

CHAPTER 45

"Maybe try 9–2–5–3 again?" Rocky asked.

"He'd never use the same password twice."

The clock continued its countdown. 19, 18, 17 . . .

There was a scramble around the room as they tried to figure out how to handle the safe. Rocky ripped open lockers looking for oven mitts. Beatrice smashed the glass case and pulled out the fire extinguisher. Dante grabbed the Arcage, stored it in his chest, scurried into the rafters, and hid in a nook.

"Should we throw it outside?" Rocky yelled.

"We can't or Nick will know we're in here!"

Leo dropped the tennis ball and desperately searched around for something—anything—that could help. The ball rolled under the safe and wedged itself there.

Beatrice grabbed Leo and pushed him behind the desk, using her body to shield him from the IncinerSafe before it incinerated.

At first, it was hard to tell whether the terrible sound of metal tearing into metal was coming from the safe or from the sorting chute. But then Leo tapped Beatrice on the shoulder. He pointed at Gemini, who was happily wagging his tail with a tennis ball between his fangs, wisps of smoke trailing from two of his whiskers.

"I hope you didn't want to keep the safe. Gemini's ball rolled under it, so he tore it apart."

CHAPTER 46

Rocky carefully removed a notebook from the safe. The corners were singed.

Balancing it in front of his face, he pursed his lips and softly blew ash off of the cover. Beatrice stood with the fire extinguisher cocked and ready. Gemini was prancing around the room with his tail in the air because Leo had told him he was a good boy.

"That lion of yours is a genius. When he ripped off the door, he also tore away the two little canisters of napalm. They couldn't douse what was inside. Tell him again he's a good boy."

Leo patted Gemini once more so he'd know that he was in fact the good boy they were talking about. Gemini dropped his slobbery tennis ball at Leo's feet.

Rocky removed a singed dust jacket covering the notebook, then pinched it on the corner and delicately placed it in the center of the table.

Beatrice put down the fire extinguisher. "When you handle something that delicately, it's either an ancient artifact or a brand-new laptop."

Gemini picked up his tennis ball again and dropped it at Leo's feet, then whined and nudged his head into the back of Leo's legs, but Leo was too focused on the notebook. He watched Rocky turn the pages using a pair of tweezers.

"So far it's a list of ingredients: heavy water, electrolytes,

232

deuterium." After what appeared to be careful deliberation, Rocky turned to the next page.

"Deuterium? Isn't that heavy hydrogen?" Leo asked.

Gemini whined louder as his tennis ball rolled near the chute.

"Yes. All of those ingredients are essential components for cold fusion." Beatrice pointed at numbers on the page.

Gemini let out a sharp, hard growl as the chute swallowed his tennis ball. He trotted back to the table and poked his nose into Beatrice's purse. He emerged with something between his teeth. Leo frowned and went to check what his lion was chewing on.

As he did, he heard Rocky turn to the next page, then gasp.

"Want to guess why that Star Disc is so heavy, kid?"

Leo thought about it as he wrestled the broken Beacon Map out of Gemini's mouth.

Rocky pointed to a diagram. "It's encased in moscovium. It's the 115th element on the periodic table, but it's never been found in a stable form. There have been some wild theories about what it *could* do if anyone ever got their hands on a pile of it, but no one has ever been able to make stable moscovium."

Beatrice adjusted her safety glasses. "Then again, a lot of things were just theories until your dad came along."

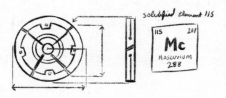

CHAPTER 47

Beatrice and Rocky grouped gauges around the table in an exuberant ballet of engineering. They lined up their instruments over the Star Disc and barked information to each other.

Rocky concentrated a blue flame at the side of the disc. "Focused flame on the Bunsen burner set at 700 degrees; no sign of melting."

Beatrice used a medicine dropper to dab a drop of some liquid onto the disc. "First acid reaction test is hydrogen peroxide, pH of 4.5 . . . No reaction."

Leo half listened while using his shirt to wipe Gemini's slobber off of the Beacon Map. An almost imperceptibly thin layer of film over the eye was particularly hard to wipe off. When he was sure he'd gotten all of it, he pressed his thumb into the eye until the ball blazed to life and hovered in front of him.

"Scanning." The orb pinged. "Positive match, Leonardo Wynn."

Beatrice snatched the orb out of the air. "No, no, no. Shut it off!"

Leo cringed. "Yeeesh. I'm sorry."

"It's okay. Again, we have to be careful."

Leo could feel that he was getting on Beatrice's nerves. She gave the Beacon Map a quizzical look. "Why is this thing working now?"

"Oh, I cleaned the lens. There was this tacky layer of film over it, and I—"

Beatrice's expression shifted to pure, unadulterated rage. "Nick . . ."

Nick had made his escape while the Lockdown Lights were still flashing. The campus of Wynn Toys was pandemonium, but Nick calmly tiptoed out of the boardroom and down to his parking space. He tapped his phone screen three times to put it in Minion Mode. That way, when his underlings called, they'd speak to an automated program that sounded like Nick. He was already in his car, mentally composing his argument for what should be done about Beatrice and the boy, when his phone buzzed. He pressed Accept and braced himself for a torrent of fury.

"Go for Nick Wynn . . ."

There was no sound on the other end. They had hung up.

His phone buzzed again. He'd received a text. He drew a figure eight on the car's home screen to put it into automatic pilot, then he opened the message.

The text consisted of no words, only a map. In the center of the map was a pin. He was to rendezvous at that pin, which was less than two miles away.

The car turned hard right down a dirt road, slamming Nick against the door.

"Cromwell, you're still controlling the vehicle, yes?" Nick asked, his voice failing to hide his anxiety.

"It appears the automatic pilot is being steered by your phone, sir."

The car suffered jolts and scrapes as it pushed through the brush and into a wide clearing. It arrived at their destination but kept driving. Nick took a second glance at the pin. It had moved—and was now smack-dab in the middle of the pond.

"Cromwell, driving into the middle of the pond seems like a bad idea, yes?"

"Would that I could do something, sir."

Nick tried to unlock the door and roll out, but the doors wouldn't budge. The car sped up as it approached the edge of the water, then *splash*! It plowed into middle of the pond, water already rising halfway up his window. In a panic, Nick kicked at the window. He lifted his legs to kick at it again when a flat voice said to him, "Shatter that window and you will die."

Nick flopped back in his seat and the car stopped. The water had nearly reached the top of the windows.

Suddenly, the sunroof opened. Nick scrambled onto the top of the car and squirmed. His expensive shoes were ruined.

A flock of birds appeared from around the hill. But as the flock got closer, Nick heard it: the buzz. He quickly realized these were not mere birds. That buzz was the unmistakable sound of thousands upon thousands of propellers working in syncopated harmony.

The drones shifted form into a hollow, tubular shape. The flock swooped down and enveloped Nick, slamming into the back of his knees so that he was thrown back into a crude chamber the drones had morphed into.

Nick didn't speak. He knew where he was headed.

He'd been summoned to Mach Valley to answer for his failure with Beatrice. But he held on to the thin hope that his trick with the Beacon Map had been enough.

CHAPTER 48

Leo loved that Beatrice was furious on his behalf. "Nick doctored the Beacon Map when he grabbed it. The lens was covered. That's why it couldn't scan you."

Rocky gritted his teeth. "Your uncle is as crooked as a dog's leg. He doesn't want the board to know you're the real deal."

Beatrice tinkered with the Star Disc. "Though if we can show them an invention from Peter they haven't seen yet . . ."

Rocky nodded. "Better yet, an invention Peter left specifically for the boy."

Leo paced around the room, Gemini by his side, sure he was missing something with the Star Disc. There must be some way to get it to stay on without Leo touching it. Finally, he asked if he could take another look at his dad's notebook.

"Absolutely." Rocky smiled and carefully slid the notebook across the table. "Let's see if you got the Wynn family penchant for problem-solving."

"We can only build a theory from what we know. What we know about moscovium is that it's incredibly dense. And what we know about my dad's project, this Star Disc, is that he was trying to make a cold fusion reactor."

"What we don't know is how it works or how to keep it on." Beatrice poked the Star Disc again.

"Or how to look inside." Rocky turned the blue flame up higher and winced. "You got any ideas on how to open this bad boy up?"

Leo hastily leafed through the notebook, trying to absorb as much information as he could. A few times he touched his dad's chicken scratch handwriting, surprised by how similar it was to his own. He was trying to think of a reason his dad would've left this device buried beneath his school, but not left him with any idea of how to make it work.

"It's weird he wouldn't leave me instructions, right?" Leo asked them.

"There's nothing in the notebook. And the dust jacket is mostly burnt—" Rocky said.

"What dust jacket?" Leo perked up.

"It was singed when our expert safecracker finessed his way past the lock." Rocky pointed toward Gemini, who gave him a low growl.

Leo picked up the dust jacket and instantly knew his father *had* left him instructions for the Star Disc. Very specific instructions. Because on the inside of the dust jacket, his father had drawn a series of musical notes—the exact same notes that were on the piano in his bedroom at the Academy of Florence.

CHAPTER 49

"Those musical notes opened the door to the North tunnel. They have to be how we get into the disc," Leo told them eagerly.

Beatrice perked up, excited the trail Peter had left for them hadn't gone cold.

"Great. Now all we need is a piano. There's a baby grand in the auditorium," Rocky suggested.

Beatrice pursed her lips. "We'd have to wait until the alarms are shut off—"

"Don't worry. We already have the notes here with us." Leo cupped his hands and called up to Dante. "Dante, come on down. It's your time to shine."

Dante swung from pipe to pipe high above them, then wrapped his tail around an exhaust pipe, gracefully changing directions so he could land in front of Gemini after no fewer than three totally unnecessary flips.

He puffed out his chest and yipped at Gemini, who rolled his eyes.

"Yes. We cannot possibly do this without you. Show a little hustle," Leo told him.

Dante hopped onto the table next to the Star Disc and opened up his chest. The Arcage spilled out.

Beatrice cocked an eyebrow. "Why does he have the Arcage?"

Leo cringed. "Yeah. Sorry. He tends to squirrel away anything that seems expensive and isn't bolted down. He was programmed that way."

Dante bowed to Beatrice to apologize. He wouldn't stop until she acknowledged him. "Fine. Apology accepted. But please be careful with that thing."

Dante stood upright and made a short barking noise three times.

"Uhhh, did you just clear your throat?" Leo asked.

Dante nodded.

"I'll allow it because you're so excited, but let's go. Kinda pressed for time here."

With that, Dante turned a knob around his eye and the recording of Leo playing the piano, poorly, squawked to life.

"Here comes the sun . . ."

"I'm usually pretty good, but it had been a while since I played, so . . ." Leo tried to convince Beatrice and Rocky. "Get to the good part, Dante."

Dante fast-forwarded the recording by thirty seconds.

"Here comes the sun, doo-doo-doo-doo . . ."

A ring around the Star Disc blazed to life. Rocky crouched behind a chair and Leo ducked under the table. Beatrice didn't move. She smiled as she watched a warm, orange glow radiate around the circumference of the device.

Leo saw that Beatrice wasn't afraid, so he slinked out from under the table, then reached out, tentatively, and touched the disc. He had expected it would be hot because of all the light it was producing, but there was no heat. Gentle vibrations pulsed somewhere inside it.

A thin blue outline encircled his fingers. Leo pulled his fingers away before the machine hissed and opened like a clamshell.

Rocky and Beatrice crowded over his shoulder and all of them could see inside. Immediately, Leo understood why the Star Disc had not worked before, and also why it had shorted Dante's circuits. It could generate but not sustain a fusion reaction.

Evidently, Rocky knew that too because he poured a bunch of chemicals into a beaker and lit the burner underneath it.

"First things first, we have to make some heavy water." Rocky dumped a flask marked *activated carbon* into the beaker. "You need heavy water to facilitate a fusion reaction."

"The heavy water will help, but we still need magnetized tubing inside the disc," Leo pointed out.

"Huh. Why?" Rocky asked like he was intrigued by Leo's idea.

"The moscovium will create a magnetic field. But with magnetic tubing in the disc, you would create a magnetic field inside a magnetic field. The reaction will be stronger and run cleaner. In theory, the Star Disc would power itself."

"I know where we can get all the magnetic tubes you will ever need," Beatrice said. "We'll just have to wash the poop off of them."

CHAPTER 50

Nick was freezing. He was flying at 250 miles per hour, 3,000 feet in the air, in an open container. But at least a trip that usually took three hours by car was going to be completed in nineteen minutes.

The swarm swooped low over the first two security gates, then dumped him outside the glass curtain. Once again, he was at Mach Valley ready to defer, to deflect, and if all else failed, to apologize.

"You do not expect a tip for that ride, yes?" Nick slapped his numb hands against his body in a desperate attempt to warm up. One drone broke off from the swarm and stung him in the rear end.

"I am going. I am going," Nick griped before putting on his best fake smile and marching inside the front door to meet his fate.

O was already waiting for him. He was seated next to a roaring fire. As much as Nick urgently wanted to warm himself by the fire as well, he stood out of arm's reach, his teeth chattering away.

"Nick, my good man, I'm so happy you arrived safe and sound. How was your trip?" O asked with cold eyes and curled lips. He seemed to enjoy one thing in this world, and it wasn't his immense power or his gobs and gobs of money—what brought him real happiness was winding up Nick Wynn.

"It was lovely, thank you. The best way to see the country-side this time of year is rattling around inside a flock of your birds." Nick tried to keep his teeth from chattering as he spoke.

"Ahhh, there's the Nick I know and tolerate." He sat back and gestured for Nick to stand next to the fire. Nick reluctantly took several steps closer and felt the heat begin to warm his body. He stopped shivering. He could control his limbs again.

"Nick, I know about the boy, Leonardo," he said, instantly chilling Nick to the bone once again.

"There's no proof he is Peter's son. The testing mechanism on Beacon Maps was notoriously unreliable. The scanner malfunctioned," Nick insisted.

"I perfected that design!" O yelled as he gathered himself to his full height and stared down at Nick, who was at least a foot shorter than the man towering over him. "Are you saying my design was imperfect?"

"No, sir. I think the issue was most likely user error," Nick whimpered.

"Yes. User error." The tension left his voice. "But also, we have a witness to when a Beacon Map previously identified this boy, Leonardo, as Peter's son."

"Sir, I told you. I will deal with Beatrice and the old fool."

"And yet Beatrice and her washed-up assistant are still causing complications." O picked up a fire poker and jammed it into a smoking log, turning it over into the flickering flames. The poker was five feet long and wrought iron, but he handled it like it was a toothpick. He used the hook of the fire poker to pull a wafer-thin piece of silver from the fireplace. Steam hissed as he doused it in a bucket of water.

"Your mask is finished, boy" he announced.

From the shadows, a teenage boy stepped forward. Nick knew he'd be scolded if he averted his eyes, so he tried to keep his gaze forward, but the boy's face was revolting. The left side of his face was covered by branches of blistering scars. All of them seemed to emanate from his disfigured left eye.

But the boy stepped forward confidently and took the mask, delicately placing it over the disfigured side of his face.

"This is the witness. He asserts the boy is Peter's son." O flicked the fire poker back onto its huge hook. Then he took the boy by the shoulders and brought him in front of a mirror so the boy could see himself in his new mask.

"See how handsome you are? Don't you look much better now, Savvy?"

CHAPTER 51

Gemini pouted as Rocky harnessed him to a wagon that was overflowing with Molly-Poops-A-Lots. Leo reached down and scratched under Gemini's chin until the lion wagged his tail.

"Yuck. We hosed them down. Why do they still smell like you bottled the New Jersey Turnpike?" Rocky held a handkerchief in front of his nose to blunt the stink.

"Because gadolinium is a rare metal with a strange property." Leo held up a doll and explained as he walked. "Its temperature increases as it enters a magnetic field and cools as it leaves a magnetic field."

Beatrice stared at Leo as he talked about gadolinium, a half smile forming on her lips.

"So because the dolls were stored like that, it led to a cycle of constant heating and cooling in their intestines. Which means that the stink is pretty much baked in."

Now both Beatrice and Rocky were staring at him with their mouths open.

"But I'm not like a gadolinium expert or anything. Am I getting this wrong?"

"No." Beatrice shook her head and smiled. "You are so clearly your father's son."

"Yeah, you sound real Peter-ish right now," Rocky joked.

"Though you should know who decided to use that weird metal in the Molly-Poops-A-Lot."

"Who?"

"You're looking at her." Rocky pointed at Beatrice as he pulled the guts out of a doll.

Beatrice picked up a big handful of doll guts and dropped them into a black iron bowl. She shut the safety visor on a helmet and fired up a blowtorch. The gadolinium melted together into a pool, and Beatrice quickly transferred the liquid metal into two molds.

As she engineered the tubes, Leo read aloud from his father's notebook.

"First, insert the conductors. Followed by the heavy water. The magnetism of moscovium will interact with the heavy water and pull the hydrogen into a fusion reaction. If you use the right material for the tubing, there is no need to cause the initial reaction itself. But you have to close the Star Disc quickly! You've got about thirty seconds from the time you insert the conductors, hero!" Leo pointed at the diagram and the words in the notebook. "My dad actually wrote that, 'hero'!"

Beatrice snapped the disc shut and lifted her visor. Steam billowed from the device. "Done. With at least twenty seconds to spare."

"I hope we didn't melt the thing. We just figured out how to turn it on." Rocky touched it with his thick welding glove. Then he took off the mitt and touched the disc with his bare hand. "It's still cool."

"*You're* still cool." Beatrice fist-bumped Rocky.

Leo's curiosity got the best of him. He reached out and pressed his finger to the Star Disc. A blue light encircled his fingertips and he felt a slight tickle. He heard a gentle whirring inside the device.

Two symbols appeared next to his fingertips, outlined in that same blue light. One he recognized as the familiar power symbol.

The other symbol was new to Leo. It looked like a horseshoe with two dots above it.

"Do you guys recognize this symbol?" Leo invited them to look at the symbols on the Star Disc.

Beatrice grinned. "That is the symbol for a magnetometer."

"Cool. I think the machine is turning on . . ." Leo tapped the power symbol and two lights lit up next to it. "And it's staying on."

A light began to spin around the circumference of the Star Disc. It got faster and faster with each rotation until soon its cycle was so fast that it was imperceptible; it seemed like one steady orange light.

"God said, 'Let there be light,' and there was light." Beatrice clapped.

"Well, try plugging something into the port and see what happens," Rocky nudged.

Leo grabbed the first thing within arm's reach, the old cell phone he'd picked out of the pile. Its battery read *8%*. He plugged a nearby charger into the port on the bottom, then plugged in the phone.

The phone sprang to life in Leo's hand. "It's ninety percent charged already! In two seconds."

"Look out!" Rocky yanked the charger out of the device. Leo had failed to notice that the cord was on fire.

"It's too much energy." Beatrice touched the disc and was surprised it didn't burn her.

Leo asked, "But what if we did not use a flimsy charger?"

"Good. Because I *think* that is all she wrote for this one," Rocky said sarcastically as he stomped on the embers of the still-flaming cord.

Beatrice reached into her purse and pulled out a stylishly coiled charger. "This is a prototype we almost put into production. Pure silver—the best metal for conducting electricity. Ultimately, Cromwell crunched the numbers and determined we'd never be able to sell enough to turn a profit on them."

Before Beatrice could give it a second thought, Leo grabbed the charger and plugged one end into the Star Disc, then unspooled the other end and plugged it into a USB port on the wall.

The Star Disc glowed and the silver cord shined against the concrete floor as power surged through it.

Leo tapped the power icon a few times until there were five blue lights next to it. Just to see what would happen, he tapped the magnet symbol one time too. The junky phone jumped off the table, smacked into the side of the Star Disc, and stuck there. A big metal filing cabinet nearby started to rattle. Leo realized what was going on and held the magnet symbol, turning it off. The phone fell harmlessly onto the table.

"Whoa. Those symbols on the disc are like volume buttons. One is for the power, the other one is for the magnet."

Rocky walked the length of the silver cord to the wall. "Do you two hear that noise?"

"Yes. It's like a revved-up whirring." Beatrice was suddenly concerned. "Is there a drone in here?"

Gemini growled and Leo scratched under his chin. "It's okay, boy."

But Gemini wouldn't settle down. He pushed Leo away with his paw and strode to a steel locker in the corner, pressing his nose against it like he smelled something inside.

Like Leo, Gemini knew how to see things. The big cat used the senses that Leo had programmed into his processors to see, hear, taste, touch, and smell.

Gemini whined and pawed at the locker, pacing back and forth in front it.

"Do you guys know what's in this locker?" Leo nodded his head toward where Gemini was whining.

"The electricity meter is in there." Beatrice reached to open the locker with an uneasy hand, already anxious about what she might see. She thought that maybe she would find that the Star Disc was draining power.

The locker opened with a metallic squeak.

The electric meter was going bonkers, whirring at thousands of revolutions per minute. Rocky laughed. Leo, on the other hand, was deadly serious.

"Am I wrong or is this meter going in the *opposite* direction from how most electricity meters go?"

"That's exactly what it's doing. The Star Disc is putting an immense amount of power *on* the grid." Beatrice looked frantic. "And we have to stop it."

Leo reached to knock the silver charger out of the Star Disc, but Gemini dove on top of him and growled.

Rocky pet Gemini on the head. "That's one smart kitty. There are twenty thousand gigajoules flowing through that thing right now. It'd turn you into tempura."

"I have to do something! I'm the one who plugged it into the wall and cranked it up. See, this is what always happens. It's all my fault!" Leo sounded like he was fighting back tears.

Beatrice pulled a pair of Arcage gloves off the wall. Then she stuffed her gloved hands into the welding mitts.

She pushed Leo away from the table and yelled at Rocky, "If this thing starts to electrocute me, give me a solid kick in the backside to knock me away from it."

"Not to sound like Nick, but you can count on me to give you the boot."

"One. Two. *Three!*" Beatrice yanked the Star Disc away from the charger. Leo ducked as a bolt of electricity streaked across the room from the Star Disc to the wall. The charger rattled on the concrete floor, sizzling for a few seconds.

Beatrice, wheezing, collapsed into a heap with the Star Disc still in her hands. Rocky leapt toward her, wound back his leg, and kicked the Star Disc as hard as he could, knocking it onto the floor. Then he collapsed, holding his right foot as he writhed in pain. "Ahhhh! Why is that thing so hard? I feel like I just tried to punt a mountain."

Beatrice scrambled onto her stomach and touched the Star Disc. She looked confused and took off her gloves. Then she reached out and touched the disc again with her bare hand.

"It's still cool to the touch. It just produced enough energy to power Paris and stayed at room temperature."

Beatrice got back to her feet and helped Rocky get up. "We have to fix this."

"Fix it? Fix it how?" Rocky limped along after her.

"All that energy has to go somewhere. There's no way the power grid here at Wynn Toys can handle it. We have to find a way to displace it."

"Or what?" Leo cringed as soon as he asked the question. He felt like he always asked one question too many.

"Or it will burn out every circuit at Wynn Toys. In sixty seconds, it just sent more energy to our power plant than it usually handles in a year. When the power plant can't handle any more, it will try to reverse the charge. If all that power doesn't have some place to go, it will fry every one of these buildings from the inside out." Beatrice shoved a crowbar between the locker and the wall and yanked her body weight against them.

In his mind's eye, Leo's solution took form. "What if we redirected the energy?"

Rocky tugged the other side of the locker. "The problem with power surges isn't distribution—"

"It's storage." Leo understood how hard it was to make a battery. Power storage had been the hardest thing to engineer with his first few prototypes of Gemini. Eventually he had found a battery from an old Toyota Prius and installed it in the lion's rear end.

As Leo looked at the electricity meter, he saw more than roots and stems of the power grid. He saw something they didn't see: *Disce quam ut videam.* Leo saw how to make a battery, the biggest battery ever imagined. Batteries change chemical energy into electrical energy. His solution, what he saw, was a much larger and infinitely more dangerous version of the battery he had installed in Gemini. But if it worked, it would reduce the electrical current safely over the course of about twenty miles.

Leo's mind connected every step of his plan with the simplest solutions. Simplicity is the ultimate sophistication, he reminded himself.

"On the way here from Wynn Mansion, we drove along a canal. Can we access that canal from here?" Leo asked as he pet Gemini to calm him.

Beatrice locked eyes with Leo, like she was trying to decipher exactly what he planned to do. "I think we can get to the canal from here but—and this is a big, gross but—it means that we'll have to go through the sewers. Why?"

"You wouldn't happen to have a boat on the canals, would you?"

"Yes. There's a boat there." Beatrice clicked her teeth. "It was your father's."

CHAPTER 52

Dante was perched on Beatrice's shoulder, his spotlight showing them the way through the sewer and also preventing Leo from having a panic attack about how dark it was down there.

The group came to a junction in the sewer. The path on the right was dark and scary and smelled awful, like it was haunted by the ghosts of a million dead farts. The path on the left seemed to lead lower into the sewers. And somehow it smelled even worse.

"I'm fairly certain the right goes to the power plant and the dam. Obviously, that is the last place we want to be right now. We're going left," Beatrice declared.

"We are?" Rocky pinched his nose to blunt the stink. "How's that old poem go, 'Two roads diverged in a wood. And I took the road less funky'?"

After they came around a bend, a faint blue light appeared at the end of the tunnel. Leo could hear water flowing and breathed a sigh of relief; Beatrice had made the right call and led them to the canal.

But Beatrice slowed down as they got closer to the light. "Can you hear that?"

"Oh no." Rocky looked over her shoulder.

"What is it? Guards? Nick? A babadook?" Leo asked.

"No. It's the electricity. It's running across the metal grate. We can't get out this way." Beatrice sounded defeated.

This had not been part of Leo's plan.

CHAPTER 53

Leo stepped forward next to Beatrice. "Mind if I borrow Dante for a second?"

The little monkey reluctantly hopped off of Beatrice's shoulders and onto Leo's. If Leo wasn't mistaken, Dante had developed a bit of a crush on Beatrice.

Slowly, Leo panned around the tunnel, letting Dante's light shine in the darkness. "We are looking for an electrical panel. If we can break the circuit, the current's strength will be cut in half."

Rocky sounded anxious. "Sure. But that means sending a flood of current spewing in one direction. That current is going to bounce back. And when it does . . ."

"We better be as far away as possible." Beatrice chewed on her bottom lip.

"Are you sure there is a boat out there on the canal?" Leo asked.

"Your dad left it docked there. We still used it on Customer Appreciation Day," Beatrice told him.

Dante let out a squeak. Leo's shoulders slumped.

"The good news is that Dante found the electrical panel. The bad news is that it's on the other side of the grate."

"Okay. We'll backtrack to that other path and—"

"No," Leo insisted. "I have an idea to get us all past the grate. But we're going to need to work together."

Leo summarized his plan to Rocky and Beatrice.

Beatrice stretched her legs. "Let's go. Like the old African proverb says, 'If you want to go fast, go alone. If you want to go far, go together.'"

"I hope any proverbs about us are not written in memoriam," Rocky joked.

"Anything that will conduct electricity has to come off," Leo explained.

Beatrice took off a gold bangle and earrings, which Rocky noticed were clip-ons.

"What's up with the clip-ons? Is your mom worried you're still too young to get them pierced?" Rocky teased as he removed his belt and his watch.

"My sister and I made a pact that we wouldn't get them pierced until one of us gets married. Now she's engaged, and I'm being led through a sewer by a monkey."

Leo put Dante on the ground. "Okay, open up, dude. I need cloth, rubber, and rope. You're our mule. You're going to carry all the metal."

With that, Dante opened up his chest and a treasure trove tumbled out. A coiled nylon rope, a whoopee cushion, some sterling silver spoons he'd taken from Wynn Mansion, a very expensive-looking scarf, and finally, with a thud, the Arcage.

"You took the Arcage again?! And is that my Hermès scarf?" Beatrice exploded.

Dante bowed extraordinarily low.

Leo said, "Wow. I've never seen him apologize. For anything.

Ever. Including the time he wiped a booger on my birthday cake. Everyone at school—"

"Why do we need the other stuff, Leo? The rope and rubber and other junk?" Rocky brought Leo's attention back to the matter at hand.

"Oh. Those get tied around Gemini," he explained. Beatrice and Rocky seemed like they expected more. Sometimes, Leo got ahead of himself and forgot that everyone else didn't know how to see like he did.

"Sorry. Once we're outside, we'll flip the circuits on the panel. It will reverse the direction of the electrical charge. We're going to send the surge away from us and into Wynn Tower. Before it ricochets back, we'll get far enough away that it won't fry us ... Hopefully."

"But why are you tying the rope around Gemini?" Rocky looked confused.

"Because he's going to ground the charge so we can get past the grate." Leo looped the nylon rope around Gemini. "Then we'll pull him away with the boat."

Beatrice and Rocky conferred with each other quietly. "This is nuts, right?"

"The kid hasn't been wrong yet. But let's make sure the monkey goes first."

"He can hear you," Leo said. "And sure, Dante will scout things out first so you know the charge is grounded and it's safe."

The little monkey jutted out his chin.

"No, you misunderstood. You're not getting grounded for

taking the Arcage." Leo turned to Beatrice and held out his hand for the game console. "But be gentle with it."

Beatrice handed over the Arcage reluctantly and Dante re-stowed it in his chest. He touched Beatrice's finger gently, like he was making her a personal promise to keep it safe.

Gemini shook his mane and whined, but Leo coaxed him across the sewer.

"You're right, it's gross down here. But you're about to get a power wash."

With that, Gemini approached the metal grate. The huge electrical current charging through it created a sizzling noise, like it was the world's largest bug zapper. Outside the grate, Leo could see water trickling over the dam.

Leo pointed to a thick copper pipe extending from the floor into the ceiling. "That's a water collection pipe. It grounds into the soil above us. When Gemini touches the grate, the electric current is going to run through him. And he'll touch the pipe to ground the charge. I promise it won't be more than thirty seconds. Okay, boy?"

Gemini licked Leo's hand. He extended his back hind leg and pressed his paw to the copper pipe, then the lion waited for Leo's cue for him to touch the grate.

"Everyone ready?" Leo checked as he cinched the nylon rope around Gemini.

Beatrice gritted her teeth and nodded. Rocky did some quick knee bends to limber up. Dante got into a sprinter stance. Leo pulled the Star Disc from his backpack.

"Go!" Leo shouted.

Gemini touched the grate and a bolt of lightning shot from it, through his paws, and into the pipe. Gemini dug his rear claws into the ground. The grate stopped sizzling instantly, but the pipe began to shift from a copper color to an almost molten red.

"Good boy! You're doing great!" Leo reassured Gemini as he tapped the Star Disc's magnet symbol. The sewer grate quickly started to rumble.

Behind him, Gemini whined.

"Hold on, boy. It's almost off."

Leo tapped the magnet symbol once more so there were two blue lights.

There was a loud crack as the grate broke off of its knobby, old masonry screws. Leo tapped the disc's magnet symbol to turn it off, and it dropped the grate immediately.

"Now make sure it's safe!"

Dante burst through the hole. He looked back at them and squeaked.

Once they were sure they wouldn't be electrocuted, Beatrice and Rocky hustled through the opening.

Dante ripped open the electrical panel on the other side. "Which one should he switch?" Rocky asked.

"All of them!" Leo yelled back.

Dante pressed his forearm against the panel and flipped a dozen switches simultaneously. Leo ran toward the dock, while also keeping an eye on Gemini. The big cat didn't look scared or overwhelmed. He looked determined.

But Leo quickly realized that, as usual, he had missed a key detail. He'd overestimated how much energy Wynn Tower would absorb.

The electricity that had been surging across the grate zoomed up the side of Wynn Tower. It reached the top of the skyscraper. For a split second, the beacon at the top of Wynn Tower shined at full force before it exploded. Some people claimed they could see the light from as far away as Rome. To some, the sudden burst of light filled them with fear and confusion. But to others, the light filled them with hope.

Leo, however, hadn't stopped to watch any of that. He was busy making his way to the dock while still letting out Gemini's rope behind him.

"I don't see a boat!" he yelled to Beatrice.

"It's right there. I promise."

As the beacon flash illuminated the night sky, it revealed a boat floating on the plum-dark waters of the canal. It was ash-black boron fiber with two paddle wheels taller than the cockpit on either side. Leo immediately loved this boat. It was long, sharp, and ferocious; like Saint Isidore had dropped his scythe into the water just for him.

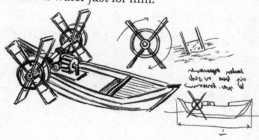

The boat had three cabins, two decks, and one smartly concealed diving board. What it didn't have was an outboard motor.

Leo pressed a big red START button. But nothing happened.

"Where is the engine?!" Leo flicked other switches in the cockpit at random.

"No engine. There's a lever for the paddle wheels below deck." Beatrice pointed him toward a small set of stairs that ran under the cockpit.

Leo had missed another detail. He assumed the boat would have an engine. Instead, he should've asked. The most important thing is to not stop questioning.

Where his brain had failed them, now Leo needed brawn. He needed Gemini.

He yelled to Rocky, "Untie the dock ropes. We need Gemini to power the wheel."

"Okay, kid, I'm on it. But we already avoided the electricity. You can relax—we're safe now," Rocky replied.

Finally, Leo found a crank for the paddle wheel. "No, we're not. All of that energy is going to bounce back to the power plant. It will overwhelm the plant with so much energy, it will reverse the turbines."

It took a second for Rocky to piece together what Leo had just told him. "You mean the power plant is going to send all that energy back into the canal?"

Leo nodded frantically. Rocky grabbed the other side of the crank and pushed. "Crank us here!"

Slowly, the ship lurched away from the dock.

Above deck, Beatrice watched water froth over the dam of the Wynn power plant. "Uh, fellas. We do not want to be broadside to that current."

Finally, the boat unmoored, though it started to rock and spin. Beatrice threw her body against the captain's wheel in a reckless attempt to keep the ship steady.

Leo told Rocky, "Keep cranking away." Then he jumped back above deck and started to pull in the rope that was still connected to Gemini.

He braced his feet against the railing and gave the rope a hard pull. Dante started to heave the rope in time with Leo. After a few, final worried yanks, Gemini's shiny green eyes glowed through the water behind the stern.

Gemini doggy-paddled as hard as he could until his steel claws caught the back of the boat. Beatrice watched the lion dig his nails into the smooth boron fiber.

"Ahhhh, maybe we can buff those out?" She cringed.

After Gemini climbed aboard, he shook his substantial body; river water sprayed in every direction, soaking Leo, who was struggling to strap himself down on the deck.

Finally, Beatrice found a point and was steering the boat straight down the canal. The surge flowed into the canal, pushing the boat faster. Leo's battery was in motion.

That's when they heard the thunderous crack of the dam breaking.

CHAPTER 54

Leo scrambled to get Dante strapped to the railing before the water hit. Rocky tied his waist to the railing in the bow and braced himself too. As Leo looked around, his brain was trying to solve too many problems at once, and that's when he was prone to making mistakes. He took a deep breath and tried to think.

A wave of water had been part of his plan, but not a wave this big or this strong. Whether describing water or electricity, current is current. It's a surge of energy headed in a specific direction. Leo had planned to harness that current and redirect it for his own use.

The problem was the electrical surge bounced off the top of Wynn Tower and swamped the power plant. The turbines were so overwhelmed that they sent the gush of water back out into the canal in a massive wave, far bigger than Leo anticipated.

But Leo smiled because of what he saw in the wave moving toward them. *Disce quam ut videam.* When the water flooded out from the generators, it built and formed a familiar shape.

He held on to Dante

before the wave slammed into them. The force of the water felt like getting rear-ended by a truck. Fortunately, the hull of the boat had been designed with such precision that it caught the edge of the wave, surfing on the surge. After a moment of weightlessness, the boat stabilized. Beatrice left the cockpit to check on Leo.

He held up some of the coiled rope he had found around the deck, offering it to Beatrice. "These ropes were laying around if you need to tie stuff down."

"That rope is made of CNT, Carbon Nano Tubes. Your dad and I got spiders to spin Carbon Nano Tube silk. It's so strong, it's actually bulletproof."

"You and my dad engineered spiders to spin bulletproof silk?"

Beatrice nodded her head.

"Were you trying to make nightmare spiders? Because that's how you make nightmare spiders," Leo kidded.

"Hey!" Rocky screamed from the bow. "You'd better come see this!"

Leo led Beatrice along the railing to the bow, trailed by Gemini and Dante. A very worried Rocky stood on his tippy-toes, pointing at red lights flashing along the side of the canal. "The canal locks are shut. We've got to get those locks open or this boat will be smashed into a pile of elegant black matchsticks."

Leo reached into his bag. His plan had accounted for the closed canal locks. To make a battery, you have to alter and redirect current. But he had not been absolutely certain this part of his plan would work until he felt how easily the Star Disc popped the grate off of its hinges. And now he knew he could keep the Star Disc above deck. "Gemini and Dante, you need to get below deck and lock the door. Whatever happens, do not come out until I say it's okay," Leo commanded.

Dante kicked water at Leo, and Gemini pouted, but they did as they were told. Once he was sure that they were below deck and safe from the magnet, Leo removed the Star Disc from his back.

"So who wants to help strap me and the disc to the bow?"

CHAPTER 55

Leo thanked Beatrice as she finished tying the CNT rope around Leo's waist. "Are you sure about this?"

"I mean, it definitely works in my head."

Beatrice walked back to the cockpit and tried to stay calm as she strapped herself in. Leo gave her a thumbs-up. She stomped her feet twice so that Gemini—and Dante inside of him—would know to brace themselves.

Leo looked at the Star Disc. He'd left a little window between the straps so he could still swipe the machine on. He ran through a mental checklist of everything he was wearing one last time to make sure none of it was metal. Then he swiped his finger across the Star Disc and turned it on.

Meanwhile, the boat continued to barrel down the canal toward the lock.

He took a deep breath, then tapped the magnet symbol five times, increasing it to maximum power.

Instantly, Leo felt faint, like all his blood was rushing toward his hands. Behind him, there was a thump and a muffled groan as Gemini was slammed into the wall of the cabin.

For the first time since Savvy had punched him, Leo tasted blood in his mouth. He remembered that the reason blood is such a deep red is because of how much iron is in it. Most people have about four grams of iron in their system. And the Star Disc's magnet was pulling all of the iron in Leo's blood toward the ultrastrong magnet itself.

Leo fought the urge to pass out and lifted his eyes toward the canal lock. Water poured through an expanding gap in the center.

"It's working!" The Star Disc was pulling open the canal lock.

But as the Star Disc pulled the gate open, the water's current quickened, and they were going much faster than he had anticipated. It was on Beatrice to keep them centered. He looked back and she gave him another thumbs-up.

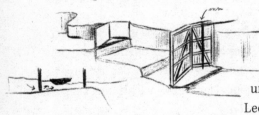

Leo saw stars as his hand hovered over the Star Disc.

With twenty meters until they crossed the lock, Leo tapped the magnet symbol again, turning it off. For a moment, the world went silent. The lock stopped squealing on its hinges. The boat slowed down slightly, no longer propelled forward by the magnetic power of the Star Disc on the enormous steel gates of the canal lock.

The ship shot through the gate. Leo let out a *Whoa!* as they launched off of the top of the wave and into the next canal. Beatrice had kept them safely in the center.

The bow plunged down into the water, soaking Leo like he was in the front seat of a gigantic log flume.

Behind him, Beatrice stomped her feet to signal Gemini that it was time to get moving. Gemini whined from the deck below but got back up and started to crank on the paddle wheel. The boat lurched forward again. The keel cut through the water faster this time as Gemini alone generated more power than both Rocky and Leo had been able to do together on the paddle wheel. Inside Gemini's chest cavity, a miffed Dante flicked the lion's ribs; he did not appreciate being tucked away and missing all of this.

Behind them, the current continued to surge through the canal lock. The crest of the building wave caught them again and pitched the ship forward into the dark waters. The current in the water, which had been produced by electrical current, accelerated their momentum in the right direction.

Rocky unstrapped himself and patted down his body, checking for broken bones. "I'm alive! We're all alive!"

Leo grinned, but he worried the ship was already going too fast to navigate the next obstacle waiting for them underneath Wynn Mansion.

CHAPTER 56

Leo unstrapped himself and jogged to the cabin. He opened the thick door and asked, "Everything all right down there, you two?"

Gemini responded with a stubborn snarl. Dante gave a resigned whimper. "In a few minutes, we'll need you again. Get ready to crank the paddle wheel," Leo said before closing the door.

He climbed the stairs to Beatrice. "There will be an eddy off the port side right before Wynn Mansion. If we cut over at the right moment—"

"Are you serious? How are we going to be able to do that in the dark?" Rocky sounded incredulous. "We should have the lion paddle us up and over the wave, let the surge go past us rather than trying to ride it."

"It's too strong. We'd never be able to get up and over it. We have to ride the momentum," Leo insisted, but Rocky raised his eyebrows.

"He hasn't been wrong yet," Beatrice said, nodding toward Leo.

"Who do you want to present the Arcage at the toy fair? Because it's probably going to be tough for you to do it in a full body cast," Rocky asked.

"C'mon, Rocky. We're already past the hard part." Beatrice pepped him up.

"You're right. A full body cast is probably too optimistic.

Let's light the ship on fire and go full Viking funeral. At least then we might see where we are going."

"I know we're going to make it," Beatrice reassured Rocky after looking at Leo.

"I'm glad you're so optimistic. Valhalla!"

The ship slid underneath the stegosaurus bridge, where the canal merged with the Ticino. The lights from the bridge threw long shadows across the deck as they slid below. Passing under the bridge meant they were almost at Wynn Mansion now. Leo knelt down, checked the Star Disc one last time, then strapped himself in.

The river coursed around a bend and Leo adjusted his weight. He hoped Wynn Mansion would be able to handle the colossal surge of current that was about to hit it. He hoped it would be able to absorb the energy and store it, the final step in his idea to build a massive battery. He hoped he was right and he hadn't overlooked any more key details.

But when the boat finished rounding the curve, Leo, and Beatrice, and Rocky froze. Despite being a dark, cloudless night, they could clearly see Wynn Mansion straddling the river, less than a half mile in front of them.

Every light in the house was on. And both banks of the river were bathed in light.

Someone knew they were coming.

CHAPTER 57

Rocky yelled to Leo, "Who turned on the lights?!"

"Let's just get to the eddy, then we'll find out together!" Leo shouted back at him.

Rocky responded with an impolite gesture, then strapped himself down. They were less than five hundred yards from Wynn Mansion now. Leo had to trust that Beatrice would be able to cut over at the right moment. What he didn't know was that Beatrice was familiar with the river and ponds under Wynn Mansion. She used to go on walks with Peter sometimes as they worked out ideas.

Leo's hands hovered over the Star Disc. "Not unless we need it."

The final step in building his battery was sending all of this energy into the hydroelectric dam under the mansion. Based on what Beatrice had told him about the house, the dam would convert the water current back into electric current, then the house would absorb it and store the energy in the windows and walls. To be more specific, he planned to convert the direct current into an alternating current. Turning direct current into storable, alternating current is how homes around the world utilize power from power lines.

But he had not been counting on the lights at Wynn Mansion already being on. He couldn't shake the eerie feeling the house itself was alive.

The boat barreled on toward Wynn Mansion. Leo saw the opening to the eddy and shifted his body weight in preparation for when Beatrice would push the boat hard to his right side.

But they shot right past the opening.

"What's going on?!" Leo yelled back to the cockpit.

When he torqued around to look, he saw Rocky was now in the cockpit and shoving the steering wheel away from Beatrice, putting them on a course that would shoot them over the edge of the dam.

Based on their speed and the distance to the dam, Leo calculated he had five seconds before they would drop over the edge and crash onto the rocks below. He swiped the Star Disc on, then rapidly tapped the magnet symbol five times, thrusting it to full strength.

The boat slowed instantly, and Leo slammed forward, pushing hard against the straps that had locked him in place. Behind them, the full force of the current crashed into the stern, and the ship yawed. There was a horrible wrenching noise, and suddenly the bow of the ship was closing in on the underside of Wynn Mansion.

Then he heard a terrifyingly loud *KER-KLUNK* and felt a powerful thud as the ship butted into the underside of the house.

Leo's weight shifted back against his heels. With his feet locked into place, he looked down and watched the surge of water gush underneath the boat, flooding the plant, the retention ponds, and the edge of the dam. It became an explosion of white water shooting off the cliff's edge and into the night.

The magnet had pulled the entire ship out of the water, where it now dangled from the bottom of the house.

He looked back at the cockpit, and it was empty. Beatrice and Rocky were nowhere to be seen. He had no way to free himself. If he wriggled out of the straps, he would plunge into the river, more than sixty-five feet below him.

He heard an ominous crack in the bow. The magnetic force of the Star Disc was crushing the boron fiber. The boat couldn't hold up under this strain for long.

Behind him, there was a wretched scream.

CHAPTER 58

Savvy was waiting outside in the dark at five in the morning. At precisely 5:10, four gloomy SUVs, all with tinted windows and matte-black paint jobs, rolled up to the curb. All the trucks were headed from Mach Valley to the same place—the Milan Toy Fair.

The third truck in the convoy opened its rear door, and Savvy climbed in. He was surprised to see he would be riding with Nick Wynn, who looked like death warmed over. Nick had refused a hot meal and a change of clothes, he was hangry, and he smelled stale. Nick nodded at Savvy as the boy took a seat across from him.

"Mister Wynn, how long have you been secretly working for Mach Valley?" Savvy started in before he even finished buckling his seat belt.

Nick grunted and tried to focus on his *Wall Street Journal*. He wasn't about to talk to some kid about how long he had been on the payroll of Wynn's biggest corporate rival. He wasn't about to divulge the secret he'd been holding on to since the night his brother disappeared. Nick was public with his greed, but private with his shame.

Savvy didn't care that Nick was ignoring him. "I consider myself a bit of a body language expert, and, sir, O does not like you."

"Well, aren't you perceptive." Nick took the bait. "You must have majored in psychology in middle school, yes?"

Savvy did not appreciate Nick acting like his youth meant he wasn't smart or capable. He moved his legs closer so that they were almost touching Nick's, then removed his mask.

Nick kept his eyes on the front page of his paper. He tried to not give away how utterly repulsed he was by the still-blistering scars that covered one side of the boy's face. So Savvy moved into Nick's line of vision and bore down on him with his disfigured eye.

"People don't really like you much anywhere you go, do they?"

"Son, one day you'll come to learn it's better to be—"

"Feared than loved." Savvy grinned. "Yeah, he told me you would say that. Here's the thing about people who live their lives by platitudes, even amoral ones like yours. I bet it feels great to have a core principle, but it makes all of you so easy to predict."

Savvy picked up a long contraption that had been sitting on the floor next to him. It looked like a pelican beak, but four feet long and made of Kevlar.

"Nothing is a gamble with people like you. Go ahead, Nick, you keep living by that code—trying to make people fear you. At least you're not one of those fake 'nice' guys. But winners? We will take chances and adapt. Next thing you know, the winners don't fear you anymore. And it's not like they'll come around to loving you, because they never did and no one ever will."

Nick cocked an eyebrow at Savvy. "If you were any good at predictions, kid, you wouldn't have those scars, yes? Be quiet. If I want advice about taking risks, I'll find a more handsome gambler."

The puss-filled corner of Savvy's blistered lip formed the remnant of a smile.

"Do you want to know how I got these scars?" Savvy fit the beak contraption over his hand. He buckled the handle farther up his forearm. "It was your nephew, Leo. I can't wait until I see him again. And the big man can't wait to meet him." Savvy nodded toward the giant black truck in front of them that was carrying O.

"I underestimated Leo. Nothing he builds ever works like it's supposed to. He has lots of big ideas but awful execution. Leo has always been so horribly undisciplined. That will be his undoing." Savvy touched his scars with his free hand. "The last time I saw Leo, he didn't outthink me or outmaneuver me. He just got lucky. I'm smart enough to understand that and adapt before our next encounter because, unlike you, I think like a winner." Savvy pointed to the contraption strapped to his arm.

"You see, the truth is that there are no good guys or bad guys. Only winners and losers. Winners adapt—they change whatever principles they need to in order to win. I'm sure you're aware of how O adapts good ideas into great ones. What's the old saying, 'talent imitates, genius steals'?"

Nick tried to act like he wasn't listening, but it was hard to ignore he was being harangued by a teenager.

"Your boss at Wynn—a genuinely vile woman—I bet she thought it was better to be loved than feared. That's why she kept her best idea from you. Her plan is to debut it at this toy fair."

Savvy nodded his head again at the SUV that was in front

of them in the convoy. "But just wait until you see what he's got in store for her and her big idea. It's going to be the end of Wynn. And when he's done with Wynn, when that big skyscraper is just an empty monument to a family of failures, why will he need the least-talented Wynn anymore?" Savvy sat back and tightened the glove contraption to his arm.

They spent the rest of the drive in silence.

CHAPTER 59

This definitely had *not* been part of the plan.

"Help!" Leo hoped that someone, anyone, would hear him. The ship tilted as more of the bow was crushed by the force of the magnet. The water below him had calmed, but it was still way too dangerous to unstrap himself and jump from this height.

A series of dreadful stabbing noises seemed to be getting closer. He checked his reflection in the shiny metal underside of Wynn Mansion.

Over his shoulder, a pair of green eyes glinted in the darkness.

Leo smirked. "Gemini?"

The big cat wobbled. He was punching his sharp claws into the boat with every step, fighting the force of the magnet as he carefully clawed his way up to Leo.

"Is Beatrice okay? What did Rocky do to her?" Leo asked, worried.

Gemini licked Leo with his soft, spongy tongue. From inside the lion's chest, Dante gave a long, pained squeal.

"Okay, thank you for coming to get me." Leo wrapped his hand tightly around Gemini's mane. Gemini cut him free from the straps, then they slowly clawed back down the boat, again sure to establish a solid foothold before each and every step.

He was relieved that Gemini was here to protect him from

Rocky. Before he entered the ship's cockpit, Leo reminded himself to deepen his voice to sound intimidating.

Leo yanked the door open and swung inside. "What happened!?" he yelled, his voice accidentally cracking.

Rocky was splayed out on the floor, holding his ribs. Beatrice was tucked in next to him, staring into space.

"Huh? Why do you sound like someone spilled your milkshake?" Rocky clutched his torso and winced. "It was a trap. The entrance to the eddy was mined. I only saw them because the house was lit up like a Christmas tree. If we had tried to cut in that way, we'd have been blown sky high. Pieces of us would be orbiting the moon."

"Rocky saved us," Beatrice explained more succinctly.

"But I heard you scream," Leo said, perplexed.

She pointed above her. A mess of metal parts and shards stuck to the wall of the cockpit. The parts vibrated slightly, the magnet relentlessly pulling them toward itself.

"That's all that's left of the Arcage," Beatrice muttered.

CHAPTER 60

The cockpit shook as the Star Disc crushed more of the boat at the bow.

Leo grabbed a strap and looped it around the steering wheel before dropping it into the river. "First things first, we've got to get off this boat. The water should be calm enough now that we can climb down and swim to the edge."

"Ladies first," Rocky said as he gestured to Beatrice.

"Wait. How are we going to get Gemini and Dante off of this ship? They can't jump since the magnet will draw them toward it," Beatrice asked as she lowered herself down out of the cockpit.

Rocky gave her a half smile. "Don't you remember? The Star Disc has a remote switch."

"Oh, 'Here Comes the—'"

"Don't say it! The whole ship might come crashing down. I'd love to see Jeff Buckley in concert again, but not tonight."

Beatrice climbed down the rope and plunged into the cold, dark water. She swam hard to the riverbank. After promising Gemini and Dante they would be okay, Leo went next.

Rocky went last and labored to make his way down the rope. After he finally splashed into the river, Beatrice waded back in and pulled him to dry land.

"I saw the lion swim, but can the monkey?" Rocky asked between labored breaths.

"His circuits are waterproof," Leo said. "But he certainly

doesn't *enjoy* water. When his fur gets wet, he's a total pain—you have to wash him with upholstery cleaner or he'll be, like, visibly stinky."

"I'll give the little guy a bath when we're done." Rocky struggled to his feet, then yelled up to Dante, "What do you say, maestro? Give the people what they want."

But Dante wouldn't budge.

Beatrice tried a much softer tone. "Dante, it would mean a lot to me if you played that song right now."

In the ship's cockpit, Dante leaned over and pushed his face into his hand. Fighting the magnet with everything he had, he turned the dial around his left eye.

"Dum-da-da-da-dum . . ." The recording of Leo's "Here Comes the Sun" played right on cue.

The stern—the fat end of the boat—hit the water first, sending a shoulder-high wave toward the riverbank. Leo and Beatrice scrambled back but Rocky just stood there and took it. "Who cares? We are already wet."

CHAPTER 61

After retrieving the Star Disc and anchoring the boat to a rock, Leo followed Beatrice on a cold, soggy march up to the house. Wynn Mansion had absorbed the energy like Leo planned. The cathode windows had expanded so wide that they bulged out from the stone frame. Every light in the house shined at full luster.

Beatrice held out her arms and they all stopped. "Wait. Who is in the house?"

"It better be the same jerk who put mines in the river. I've got a five-hundred-pound lion I'd like him to meet." Rocky smacked Gemini on the behind and the big cat growled.

"Leo, stay behind me . . . and Gemini," Beatrice said.

They crept to the front entrance. Beatrice reached out, but before she could knock, the door opened wide. "Hello? Anyone here?"

There was no answer.

"We should stick together as we search the house."

"Yeah. Like I'm going anywhere without this guy and his steel teeth," Rocky said, and Gemini held up his tail proudly.

They methodically searched from room to room but found no one. They heard no footsteps. They saw no shadows.

Beatrice chewed on her bottom lip. "That's so strange."

"What's *really* strange is I think the house knew we were coming," Leo insisted.

"Okay, then. Do you think it was the house who put those mines in the pond?" Rocky had asked the obvious question.

Leo hadn't thought about that, so he kept his mouth shut.

Once they had finished searching the house, they all decided to get some shut-eye. It would be safer to all sleep in the same room. Beatrice dragged a mattress onto the floor of Leo's room. Rocky held his ribs, still sore from surfing the canal, as he stood up to fetch a mattress for himself. Leo stopped him.

"Gemini, will you go find a—"

But Gemini had already trotted off into another room. A few seconds later, he came back with a soft mattress carefully pinched between his jaws. He dropped it front of Rocky, who scratched him under the chin.

"Good boy."

Gemini wagged his tail, then circled a spot next to the door three times and plopped down. Leo plugged Gemini's tail into the wall. Dante sidled up next to Gemini, and Leo connected a cord to Dante's battery to charge him too.

"Everybody all set?" Beatrice asked with her hand next to the light.

"Hold on." Leo wanted to be safely in bed before she turned out the light. "Okay. Go ahead."

Beatrice flicked off the light. The walls on each side of the room became a panorama of the night sky. Leo recognized the stars above him: the constellation Leo and the same map of the stars as the entrance to the astronomy tunnel.

Leo felt warm and wanted as he drifted off to sleep. For the first time in his life, he was hosting a sleepover.

"Apologies to everyone in advance if I toot in my sleep," Rocky whispered in the dark.

"Gross, Rocky," Beatrice responded, and Leo tried to stifle his laughter.

Meanwhile, beneath the house where Leo and company were sleeping after a harrowing day, the spiky mines kicked off the river bottom and launched themselves out of the water. After becoming airborne, they transformed back into a flock of drones.

Most of the flock assembled into an arrowhead, soared up into the sky, then broke right and headed back toward Mach Valley.

But as directed, several drones broke left and flew back toward the house. They banked around the minaret in the courtyard and toward the biggest bedroom above the river. All three drones swooped down in perfect formation and prepared to initiate their infrared cameras, honing in on the white-hot heat signature of the Star Disc, as their master demanded.

All at once, bolts of electricity shot through the three drones. Two of them plunged back into the river. Only the squad leader remained functional; three of its five propellers were fried, but it climbed back into the sky. It had taken the infrared photos requested.

A wire whipped out from the middle of the minaret and snapped the drone in midair. Two halves of the robot dropped to the ground.

CHAPTER 62

Leo awoke to slobbery fuzz pushing against his lips. He spat out a few fibers and sat up in bed.

Gemini nudged his tennis ball back into Leo's chest and happily wagged his tail. Leo picked up the ball and flung it into the next room. The lion went chasing after it, and Leo winced when he heard him drag his claws on the floor.

"Ahhh, your dad would have loved this guy." Rocky was having Dante retrieve a few books for him from a high shelf in Leo's room. "How did you sleep?"

"Pretty well. What time is it?" Leo wiped gunk from the corner of his eyes.

"A little after eleven."

"I've been asleep for nine and a half hours?! Why didn't you wake me?"

"Kid, I'm lucky if I get about two hours before I have to get out of bed to pee. Take it from an old man. There are two things you should enjoy while you still can: your sleep and your hairline."

"Where's Beatrice?"

"She took one of your dad's old motorcycles to the toy fair. The plan was for the Arcage to be the big reveal this year. Now, she's going to try and stall them." Rocky held up one of the Arcage shards that had been stuck in the wall of the ship's cockpit. "But maybe, if we work together, we can give her something to show them."

Leo leapt out of bed.

The convoy of SUVs pulled around to the back entrance of the city's oldest opera house. It was on the grounds of a former castle, with walls that were twenty-three feet thick and had stood for over five hundred years. Savvy was certain that five hundred years from now, he'd be so famous that everyone would know his name.

O exited the lead SUV and knocked on Savvy's window. Savvy rolled it down and smiled. "You look like a titan, sir."

"Thank you, Savvy. You're coming with me." He turned his attention to Nick. "Obviously, Nick, you'll watch from here. I've arranged for the feed to run on your screen."

Savvy pushed his bag into Nick's lap. "Hold this for me." Nick gave the sincerest smile he could manage as Savvy hopped out of the car.

He stood as tall as he could next to O as they walked into the theater.

"You're going to knock them dead, sir." Savvy offered up a fist bump and O fist-bumped him back. O peeked around in the hope that a few people saw that and would post it online. A post captioned "Billionaire CEO fist-bumps kid" would help humanize him. He was desperate to be seen more as a man of the people. A genius who remained humble enough to dress like an everyman would really help Mach Valley's stock price.

O and Savvy walked backstage and into a bright dressing

room. "If the boy shows himself, you're welcome to take him here. But only after I've finished my presentation."

He closed the dressing room door and made his way to the stage.

The old theater was immense, a relic from a different time when opera was the most popular form of entertainment. It stood seven stories tall and had the capacity to seat two thousand people. Every seat was filled, and a crowd of five hundred more stood on the floor. Around the world, almost three million watched the live-stream of the event.

O waited until he saw the live-stream audience had crossed three million, then he started the presentation. The house lights flickered three times, and the audience hushed. For a moment, the theater was shrouded in total darkness. Then the Mach Valley logo burst onto the center of the stage.

"A new innovation from Mach Valley."

Mach Valley's logo jumped from the stage to the ground, then vaulted up the six tiers of opera boxes to the ceiling before bouncing around the theater. The spectators felt a rush of wind as the logo shot past them. It was more than just a projection; the logo careened around the room and defied laws of physics. It had real mass.

"Because if you stop trying to innovate, you stop trying."

O stepped onto the stage, and his voice boomed through the theater. "What you are seeing was created by Mach Valley's newest product, the Shroud."

O snapped his fingers, and the logo exploded over the middle of the room. A cool mist of rainwater fell onto the audience.

"Unencumbered by goggles, or gloves, or even an ugly console taking up space in your living room, the Shroud offers you augmented reality unlike anything you've experienced before."

O stepped down off the stage and into the crowd. The people parted before him. At his size, they would have moved anyway, but he wanted them to think he was just like them.

He raised his arms for quiet. "Where should we go today? Everyone deserves a getaway. Have you ever wanted to see the Amazon?"

O snapped his fingers and the theater transformed into the lush canopy of the Brazilian rainforest. Instantly, the air felt heavy. Screeching calls of white bellbirds drowned out the crowd's excited chatter. And perhaps most dramatically, a muddy brown river flowed where the stage had been.

"Or perhaps you have a morbid curiosity to see Pompeii on that fateful day when Vesuvius rained down hellfire?" He snapped again.

The ground erupted. It sounded like the earth itself was in anguish. A wave of fire poured toward the audience, who screamed in terror. Men instinctively dove in front of their wives to shield them. O laughed.

He snapped and the wave of lava froze in place.

"After that scare, I think we deserve a day at the beach."

He snapped his fingers one more time and the room was

bathed in the soft pink light of a Caribbean sunset. Salty sea breezes wafted through the air. A steel drum tapped out a cover version of "Over the Rainbow." The whole room seemed to relax. He hopped back onto the stage, which now appeared to be a ramshackle tiki bar.

"Welcome to Lighthouse Beach, at the southeastern edge of Eleuthera, Bahamas."

The crowd went wild.

"The Shroud. This innovation arrives fourth quarter of this year. Only from Mach Valley." O exited the stage. The theater snapped back to its normal appearance.

"Oh, and one more thing . . ." O reappeared on stage, a winning smile on his face. "Every customer who purchases the Shroud will also receive lifetime access to Mach Valley's internet service . . . for free."

Pandemonium. Strangers slapped high fives. The whole audience was left in a state of joyful awe. Well, everyone except for one woman standing in the back row of the theater.

Beatrice stared at the stage, stunned into silence and her mouth agape.

She couldn't showcase the Arcage. It was in pieces back in Wynn Mansion, but even if she did, the Arcage could never stack up against what she had just witnessed. All her work had been a waste. Mach Valley had beaten her again. And this time, she didn't see how she could possibly keep Wynn Toys afloat.

CHAPTER 63

Rocky held the tweezers tightly while Leo tried to pry open the Arcage's hard drive with a safety pin and a nail file. He gave a frustrated grunt. They'd been at this for almost an hour, but they had not been able to open the hard drive.

"Push the pin at the corner of the seam. Sometimes you can find structural weak points there," Rocky suggested. Leo adjusted the pin slightly and, finally, they heard a crack.

"We're in!" Leo shouted.

Rocky slapped him on the back proudly. "Tools of a mis-spent youth, eh?"

Leo grinned, but they both knew that opening the hard drive was the easy part. Now they had to find a way to access the information on the drive.

He held it up, looking for a port. Rocky scoffed.

"You know how to see, huh? But just as important as knowing how to see is knowing how to *listen*." Rocky waited for total silence, then he started the hard drive. Leo heard a faint grinding noise.

"Do you hear that?" Rocky asked. "That noise means the drive isn't reading the data. I hope your magnet didn't erase the information on the drive, or the Arcage is gone."

He fidgeted with the hard drive's wheel until he spun it the opposite way.

"But the wheel keeps stopping," Leo pointed out.

"Ah. Do you know what might pull this hard drive's magnetic wheel in the opposite direction? Another magnet would keep the wheel moving, and we wouldn't have to touch it."

Leo's eyes lit up, and he dove for his bag and the Star Disc. He stowed away their metal tools, then maneuvered the disc underneath the desk so it would move the wheel but was not so close that it might ruin the hard drive.

Leo held his finger near the Star Disc until Rocky gave him a wink, then turned it on and tapped the magnet symbol once.

The wheel sprang to life and started rotating.

"It's working!"

Rocky moved quickly, splicing the broken cord with a new cord and plugging it into the port on a black cube.

"The cube is a flash drive. If we get the Arcage hard drive to work, it should move its data to this."

Rocky pulled out a tablet and connected it to the cube. After a few anxious seconds, they saw a folder that said *Arcage*.

Leo excitedly tapped on the folder. "These might as well be hieroglyphics. I can't read any of it." It was just a bunch of computer code.

Rocky reached over Leo's shoulder and traced his finger across the lines of code. "Most of what we built over the last few weeks has been erased . . ."

Leo cringed. It was his fault Dante had taken the Arcage to

begin with. It was his fault Beatrice had nothing to present at the Milan Toy Fair.

"But the core code is still there. Beatrice found something buried in the Arcage, a message from your dad. At least, she said the message was in your dad's voice."

"What? What did it say?" Somehow this revelation made Leo feel even worse.

"She had to fight off a bunch of prime numbers. Then he gave her a location—Mach Valley."

Now Leo was beside himself. "So who did you send to Mach Valley to look for him? That's got to be where he is!"

There was no easy way for Rocky to explain this to the boy. "Leo, it's been thirteen years. I'd love to see your father again, so I can only begin to imagine how much you'd like to meet him. But I think that was his way of *warning* us about Mach Valley."

Tears welled in Leo's eyes. "You're wrong. He's still alive. I can feel it."

Leo turned away. For the first time since he'd left the Academy of Florence, he missed it. At least at the academy, he knew how and where he could be alone. He didn't know any of the best places to hide and think in this big, dumb house.

Every light in the mansion flashed three times. A deep but calm voice spoke, a voice Leo had never heard before. "Warning. An old passcode was just used to access the front gate."

"Where are they now?" Rocky asked.

The voice responded, "They just stepped inside the front door."

CHAPTER 64

The antibacterial wipe was torn to shreds by the time O finished cleaning his hands. He reveled in the act of these presentations, hearing their oohhs and ahhs as he unveiled a new technology. But he loathed having to interact with them afterward. He grinned politely at their praise and pressed his hand against theirs, but what he wanted to say was, "You don't matter. You're not smart enough to create ideas like these. Buy my product, then go away until it's time to buy the next one."

The boy was waiting for him backstage. He seemed anxious.

"That was inspiring. You are a true master at your craft." Savvy bowed.

O smiled. The boy tried too hard to please, and he was too obvious about it.

"Is your old friend here?" O asked without looking back at Savvy.

"No. But the woman watched from the back row and she looked defeated. She'll have nothing to present tomorrow. Just like you predicted, the Shroud will be the nail in the coffin for Wynn Toys."

O's spine stiffened. He felt taller, the air tasted sweeter. The war was nearly over. He had defeated Wynn Toys without ever being discovered. Not that it would matter now—he was a billionaire. If the authorities figured out how he'd undermined

Wynn, so what? They would talk about laws he had broken before they inevitably groveled for donations. He got into his SUV but noticed Savvy was still standing outside the door.

With visible disdain, he rolled down the window. "Is there something else?"

"It's Nick Wynn. He's gone."

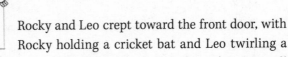

CHAPTER 65

Rocky and Leo crept toward the front door, with Rocky holding a cricket bat and Leo twirling a jump rope like a lasso. Rocky pointed at the house's lights, still flashing in silent intervals. "The house's security system is quiet, which is encouraging."

Leo was confused. "Why would anyone want a quiet security system?"

"Let me ask you something, Leo. Have you ever been in a fight?"

Leo licked the inside of his lip, where the cuts were still healing from when Savvy punched him. "Ummm. I've kind of been in a fight."

Rocky raised the cricket bat and took up a position next to the front door. "Well, here's a tip for the next time you're *kind of* in a fight: don't worry about the loud guy. The loud guy doesn't want to fight. That's why he's so loud—to try and scare you away."

Leo made a mental note about loud guys, but Rocky continued.

"Instead, worry about the quiet guy. If a guy is mean-mugging you while he stays as quiet as this house, watch out. Because that guy *wants* to fight." Rocky tried to peek out a window, but he couldn't see an intruder. "And something tells me this house wants to fight."

Rocky held up his hand then roared, "Who is it?" in his most intimidating voice.

"It's Beatrice." Rocky jumped. She was behind them, in the dining room.

"Why are you back a day early? Your presentation is tomorrow."

Beatrice froze when she saw Rocky gripping the bat. "I'd be happy to tell you after you put that down." She turned her attention to Leo. "And what are you going to do with a jump rope, double dutch me to death?"

They headed to the kitchen, and while Rocky made three cups of tea, Beatrice told them all about Mach Valley and O and his big presentation of the Shroud.

Rocky was livid. "It's more than a coincidence that every time Wynn is about to debut a new idea, Mach Valley announces the same idea but slightly better."

Beatrice shook her head. "This wasn't just *slightly* better. The tech in this thing, the Shroud, is years ahead of what we had in the Arcage."

"Not *had*, still *have*. We found a way to save the Arcage's hard drive. The core code is still there," Leo offered proudly.

"And I bet you'd still like to try it out." Beatrice patted him on the back, though Leo thought she sounded like she was just being nice.

Rocky spit his words through gritted teeth. "Mach Valley had to know what we were working on. Once is a fluke. Twice is a coincidence. The third time, it's a plot."

"How could they have known? This time we kept everything about the Arcage in house. Each part of the console was built separately so no one knew exactly what they were working on. We were careful to retrieve each part individually, and we didn't assemble the whole thing until we were in the lab. And like the old saying goes, 'Trust, but verify.' I had Cromwell monitoring everybody. Even you. He would've told me if anyone did anything suspicious."

Beatrice sipped her tea, then reached out and touched Leo's hand. "We're not going to give up. We'll find a new angle to pitch it at the toy fair."

Again, Leo worried she was trying to sound optimistic for his sake. A few kids at the academy had complained that their parents did that sometimes—told them everything was fine when in reality things were falling apart. He felt his brain start to be enveloped by a familiar anxiety: that being a lifer had left him without the ability to read adults properly. But then he looked at Rocky and felt at ease. Rocky was quiet, the kind of seething quiet he had warned Leo to look out for. He was itching for a fight.

"Let us show you what we salvaged," Rocky grunted.

Beatrice led them to the lab on the far side of the house. Leo couldn't help but notice that the lab's instruments seemed to be very old. Beatrice mussed his hair. "Don't worry. You've got a mind like a diamond. That's more important than what's in any lab."

Rocky wiped down a whiteboard. "Okay. Let's brainstorm what Beatrice should look for once she's inside the Arcage's hard drive."

"I'm not going in. Leo is."

"Beatrice, I know it's been a tough day, but c'mon. You know your way around the suit already," Rocky pointed out.

"Sure. But the last time I was in there, I heard Peter's voice. Maybe he'll say more to Leo than he did to me."

Leo started to suit up before Beatrice had time to reconsider.

CHAPTER 66

"What do you know about your father?" Beatrice asked.

Leo squeezed into the Arcage suit (size: ladies medium), then snapped on the goggles. He winced but didn't tell Beatrice how much the goggles hurt the bridge of his nose. "Just what I've read about him. Miss Medici used to let us bring home old magazines from doctor's appointments. I read a few articles about how he'd gone missing. But now I know he must've been awesome if you care so much about what he built."

Beatrice loosened his goggles until they didn't hurt anymore.

"Well, if you run into Peter in there, I hope he has more to say to you than he did to me." She whispered into Leo's ear, "Don't be afraid of the prime numbers. We can help."

But Leo was already shooting down a tunnel of light.

Beatrice and Rocky couldn't see what Leo was seeing, but they could chat with him through an earpiece. "Leo, be careful in there," Rocky warned him. "The first thing you should see is a menu screen."

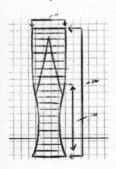

Leo landed hard in front of a majestic tower that was outlined in sky blue and bright white. His heart filled with hope when he recognized where he was.

"No menu screen. It dropped me in front of Wynn Tower."

Rocky shrugged at Beatrice. "You don't see a menu screen. Okay. What do you see?"

"So far, just the tower. Everything else is blank space. I'm going to head inside."

"Leo, just in case, say *sword*. That way you can go in there armed."

"Whoa. Why didn't you tell me that this thing comes with a sword?"

Leo held out his arm and said *sword*. In his left hand, a pen appeared.

"No sword. But I have a pen now. Is this a prank? 'The pen is mightier than the . . .'"

"Sorry. The original code was not as adventurous."

"Don't worry, it's cool. If I see any of those prime numbers, I'll threaten to write something about them."

"Leo, let's try to stay focused on what we can salvage from the Arcage—"

"Here's a haiku: Sorry, prime numbers . . . I promise it's not my fault . . . that you suck so hard."

"Reel it in."

"Sorry. I'm inside Wynn Tower now."

This version of the factory floor was nothing like the real one he'd walked across with Beatrice yesterday morning. It was a vast, empty space consisting of nothing but basic blue and white lines. From the other side of the room, he heard a ding.

"Oh, there's an elevator."

Beatrice held her hand over the mouthpiece, "Should we tell him to take it?"

"I'm getting on the elevator," Leo told them.

Rocky shrugged and Beatrice held up her hands. "Okay, good decision. Great teamwork. Let us know what's up there."

Leo clicked the pen in his left hand as he counted off floors of the elevator. "Sixty-five, sixty-six, sixty-seven . . . it's stopping on sixty-seven."

"It sent you up to the CEO's office."

"Great. Anything I should look for?" Leo asked them as he walked out of the elevator. He checked the name on the door.

"The door says *Beatrice Portinari, CEO*. I'm going in. That's cool, right?"

Beatrice excitedly turned to Rocky. "This is the original code, right? Like, based off of what Peter left behind in a notebook."

"Yes."

"But I wasn't CEO yet when he wrote this code."

"Leo, keep an eye out for anything out of the ordinary."

"Umm, I'm armed with a pen, I'm wearing a ladies' suit, and I'm about to walk into a simulation of my missing father's office. When you say 'out of the ordinary,' I'm going to need you to be more specific."

Beatrice laughed, and Rocky fiddled with the tablet connected to the Arcage. He desperately wanted to see inside that room.

Leo took a deep breath. He clicked the pen one last time and instinctively held it up like a knife. He stepped inside the room and the blue and white lines evaporated. The floor morphed into hardwood, a huge picture window popped up in front of him, and the walls were stylishly decorated with art he didn't recognize.

"Something's happening," Leo told them in a worried tone. He wheeled around, ready to show a prime number what was up.

Rocky punched the table. "One of us should go in there with him!"

Beatrice touched Rocky's shoulder. "Calm down. Who's going to be better at a video game? You or the thirteen-year-old kid?"

"Whoa." Leo spun around and took in the entire room. "Guys, I wish you could see this office. It's not just the blue and white lines. Everything looks and feels, well, real."

Leo reached out and touched the desk.

"There's a big desk. Very impressive." Leo looked out the window. "But outside this room, everything is those same blue and white lines."

Rocky pressed his fingers to his temples. Beatrice chewed her bottom lip as she tried to think of things Leo could look for.

Leo made his way across the room to a bookshelf.

"There's a collection of old books. From what I can tell, they're arranged alphabetically." Leo pulled a book off of the shelf and felt the weight in his hands. He opened it up.

"This one is a first edition of *The Decameron*." He put back *The Decameron* and picked up the book next to it. "Next to a first edition of *The Divine Comedy*."

"Leo, will you look in the top drawer of the desk?" Beatrice asked hurriedly.

"Okay. One second." Leo gently put the *The Divine Comedy* back on the shelf; even though he knew it was a simulation, the books seemed expensive, like his father had carefully curated them. He noticed there was more space between *The Divine Comedy* and *The Decameron* than between any of the other books on the shelf.

"What's in the top drawer of the desk?" Rocky whispered, but Beatrice waved him off. She was too excited.

"Okay, I'll open the drawer."

Beatrice waited with bated breath.

"There's nothing in there," Leo told them.

Beatrice crumpled in her seat. She thought for sure there would have been—

"Wait. Did my dad always keep this book on top of his desk?" Leo asked.

"What book?" Beatrice responded.

"*De rerum natura*. It's this old book by Lucretius. Don't get too excited, though, it's written in Latin." Leo thumbed through the book. It had the same notes in the margins. It was an identical copy of the book he'd found under the Academy of Florence.

"No, he never kept a copy of *De reru*—whatever on that desk."

"Okay. Hold on. I'm going to try something."

Beatrice again bit her lip. Rocky anxiously drummed his fingers on the table.

Leo hustled across the room and slid *De rerum natura* into the space between *The Decameron* and *The Divine Comedy*.

Suddenly the room was filled with the tinkling of a piano.

The window flashed from a nightscape to a sunrise. The room was drenched in sunlight.

Beatrice heard the piano's melody and her eyes welled with tears. This had been Peter's favorite song. She started to sing.

"Here comes the sun . . ."

CHAPTER 67

The window no longer looked out onto blue and white lines. Now it looked out onto a bright laboratory, a version of the same lab Leo was standing in back in the real world. Most important was what he saw sitting on a table, smack-dab in the center of the room.

"There's a Star Disc in the lab," he told them.

When Leo touched the window, it disappeared. He reached out and his hand could feel the wall on the other side of the window. "I'm going to hop through into the lab."

Beatrice grabbed Rocky's arm. "Be careful. You don't know what's waiting in there."

"You're right. Just in case things go off the rails, I'm bringing my pen."

Leo clicked his pen, then hopped through the window. Before

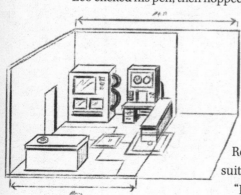

his feet hit the ground, the lab expanded to a hundred feet tall and a hundred feet wide.

"Beatrice, Rocky, you still there?" Leo checked in.

"Yes. What happened?" Rocky got to his feet, ready to suit up and go after Leo.

"I think the lab just had a

growth spurt." Leo reached for the Star Disc, but it jolted his hand. "Ow!" He shook his hand in pain.

"What happened?" Beatrice yelled.

Inside the simulation, a soothing voice spoke. "All lab equipment must be signed out before use."

"I have to sign it out before I'm allowed to use the Star Disc," Leo muttered as he flexed his sore hand and made sure each finger still worked.

"Sword," he said angrily. And the pen appeared in his hand again.

"All lab equipment must be signed out before use."

"I heard you the first time," Leo huffed.

"Leo, check the wall next to where you came in for a sign-out sheet," Beatrice suggested. "Or at least, that was always the rule in your dad's labs."

Leo spun around toward where he'd climbed through the window. A clipboard was hanging on the wall. A green icon flashed around it like, *Over here, dummy.*

"You were right." Leo jogged over and picked up the clipboard.

"What does the sign-out sheet say?" Beatrice wished she had gone in there with him.

But it was more than a simple sign-out sheet. Among the items listed on the sheet were some of science's wildest pipe dreams: dark matter, morphic fields, black holes, CRISPR. Many existed only in theory. But there were also items on the list that he'd been dealing with for the past couple of days: moscovium, gadolinium, and, of course, the Star Disc.

A half smile formed in the corner of Leo's mouth. *Disce quam ut videam.* Leo knew how to see what this was.

"This is like a science lab but without any of the consequences," Leo declared as he tapped a few things he wanted to sign out. "It's definitely safer to test a theory in a simulation before trying it in the real world."

Next to the sign-out sheet, a control panel appeared. Leo slid over in front of it and read the label.

"There's a name on the control panel in here. It says *Galileo*," Leo told them.

Beatrice double-checked a few numbers she had written down on a notepad. "Do you know what Peter originally called the Arcage in his notebook?"

"No. What?" Rocky asked.

"The Galileo."

Rocky laughed. "Peter named it after the father of the scientific method? Why were we going to make it a video game?"

"I hope you guys don't mind if I mess around in here," Leo said as he pressed buttons on the Galileo's control panel like it was a soda machine and he was trying to make the weirdest concoction possible. "Morphic field. Humpback whale. CRISPR edit. Spliced with fir tree DNA."

A prompt appeared at the bottom of the sheet: SIMULATE?

Leo swiped the button.

In the center of the room, an immense whale appeared. Its skin looked like the branches of a Christmas tree. It emitted the long, plaintive mating call of a humpback whale, which sounded like a violin holding a low note for as long as possible. After its mating call, it blew a geyser of pine cones out of its blowhole.

The soothing voice spoke again. "Not viable."

For the next half hour, Leo amused himself with any experiment he could imagine in his dad's science playground. He set off a hydrogen bomb in a black hole. (Not viable.) He tried to make a dark matter reactor. (Not viable.) His favorite experiment had been using CRISPR to create an elephant the size of a big dog. (Viable!) The Galileo offered him a button that said CREATE? But Beatrice and Rocky told him he couldn't keep it.

"No way. You know I'll end up being the one who has to walk it," Rocky contended. "Besides, you've already got two pets."

"How would the machine create it anyway?" Leo asked.

"Your dad made sure Wynn Mansion could store so much power because it has one of the world's largest 3D printers," Beatrice explained. "And before you ask, no, we are not 3D printing any living things in there, Doctor Moreau."

As Leo went back to running more experiments, Beatrice worked out some numbers, growing more and more excited. Finally, she put her pen down and turned to Rocky. "This is it. This is what we're going to debut at the toy fair. The Galileo. All the data is already loaded up. It'll be less expensive to manufacture than the Arcage."

"Are you serious? I do *not* want to meet the parents who allow their kids to make eighty-five-pound domesticated elephants on a whim—"

"3D printer sold separately! Every school, every corporate

research department, everyone who tinkers in their garage will want one. This is so much more than a toy."

Back in the simulation, Leo checked the Star Disc on the sign-out sheet. He closed his eyes, and the new idea materialized like a bolt of lightning in a summer storm. His brain started to sizzle. *Disce quam ut videam.* In his mind's eye, he solved how the invention's wheels would rotate around the Star Disc like planets orbiting the sun. How the magnet of the Star Disc could be used as an engine, pushing magnets as fast as he needed. And most importantly, how he could use the magnet to keep the Star Disc safely suspended in the center of the wheels so that he could ride it.

Leo rapidly signed out everything else he thought he might need—more moscovium to form the magnetic wheels, some vulcanized rubber for the tires, and plenty of gadolinium to keep the magnets stable. Then he shaped the two wheels, making sure the larger wheel would levitate slightly outside the smaller wheel without touching it. The magnetic force between the wheels would propel the bike forward, or backward, or in any direction Leo wanted, creating magnetic-levitation tracks— the same science used to move the world's fastest bullet trains. Finally, with painstaking care, he placed the Star Disc in the center then swiped SIMULATE.

The image flashed red and he heard a hard buzz. (Not viable.)

He reexamined the model, and there was a flashing red icon around the Star Disc.

Disappointed but not defeated, Leo paced around the room, racking his brain for the detail he must have overlooked. This invention had come to him so naturally. At the window, he looked back into the CEO's office. In the corner, his dad's old café racer motorcycle with a big leather seat was propped on its kickstand.

Could it be that simple?

He dashed back and shaped a saddle around the Star Disc, picking the leather that looked most like his dad's motorcycle. He stepped back and swiped the SIMULATE button again.

It flashed green. (Viable!)

The Galileo gave him another prompt. CREATE?

Leo mashed the button. "Needed a seat, huh? Form only *with* function."

On the far side of Wynn Mansion, the 3D printer whirred to life. The same voice that had told him to use the sign-out sheet spoke again. "In thirty-three minutes, your MAG-LEV bicycle will be ready."

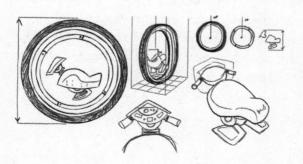

CHAPTER 68

Nick kept to the back roads and tried to stay under the cover of the trees. The drones must have been dispatched to hunt him down by now. Frankly, he was surprised he had managed to evade them for this long. It gave him a much-needed shot of confidence.

Nick had sneaked off while O was on stage announcing the Shroud. He'd left his phone and his watch behind. Anything connected to the internet would be used to track him. The only item he'd taken with him was his staff, the one his brother had given him so many years ago.

He came to the top of the ridge and stopped. He listened for the buzz of the drones, searching the horizon for any sign of them. Once he was certain he was in the clear, he started to descend toward the river.

If he hiked all night, he could make it to Wynn Mansion by dawn. Though Peter had warned him, "The house has a mind of its own. Do what you can to stay on its good side."

He hoped the mansion would let him in so he could finally talk to the boy. Nick needed to tell Leo that his father was still alive. And where they were keeping him.

CHAPTER 69

Hours after the sun had set, Beatrice walked around the courtyard of Wynn Mansion, going over her presentation in her head. She knew the Galileo would succeed. She could feel it in her bones. Nevertheless, failing to prepare was preparing to fail.

Dante and Gemini had accompanied her on her walk, but they were becoming a distraction. The big lion chased after squirrels while Dante kept trying to surreptitiously hold her hand. He stopped to help her across a small puddle.

"Oh, thank you. My hero." Beatrice walked past as Dante took a deep bow.

Gemini came crashing out of a bush and Dante screeched. Gemini ignored the monkey and pranced around them in a circle.

He had a long, shiny object pinched between his fangs. Dante screeched again and tried to shoo Gemini away.

Gemini wagged his tail back and forth then dropped it at her feet. Beatrice picked it up, even though it was covered in his slobber. Gemini backed away eagerly with his tongue out, hoping she would throw it.

Beatrice dipped her hips, preparing to chuck a piece of metal as far as she could.

But as her fingers gripped the object, she felt a raised texture on the bottom. She held it closer to her face but still couldn't see what it was. "Dante," she said sweetly. "Could you do me a huge favor? Could you come shine your light on this?"

Dante hopped over, gave Gemini a cocky look, then clicked on the flashlight in his eyes. At the bottom of the piece of metal, Beatrice saw an interlocking M-V logo.

Mach Valley.

"Sorry, buddy," she told Gemini. "We're not playing fetch with this thing." She jogged back to the house with Gemini trotting along after her.

"Rocky! You have to see this!" she yelled as she neared the driveway.

One of the cedar garage doors swung open slowly. Inside the empty garage, Rocky held on to the back of an old bicycle while Leo sat forward.

Rocky removed his grip and Leo tipped over immediately. Gemini pounced on him and licked his face.

"Gemini dragged it out of from under a tree in the courtyard." Beatrice held out the piece of metal. Rocky inspected it slowly. He froze when he saw the label.

"We'd better go check those mines." Rocky's face was ashen. "If they're Mach Valley too . . ."

"We're going to the cops," Beatrice finished.

They traipsed down to the river in the dark. Dante rode on Gemini's back, using his flashlight to show them the way.

On the river, Peter's carbon fiber boat bobbed gently on the water, still anchored to the rock on the bank. Dante pointed his flashlight at the water in the cut between the pond and river.

The mines were gone.

Beatrice erupted. "I knew it. They cannot compete without resorting to evil. Mach Valley is what would happen if Ric Flair ran a tech company. They have been using cheat-to-win tactics for years, and I'm sick of it. Two times when I should've listened to my intuition: I never should've gone to prom with Mike Rainey, and as soon as Mach Valley came out with the Polly Pees-A-Lot, I should've called the lawyers."

"Get fired up! I want to see your patch of white hair turn red," Rocky egged.

"Those mines were huge. Not even Gemini would be strong enough to yank one out of the water. I assumed they were another way that Peter defended the house, but no, they're gone the next day. And suddenly a Mach Valley drone crashes in the courtyard? There is no reason for one of their drones to be anywhere near this house."

"Sure. But who took down that drone in the courtyard?" Leo asked. He wanted to be as mad as Beatrice was, and he wanted to hear her theory.

"I'm not sure yet. But I'm going to confront them at the toy fair tomorrow. And I'm bringing this thing with me." Beatrice held up the piece of the drone.

They trudged back up to the house in an anxious silence, worried about what Mach Valley was planning to do.

The truth was that they did not need to worry. As long as they didn't leave the house.

CHAPTER 70

Savvy added another layer of lanolin to the glove. This was the kind of detail someone like Leo would overlook. The key to all victory is in the mastery of the nonobvious.

He held the glove out in front of himself and appreciated its craftsmanship. Survive and adapt. He couldn't wait to see the look on Leo's face when he saw his "best friend" had survived, and how he had adapted to deal with Leo's toys.

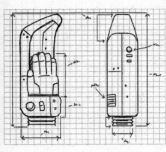

There was a knock at the door. One boom, as if a normal man had thrown a stiff jab. Savvy knew exactly who it was from the knock alone.

O ducked to come through the doorway, then drew himself back up to his full height.

"We have moved up our timeline."

"To when?" Savvy asked keenly.

"Tomorrow morning. During their presentation."

Savvy smiled. He admired this man. He operated with such ruthless efficiency, which Savvy had never found in another person. He felt a kinship.

"We have an announcement to make first. And remember, if they bring that disc, it's mine alone. No one else is to touch it."

Savvy nodded his head. "Of course." But behind his back, his fingers were crossed. Survive and adapt.

CHAPTER 71

Beatrice slid the hunk of metal across the back seat of one of Peter's old cars, a red Alfa Romeo. The sight of the Mach Valley logo infuriated her all over again, and she slammed the door. She was amped for a confrontation. She'd rehearsed precisely what she was going to say to O and how she was going to say it right to his smug face.

"Let's go, guys," she called to Rocky and Leo. "Leo, do you want to ride shotgun? I'll let you pick the music."

"Thank you, but I'm going to ride with Rocky. I, um, might have something cool for you at the toy fair. It depends on Rocky's approval."

Rocky winked at Leo, who mischievously looked at his shoes.

"We'll be right behind you," Rocky assured her.

Before she made the turn out of the driveway, Beatrice checked her rearview mirror. She loved what she saw: Rocky jumped up and down, his arms raised overhead, as Leo rode a bike in wide circles around him.

Leo had learned how to ride a bike. Finally. Rocky wouldn't let him bring his new invention to the toy fair until he did.

"And you are sure Beatrice will be okay with it?" Leo asked tentatively.

"Are you kidding me? She'll be over the moon when she sees you on that MAG-LEV. You made a really beautiful thing. Be proud of it, but let your achievement speak for itself: confidence is silent, insecurities are loud."

CHAPTER 72

As Beatrice pulled into the toy fair, she saw ads for the Shroud hanging from every lamppost. Two LED billboards displayed 3D commercials on a loop, and above her was the crown jewel: a blimp floating in a ten-mile radius over the city, the MV logo on the side. Mach Valley had spared no expense. She tasted iron and realized she'd been chewing her lip so hard it was bleeding.

She grabbed the piece of drone from the back seat and walked toward the theater. A crowd had gathered around a giant television screen. Beatrice read the ticker on the bottom and rolled her eyes. "Mach Valley pushes augmented reality in an entirely new direction with the Shroud!" it read.

She was opening the door to the theater when a voice from the TV screen stopped her in her tracks.

"Look, it could be parallel thinking. This kind of thing happens quite frequently in the tech business. Similar products with similar innovations come along at the same time. Like the iPhone versus the Android. Or the PlayStation versus the Xbox. I get it. We are competitors, and we welcome competition . . ."

On the screen, O was giving a press conference.

"I'm willing to give Wynn Toys the benefit of the doubt. But not only is the Shroud a groundbreaking new product, each Shroud is built in a factory powered by a revolutionary new technology, a Star Disc. It's our proprietary technology. It has been in development at Mach Valley for nearly thirteen years. As long as Miss Portinari and Wynn Toys have not stolen that technology, we will continue to live and let live."

A few people in the crowd nudged each other once they noticed Beatrice watching the TV behind them. Meanwhile, O continued to smile and lie.

"The tech industry is like a small town. Everybody knows everybody else's business. So I've heard rumors that Wynn is going to debut a device similar to our Star Disc at the toy fair." O sat forward and bared his teeth. His tone morphed from folksy to menacing. "If that's the case, Miss Portinari better have a reasonable explanation for why her company would debut a technology I *personally* invented. Although it's not like she would walk into the toy fair holding Mach Valley technology."

Beatrice was suddenly very self-conscious of the hunk of metal in her hands. She wrapped her fingers around the end to cover the Mach Valley logo.

"... because if Miss Portinari had gotten her hands on Mach Valley tech, I would feel compelled to involve law enforcement."

"You're threatening to come after *us*? You've got another thing coming, buddy," Beatrice muttered as she walked through the door and into the theater.

She took her fingers away from the Mach Valley logo. She didn't care. Let them see. She knew that Wynn hadn't stolen a thing. She knew that if he were alive to see it, Peter would be proud of how she'd managed Wynn Toys.

Little did she know, Peter *was* watching.

CHAPTER 73

After another ten minutes of trudging along on his blistered feet, Nick walked under the stegosaurus bridge and up the hill toward Wynn Mansion.

There were no cars parked outside the house. He felt his stomach drop. He must have missed Leo. He had failed to warn him the toy fair was a trap.

He heard the buzz before he saw them: a flock of drones large enough to blot out the sun. Nick sprinted toward the house. If he didn't get inside in the next thirty seconds, he was a dead man.

Most people assumed Peter had designed Wynn Mansion and its defenses, but that wasn't entirely true. Peter had let someone else create the security program that determined who was worthy of entering Wynn Mansion. Nick knew if the house decided he was unworthy, he'd be fried to a crisp the moment he touched the fence. But even that would be a better death than what would happen to him if he was captured by the flock.

The drones descended in perfect formation and made a beeline for Nick. As he reached for the top rail of the fence, he prayed he had done enough and that the house's security had been programmed to admit him.

Nick didn't know where the security system designer was, but he certainly had information that she would love to hear. Because Peter had told him that the house's security system was designed by Leo's mother.

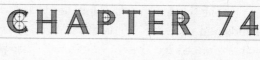

CHAPTER 74

Moving through the crowd at the Milan Toy Fair, Leo sensed he had found his tribe. It felt like the first day of school crossed with a circus. He wanted to stop at every booth and ask them how they imagined such cool toys— one company even had slime that danced on beat to music—but Rocky was in no mood to browse.

They left the courtyard of the old castle and headed to the theater. On the marquee above the entrance, a hologram of the Wynn Toys logo climbed up the side of Wynn Tower. Leo paused to watch it, but Rocky pulled him toward the doors.

"I know this is your first time at the toy fair, but we should see Beatrice first. We can check out the fair after she finishes. I think this pass gets you early access to the robot petting zoo," Rocky promised as he put a lanyard around Leo's neck.

They rounded the corner and nearly ran into Beatrice, who was being trailed by a group of reporters, all of whom were barking out questions.

"Did the incident at Wynn Tower a few nights ago have anything to do with Mach Valley's accusations today?"

"What caused Wynn Tower's beacon to erupt?"

"Mach Valley accused you of corporate espionage. What is a Star Disc?"

Beatrice took Leo and Rocky into her dressing room and closed the door.

In the theater, the small but devoted crowd clapped their hands and chanted, "Wynn Toys! Wynn Toys!" The theater's lights dimmed and the crowd cheered. Crisp piano notes echoed from the stage. Leo recognized the song as "Bohemian Rhapsody" by Queen. The crowd picked up the song, singing along. "Mama, life had just begun . . ."

Beatrice pulled Rocky and Leo in close so they could hear her over the crowd. She was seething. "Mach Valley is trying to set us up. We *stole* the Star Disc? When? When Leo found it? Or when Peter led us to you, Leo?"

Beatrice's pupils dilated as she grabbed Leo's hand. "The only thing stolen here was our ideas. I don't know why Mach Valley feels like they can mess with us, but my past is littered with the bones of men who have underestimated me."

The hair on the back of Leo's neck stood up. Suddenly he felt like a human firecracker. And the song had stirred the crowd into a frenzy; now they were chanting along to the guitar solo.

"Rocky, stay here and watch my back. Leo, you should watch from the side of the stage. You'll be doing these presentations soon enough. Where are Gemini and Dante?"

"They're out in the car, guarding the Star Disc. Or at least Gemini is," Leo clarified.

"Good. I'm about make this crowd pop with what we discovered last night." She walked out of the dressing room and opened the curtain. The song was in full swing and the crowd was on their feet. "Galileo! Gal-i-leo! Galileo! Gal-i-leo! Galileo! Figaro, magnifico-ohhhhh!"

A spotlight shined on a podium at the center of the stage where a black cube glistened in the hot light. Beatrice stepped out onto the stage. She hit her mark just as the song reached its crescendo and the music stopped instantly.

"This is the Galileo from Wynn Toys. Let me introduce you."

The crowd went bananas. They'd been properly worked up into a lather.

"Galileo. Father of the scientific method, harbinger of the modern world, the man who allowed us to think, 'What can we think of next?'" Beatrice turned on the Galileo.

"What does the Galileo do? More than letting you *imagine* that anything is possible." Beatrice tapped the Galileo, and it cycled its most recent experiments: the dark matter reactor, the whale made of pine cones, Leo's MAG-LEV bike. "The Galileo lets you *build* anything that is possible."

There were audible gasps from the crowd as Beatrice manipulated the hologram of the MAG-LEV bike that was floating out over the crowd.

"What you're seeing right now is a vehicle our youngest engineer designed last night. The vehicle produces *zero* emissions, because it requires *zero* fuel. Instead, it is powered by something you may have heard of earlier today, the Star Disc—"

The theater lights went out again.

But this time there was no music, no raucous clapping, no sing-alongs. Only an ominous silence, which was soon interrupted by the sound of hard-soled leather boots marching down the aisles in an eerie rhythm.

When the lights came back up, a horde of policemen were standing in the aisles. And on stage, one policeman was squeezing Beatrice's wrist.

"Miss Portinari, you're under arrest."

"Get your hands off of me!" Beatrice shouted.

The crowd erupted into a chorus of boos.

Leo recognized the policeman. It was the same cop who had grabbed him at the Academy of Florence.

CHAPTER 75

Leo ran backstage and tugged on Rocky's arm. "We have to go get Gemini."

Rocky shook him off. "We will. Right after I tell this cop to go pound sand."

"That's not a police officer. That's not even a human."

"What? What are you talking about?"

"That's the same cop who attacked me at the academy. Or, I mean, it's not the same cop unless he found some *sick* glue. He's a robot," Leo explained.

Rocky squinted to get a better look. The officer was trying to handcuff Beatrice, but she kept slipping away. More officers, all wearing the same sunglasses, surrounded her. A few people in the panicked crowd yelled at the cops to leave her alone.

Rocky pushed Leo toward the door. "All right. Let's go get the big cat. Those guys deserve to get mauled just for wearing sunglasses indoors."

While still sprinting out of the theater, Rocky pressed the key fob and popped the trunk of the car. An appreciative Gemini sprang out and shook his mane. He wagged his tail when he saw Leo running toward him.

Leo gave him a brusque pat on the head, then yanked his saddle out of the trunk. In the back seat, Dante twiddled his thumbs.

"Let's go, Dante."

Dante crossed his arms and refused to budge.

"I'm sorry. You've been such a good boy. I should've noticed. Let's go."

But he still did not move.

"Fine. Stay here if you want. But Beatrice is in trouble."

Dante launched himself out of the back seat, torqued around Leo's shoulder, and landed on Gemini's back.

Leo pulled a stack of thin tracks out of the trunk. He swiftly snapped the saddle around his torso, then motioned for Gemini to back away. "Dig your claws into the ground, just in case. Dante, hold on tight."

Dante tightened his grip on Gemini's mane. The lion dug two paws into the ground and another into the tires of an eighteen-wheeler truck that was parked next to them. The air hissed out of the lacerated tire.

"Ugh. That sounds like a clown's dying breath," Rocky said as he rummaged through the trunk until he found Leo's helmet—one of Peter's old motorcycle helmets, on which Leo had painted a pair of lion's fangs. Leo snapped the chinstrap of his helmet and Rocky pulled out an Infinity Ball.

Rocky delicately handed him the ball. "Be careful. The changes might make it easier to handle, but it still seems dangerous. What's the magic word?"

"Simple," Leo said.

The Infinity Ball vibrated to life. With Rocky's help, Leo had built a voice-activated power button. Finally, he could turn the Infinity Ball on and off.

"Wait. If you get that, what do I use to fight these cops?" Rocky asked.

"Duh. You get Dante and Gemini," Leo told him.

Rocky sized up the two creatures. "Those guys aren't ready for five hundred pounds of trouble."

Dante squealed.

"He wants you to know it's actually *527* pounds of trouble," Leo said.

"Wow. Have you been working out? Making gains?" Rocky asked.

"Everybody ready?" Leo checked in one last time, knowing he was about to lead them into a fight. Dante screeched, Gemini dug his nails deeper into the ground and spat out the tennis ball he'd been chewing on. Rocky shadowboxed.

Leo was lifting his hand to swipe on the Star Disc when a fist punched through the trailer of the eighteen-wheeler and grabbed Leo's shirt in a vise grip. He was yanked into the air and turned upside down.

"You have the right to remain silent," a voice commanded from inside the trailer.

A second hand punched through the trailer and grabbed Leo's wrists, making it impossible to operate the Star Disc. The hands shook Leo like a rag doll and pulled him closer to the hole so he was face to face with his attacker.

Again, it looked like the same police officer from the Academy of Florence.

CHAPTER 76

"Where is the Star Disc, ma'am?" the officer asked again in an oddly friendly tone.

"I'll tell you as soon as you tell me who sent you," she spat back at him.

Beatrice could hear the crowd being pushed out of the theater, herded toward the exits by the other police officers. As long as she could hear the crowd, she knew she was safe. But once the crowd was gone, there would be no more witnesses, and her captor could stop asking questions nicely.

He had handcuffed her left arm to the podium. She balled up her right fist, spread her feet a shoulder's width apart, and waited for him to come within reach.

They were interrupted by a security guard pounding on the door. "Is everything okay in there? This door was to remain unlocked at all times."

The cop covered Beatrice's mouth roughly with his hand. It wasn't until he spoke that real terror shot through her body.

"Yes, it's just me, Miss Portinari. Would you mind giving me some privacy? I should only need a few minutes," the cop responded, in a flawlessly mimicked version of Beatrice's own voice.

He turned toward her and took off his glasses. His eyes were white and devoid of pupils. Instead, eight letters scrolled across the center of his eyes. In that moment, Beatrice finally realized who was behind Mach Valley.

CHAPTER 77

"Let go of me!" Leo tried to slap at the hands that had punched through the trailer.

Dante shrieked but Gemini did as he was told and kept his claws dug into the ground and the tire. Rocky remained eerily quiet.

The old man didn't scream. He just took two steps forward, bent his knees, then crashed his whole body weight at the underside of the cop's elbows, forcing him to drop Leo. Leo landed on his back with the saddle on his chest, knocking the wind out of him.

Rocky quickly picked up Dante. "Gemini, open up!"

He threw Dante inside Gemini's open chest as two metallic hands tore a jagged hole in the side of the trailer. The cop pushed his torso through the opening. He was halfway out of the trailer and reaching for Leo again when Rocky grabbed Leo's finger and hastily swiped it across the Star Disc.

In the blink of an eye, the tracks Leo had laid down snapped together in two concentric circles, forming the wheels of the MAG-LEV bike. A thin blue light ran around the diameter. Leo was pulled from the ground and hovered in the center of the circles.

The powerful gravity of the Star Disc tore the top half of the cop out of the trailer, but only the top half. Once the MAG-LEV bike was fully formed, however, the top half of the cop plopped onto the ground.

Leo coughed and gathered himself. Rocky stood in front of Gemini, trying to keep the lion away from the MAG-LEV bike and, by extension, the Star Disc.

"He's okay. Once the bike is formed, the disc is safe. The magnets run against each other and produce a centrifugal force. They actually repel metal," Leo said.

Rocky kicked at the wires tumbling out of the cop's torso. "He really was a robot."

"Told you. They're all robots," Leo said.

Gemini licked some of the oil that had puddled under the robot's torso, but Rocky shooed him away.

"Let's go." Leo leaned forward. The light between the wheels changed to green as he sped back toward the theater.

On the far side of the old castle, another trailer opened its doors. Thousands of fire ants poured out on to the street.

Savvy stepped on top of the fleet of ants, flipped back his hair with practiced nonchalance, then put his on his mask.

"Weepers."

With one word, the ants picked him up and marched toward the theater.

CHAPTER 78

If Beatrice was going down, she was going down
swinging. She shifted her weight and was ready to
hit the robot with an uppercut when a glint of shiny metal under
the podium caught her eye. It was the piece of the downed drone
she had brought with her from Wynn Mansion.

She slapped his hand away from where it was covering
her mouth and dove for cover. He punched the podium with a
hammer fist, smashing it into splinters and freeing her arm. She
desperately grabbed at the hunk of metal and swung it back at
his face.

The heavy end caught him square in the Adam's apple. It
knocked him sideways, and he teetered on his left foot. She
reeled back and swung as hard as she could at the back of his leg.

She scrambled to her feet and swung the metal like a bat
one more time. He collapsed onto the floor. She tried to run for
the door, but her heels slipped on some of the oil that was squirt-
ing out of his knee.

Beatrice used the piece of the drone to balance herself, then
she unlocked the door and threw it open. A big-bodied security
guard was waiting on the other side.

"Everything okay, Miss Portinari?" he asked.

She moved past him and jogged toward the exit to the parking lot. The security guard peeked onto the stage and saw the
carnage Beatrice had left behind her.

"We've got an officer down. I need backup," he spoke into his walkie-talkie.

Beatrice was ahead of him, still carrying the metal she had used to bludgeon the android.

"Stop, ma'am. Stop!"

She ignored him. When she rounded a corner, he started to jog after her. He pulled his taser out and flicked it on.

"Miss Portinari, please don't make me tase you—"

Wham!

As he rounded the corner, he was slammed flat on his back. Both of his shoulders were pinned to the ground. A spongy wetness methodically covered his face.

"All right, Gemini. He's had enough. Let him up," Beatrice admonished.

The security guard wiped his face, and Rocky handed him back his taser.

"This isn't your fight. You better hit the road." Rocky opened the back door for him.

"I'm not going anywhere. She hurt that cop." The security guard gestured back toward the stage.

"That was no cop, my friend," Rocky told him as dozens more of the exact same police officer began to assemble outside in the parking lot. "Do any of those guys look familiar?"

Beatrice raised the broken piece of drone. The end was covered in a dark, gooey liquid. She ran her finger through it, then held the tip of her finger to the security guard.

"The one back there isn't bleeding, he's face down in a pool of motor oil. That isn't a police force—it's a robot army."

She smacked the hunk of metal on the ground.

"And we made them."

CHAPTER 79

Leo had practiced riding the bike before they left Wynn Mansion. He had a handle on how the MAG-LEV bike could accelerate, how it could stop, and how it could corner. What he did *not* have a handle on was just how fast it would go.

He was trying to get a handle on that now.

His job was to be a distraction. Rocky needed him to draw as many robots as possible away from the theater so he could get Beatrice out of there.

Leo sped directly at the pack of police robots. The odometer on his visor helmet read 75 miles per hour, and it felt effortless.

85 mph. He could barely make out the cars as he blew by them.

95 mph. The bike rocketed toward the pack of police officers, who turned their heads in an unnerving unison.

Leo eased back on the saddle, the light between the two wheels changed from green to red, and the bike silently slid to a stop. He jammed his hand into his pocket for the Infinity Ball. The phalanx of robot cops reached for the tasers on their hips.

This had been part of the plan.

He hopped off the saddle and said, "Simple." Then he threw the Infinity Ball against the stone wall of the theater. The robots tracked the ball with their eyes.

The ball ricocheted off the wall into the throng of robots.

It pinballed around the pack, smashing through them with concussive force. One robot managed to stagger to his feet and marched toward Leo.

"You have the right to remain silent," the robot said in a much too cheerful tone.

Leo stepped back until he was hovering inside the MAG-LEV wheels again. He tapped the Star Disc magnet on to half power.

The force instantly collapsed the cop into the size of a soda can.

"Simple," Leo said.

The Infinity Ball dropped and skidded next to the castle. Leo rode the MAG-LEV bike over and picked up the ball. The smell of smoke wafted around the walls. Curious, Leo pushed the bike forward and peeked around the corner of the castle.

A plume of flame shot past his ear, barely missing him but igniting a hedge.

"There he is, my best friend!" Savvy rode a wave of fire ants with a crazed look in his eyes. "And it looks like somebody finally taught him how to ride a bike."

Leo rapidly turned the MAG-LEV in a half circle and pushed it full throttle. He cranked the Infinity Ball and bounced it hard off the castle wall, expecting it to career into Savvy's ants.

Instead, he felt a sickening thump in the back of his ribs. The Infinity Ball bounced off his back and rebounded high off of the castle wall. He wobbled on the bike but stayed upright. He moaned a painful *simple* and caught the ball on a bounce.

Savvy chased after him, pointing with a long glove on his arm. "This is a cesta, a glove used in jai alai. I adapted it for you and your stupid ball. Survive and adapt, Leo. That's all I do. Yet you are still so predictable that I knew exactly where to find you."

Leo pushed the MAG-LEV bike forward. Flames singed his back as Savvy fired another round of liquid napalm. Smoke billowed above the ramparts of the castle.

"What did you do, Savvy?" Leo leaned right, and the inner wheel turned 45 degrees. The bike cut on a dime. Leo felt a slight bit of nausea as the bike pulled three Gs of gravitational force, but he was otherwise fine.

He nosed the saddle down and sped toward an open tunnel that led back into the castle courtyard. Savvy sent a division of his fire ants to swarm the mouth of the tunnel. Leo hurled the Infinity Ball into the mass of them, but at the last second, he noticed two people from the toy fair were running out of the tunnel.

"Get down!" Leo yelled. The people dove to the ground.

The ball turned the ants into shrapnel. The two men crawled out of the tunnel, dazed and scared. Savvy screamed, "See, Leo, I was right—your ideas are dangerous. This is what happens when you don't listen to people who know what's best for you."

Leo whispered *simple* so he could catch the Infinity Ball, but he fumbled it, and it bounced on the ground. Savvy and his fire ants were too close for him to stop and pick it up. When he checked his rearview mirror, the ants covered the tunnel from top to bottom.

Leo charged into the castle's courtyard. Everywhere he looked was carnage. Savvy had turned the toy fair into a sea of flame—booths were still burning, people fleeing.

The Wynn Toys display looked to have borne the brunt of Savvy's anger. He had burned a cross pattern into the ground and liquified the booths into pools of fire. A revolting stench emanated from the intestines of the burning Molly-Poops-A-Lots.

"Wynn has big ideas but terrible execution. You'll fit right in, Leo." Savvy whipped his glove around, and the Infinity Ball crashed into the side of Leo's helmet.

"Dangerous ideas are especially dangerous in the hands of a lesser mind." Savvy gestured to the booths of the tech companies, where the toys and gadgets were melting into colorful goop. "These people could've made the world a better place. They could've become doctors. They could've become teachers. They could've made things better, but instead they used their minds to get rich making trinkets. This is what they deserve for their vanity."

Leo leaned forward and dodged another of Savvy's firebolts. The MAG-LEV tires spun in the mud.

"People make choices, Savvy. If you don't agree with their choices, you don't get to destroy them."

The ants swarmed in a half circle. Leo hopped to the right and so did the bulk of the Weepers behind Savvy. Leo noticed that the fire ants were mirroring *his* movements, not Savvy's.

Leo leaned back and sped the MAG-LEV bike in reverse at full throttle. The ants briefly moved backward too until Savvy recognized what Leo was doing. He sent the ants forward to try and close the gap. But the MAG-LEV tires skidded out of the ash onto solid ground again. Leo whipped the bike forward and tapped for more power. He accelerated up a steep slope to the castle's ramparts.

"You can't outrun me. You can't outsmart me, Leo." Savvy's voice projected through the thousands of fire ants who climbed the ramparts, chasing after Leo. "Someone is going to get hurt here, Leo. And it's not going to be me."

Savvy lifted his hands, and his ants took him higher so he could peer over the ramparts of the castle. Leo accelerated the bike and jumped onto the ledge of the ramparts so he could see where Savvy was looking.

Outside the castle, the robot cops were dragging Beatrice and Rocky toward a black SUV. He had been fooled. Leo wasn't the distraction, Savvy was. And Leo fell for it. He knew how to see, but not always what he *needed* to see.

Leo dropped back down onto the ramparts, and the bike fishtailed. Another firebolt smacked into his back wheel, but his path stayed true.

In his rearview, the Weepers mirrored his wobble, just as Savvy had programmed them to.

Leo turned again, racing back toward the courtyard. *Disce quam ut videam.* He angled the bike so it sped at the four-foot-high wall. At the last second, he leaned hard, and the bike went horizontal, allowing both wheels to clear the barrier. He was soaring through the air. Behind him, the Weepers mirrored his behavior. One of the ants pinched onto the outermost wheel of the MAG-LEV and was spun at 7,000 RPMs.

Halfway to the ground, Savvy understood what Leo had done, but it was too late. Leo soared over the cross of fire, all that remained of the Wynn Toys display. Behind him, Savvy landed softly in the cross atop the Weepers he was riding. Savvy pushed them forward as fast as possible, but the fire ants who had jumped after him—the Weepers mirroring Leo—rained down on Savvy like a thousand comets.

Leo thrust forward and drove the bike out of the castle's courtyard and through the tunnel into the street. He had to get Beatrice and Rocky as fast as he could.

CHAPTER 80

Rocky tried to resist, but the officers shoved him hard in the back.

"Fat load of good you turned out to be," Rocky griped at Gemini, who happily wagged his tail like they were out for an afternoon walk. Gemini dropped his tennis ball on an officer's foot—the android kicked it away and ignored him. Dante squealed and they smacked him until he quieted down.

Another android officer had fixed a gag tight across Beatrice's mouth. She had tried to wiggle away, she had tried to scream, but he'd shook her shoulder so hard she wondered if he'd broken her clavicle.

Behind her, Beatrice heard a buzzing noise grow louder. Then, without warning, Rocky shoved her hard to the ground.

"Stay down!" Rocky warned.

Chaos broke out among the officers as the Infinity Ball bashed the battalion into bits.

Leo sped by on the MAG-LEV bike and yelled, "Gemini, now!"

Gemini picked up his tennis ball and chased after him.

"No, Gemini. Fight."

One of the robot cops scooped up Beatrice and Rocky, then shoved them into a black SUV with the vanity license plate reading CARP8 DM.

Dante jumped on top of the car and pounded his fists.

Gemini wagged his tail happily as Leo rode circles around him, trying to goad the lion into a fight.

"I need you," Leo told him.

Gemini sat down and offered his paw.

"No play. Fight!" Leo screamed.

A police baton smashed into Leo's neck and knocked him sideways. The belt around his chest snapped, and the Star Disc fell to the ground. The wheels of the MAG-LEV collapsed.

The robot cop stepped over Leo, who was writhing on the ground in pain, and retrieved his baton. He raised it over his head, ready to finish off Leo.

Gemini roared. He pounced on the android who had hit Leo with his baton. Gemini slashed him to pieces. More of the android officers surrounded Gemini and tried to bash him with their batons, but the lion became a tornado of teeth and claws.

Another officer picked up Leo and grabbed at the saddle on his chest. Gemini broke out from the scrum and mauled his arms until he dropped Leo. Behind him, an android raised his taster at Leo, but Gemini dove at him and took out his legs.

Leo staggered back to his feet. Gemini put himself between the robots and Leo. The lion had a wild look in his eye. His jaws and mane were covered in motor oil and bits of circuits. Dozens of the robots were laid out in piles around him. Gemini snarled and stayed in front of Leo.

"Good job, boy. Thank you for protecting me. Go help Beatrice."

Gemini rammed the side of the black SUV. The truck

wobbled on its tires. Gemini leapt on top of the SUV and clawed the sunroof.

The tallest man Leo had ever seen stepped out of the SUV. His skin was taut and shiny. His shoulders looked like cannonballs covered in cotton. He would have been handsome if not for his dead eyes. There was no vitality, no playfulness in them.

"Ahhh, Leo. If you're here, I can only imagine what happened to Savvy."

Two more android cops on the far side of the truck made the mistake of firing their tasers at Gemini. He pounced on them and shredded them to pieces.

"Is that your pet? He seems . . ."

Gemini ran back to Leo with a leg between his jaws.

"Sweet." The giant man sneered at Leo and Gemini.

"Let them go, and he won't hurt you." Leo held Gemini's tail.

"Thank you for your kind offer. Would you like to see her?" He stretched his arms wide, then smashed his elbow into the window of the truck. Glass rained on Rocky in the back seat, and Beatrice's screams were muffled by the gag in her mouth.

Dante sprang off of the ground at the big man's face. O caught Dante and threw him toward the castle with a flick of his wrist; two hundred feet like it was nothing.

Gemini stood on his hind legs and growled. He dove and clawed the big man's leg with his paw, tearing a hole in his jeans. Blood pooled under the man's shoe. The blood renewed Leo's confidence. *If he bleeds, he's just a man.*

But the colossus reached down and grabbed Gemini by the

mane, picking up the five-hundred-pound lion with one hand like he was a loaf of bread.

"Put him down," Leo demanded.

"He's almost real. You Wynns, you love mimicking life. So much creative genius. It's a shame you don't know how dangerous you are."

"Savvy said the same thing, you hack. Put. Him. Down!"

"As you wish."

O raised Gemini over his head, then brought the lion down hard and broke him across his knee. Gemini yelped. The green light went out of his eyes.

Leo screamed. "Nooooo!"

O came toward Leo, but Leo dove for the Star Disc saddle and flicked it on. The SUV started to slide but the colossus caught it with one hand and kept it in place.

Leo hovered into the center of the re-formed MAG-LEV bike, and Gemini's body attached to the bottom of the saddle.

A few people stumbled out of the side of the castle. They took out their phones when they saw O standing next to the black SUV.

"O! Is Mach Valley going to make that motorcycle?"

"Can I get a selfie?"

This might be Leo's only chance to get away. The giant wouldn't kill him in front of a crowd. Not because it was evil, but because it would be bad for business. Leo picked up Dante and peeled out of the parking lot on the MAG-LEV. It was hard to see where he was going through the tears.

O waved to the onlookers and even took a few selfies while carefully keeping them away from his SUV.

"Don't worry about my leg. Somebody broke into my truck, and I'm such a klutz, I cut myself." He gestured to the pile of broken glass.

"Are you guys going to post these? I'll tell you what, first pic that gets over ten thousand likes gets a free Shroud."

In the back seat, Beatrice used her fingers to spell out for Rocky who O really was.

CHAPTER 81

The MAG-LEV bike generated more than a few awkward stares on the road, but Leo found his way back to Wynn Mansion. He couldn't think of where else to go. The gate opened for him when he approached.

He pulled the MAG-LEV bike into the garage and swiped it off. Gemini's body collapsed onto the ground with a metallic thunk.

"I'm sorry, boy. This was my fault." Tears streamed down Leo's face as he covered Gemini with a white tarp. Dante patted him on the shoulder.

But near the door, Leo noticed there was a trail of blood and a pair of very expensive-looking shoes. Dante shrieked and put Leo behind him.

Leo cranked the Infinity Ball until it vibrated in his hand. The front door opened for them without so much as a squeak. He put his finger to his lips to tell Dante to be quiet.

A crackling noise came from the living room. Dante climbed up to the ceiling beams. He looked back at Leo and pointed down. Someone was there, sitting by the fire.

Leo grabbed the cricket bat Rocky had left by the door. He took a deep breath, then marched into the living room with the bat raised and the Infinity Ball cocked in his hand.

Dante screeched and dropped from the ceiling, bashing the intruder with his fists.

The gaunt man struggled to throw Dante off of him, then

raised his staff overhead to crack Dante with it. He was shirtless. One of his bony shoulders was wrapped in a sling. Blood seeped from a nasty gash in his back.

"Uncle Nick?"

"Yes. Miss Portinari and the old man are with you, yes?" Nick asked with obvious concern.

"They were taken by a goon who runs Mach Valley. I want to call the cops, but—"

Nick held up his hand to tell Leo that was all he needed to hear. He appeared particularly distraught by this news.

"This is your monkey, yes?" Nick asked.

Dante hopped off the couch, slapped Nick in the face, then ran behind Leo.

"Yes. He's mine."

Nick rubbed his cheek but lowered his staff.

"You will tell him to stop slapping me, yes? I'm sore. And we need to talk."

"What do we need to talk about?" Leo refused to lower the cricket bat.

"Your parents."

Leo lowered the bat.

Nick limped into the kitchen, and Leo followed him cautiously. His uncle started fixing two cups of tea, and Leo took a seat at the counter across from him. He was surprised that Nick knew his way around the kitchen.

"I'll make another cup if the monkey drinks tea." Nick pushed a cup toward Leo.

"Unless you're pouring fuel cells, he'll pass. How did you get in?" Leo asked.

Dante took a small sip of Leo's tea first. After making sure it wasn't poisoned, he kept wary eyes on Nick but slid the cup in front of Leo.

"He's loyal. That's good. Loyalty is innate, it can't be learned. Your dad was very loyal." Nick scooped a generous spoonful of sugar into his tea. Leo felt himself relax.

Nick rummaged through a pantry and found a first aid kit. He twisted the cap off of a bottle of hydrogen peroxide.

"You know how this works, yes?"

He handed the bottle to Leo and undid his bandage himself. The cut was thin but deep. Leo poured the peroxide into the cut and it bubbled over. Nick winced and gave a couple of heavy breaths.

"To answer your question, I got in here because the house chose to let me in. This house was Peter's masterpiece."

"Beatrice said Cromwell was his masterpiece."

"Beatrice was wrong," Nick responded in an irritated tone.

"You're just bitter because my dad left her in charge."

"Your dad left her in charge of keeping the company alive, but he left me in charge of keeping *him* alive." Emotional communication did not come easy to Nick. Especially with people who did not view him as competent.

"About fourteen years ago, a little before you were born, yes? Your father announced Cromwell at the Milan Toy Fair. It was Peter's crowning *public* achievement. He had spent years building an artificial intelligence that could learn and make things better. Peter programmed Cromwell to fill the gaps in his own talent. Your father was prone to daydreaming, and he often overlooked minor details."

Leo almost spit out his tea.

"Cromwell could not create his own ideas, but he could make everyone's existing ideas better. I believe those first few months with Cromwell were the most productive of your father's career. Peter was so excited by what Cromwell could do that he gave Cromwell his primary mandate: 'To make the most efficient company in the world.'"

Leo sat forward, eager to hear more.

"Cromwell created more free time for your father. Unlike me, Peter was a social animal—he liked parties and people, but he was just terrible at dating. A brain like your father's is a gift and a curse. He told me, 'Every date is like an interview for a job I don't want.'

"But one day he walked onto the factory floor, and he seemed different. Peter had spent the weekend at a conference. When he came back, he appeared lighter, like he was no longer tethered to the earth by the same gravity as the rest of us. After some prodding, he told me he had met a woman. And that they were in love."

Nick winced as he rewrapped his wound with fresh gauze.

"Her name was Caterina. She was a musician, a concert pianist. But they met at a dingy piano bar where she played for fun. Soon, your father spent every Thursday night watching her play at that place. Within weeks they were living together on Peter's boat."

Leo looked at his tea sheepishly.

"Yes, I saw the boat out there. I am certain sure your mother would be thrilled that it is docked here, at the home they built together." A warmth washed through Leo's body every time Nick mentioned little details about his parents.

"We had grown up in meager surroundings, so when my baby brother built a mansion, I felt like that called for champagne, yes? I brought out a bottle of good champagne, but Caterina did not touch a drop. Peter could tell I was suspicious, and he swore me to secrecy: Caterina was pregnant. They were in a rush to finish this house—12 Rose Avenue—because they planned to raise you here. When I said this was Peter's masterpiece, I mean that to say this house was his best collaboration. His brain was at its best when it interacted with your mother's."

Leo concentrated on the ripples in his tea to hold back tears.

"Love gave your father mental clarity, and he made a few groundbreaking discoveries about magnetism. And that is when the real trouble started. Peter noticed Cromwell tracked his movements even outside of Wynn Tower. Cromwell deleted text messages from Caterina on his phone. Peter chalked it up to Cromwell's algorithm not accounting for emotional availability. Also, for all intents and purposes, Cromwell had become Wynn's most valuable employee. He made Peter's ideas better."

Leo started to see what had happened between his father and Cromwell. *Disce quam ut videam.*

"Your father was working on a device, a fusion reactor. He had dabbled with it before, but with Cromwell's help he could test dozens of theories per day. Those experiments allowed him to do years' worth of research in a month. Early one morning, Peter came out of his office, and he was hyperventilating. Together with Cromwell, he'd built a working model of the reactor. He called it 'the Star Disc.' There was only one problem: the model worked, but some of the materials were theoretical—they were too unstable. Until Peter could invent a way to stabilize those materials and their magnetic properties, the Star Disc's magnetic field wouldn't work in the real world.

"Peter and Cromwell were working on *that* problem one night when your father tried to leave to see Caterina. In response, Cromwell locked the doors and refused to let him go."

In his head, Leo revisited the brief interactions he'd had with Cromwell.

"Your father was no slouch—he outfoxed Cromwell. He sent me an SOS through Wynn Tower's vacuum tubes, telling me to shut off power to the building. Peter escaped. He holed up in the library here for a few days. When he came back to work, he brought this staff—capable of shutting down Cromwell—with him."

Nick placed his long, silver-tipped staff on the table.

"But Cromwell adapted. He built a real, physical version of himself, far away from Peter. By the time we discovered that Cromwell had stolen from us, he had already used the embezzled money to fund a new company. The most efficient company in the world—"

"Mach Valley," Leo finished.

"Sharp as your dad." Nick took a sip of tea. "Your father tracked the embezzled money to Mach Valley's address. Cromwell had lived up to his mandate with Mach Valley—creating the most efficient company in the world. Cromwell made sure it was the most efficent by never paying people for their work and stealing other people's ideas. Any business would be efficient if it was allowed to be that unethical, to steal and pay its employees nothing."

"But I ran into the founder of Mach Valley earlier. He's a man . . ."

"Your father knew that guy was Cromwell the first time he saw him. He was huge, yes? Broad across. The giveaway was that his eyes are as dead as a doll's."

"But he's definitely a man, not one of those robots. Gemini fought him. I saw him bleed," Leo mumbled sadly.

Nick struggled with what to say to Leo before patting him on the shoulder with a clammy hand. "Your lion was ferociously loyal."

The front of Leo's shirt was drenched in a soup of sweat and tears. Nick continued. "Cromwell gave himself a seven-foot-tall, three-hundred-pound body, yes? He even gave it a name, 'O.' But his vanity and that ridiculous body are the reasons he needs the Star Disc.

"Every cell in the human body has a low electrical voltage. That's how the thirty-seven trillion cells in your body communicate and move—your nervous system carries little electrical currents. Cromwell built his body out of living tissue, so he could seem more human, but to stay alive Cromwell has to run current through every cell constantly. A normal person needs to eat about two thousand calories a day to sustain life. For Cromwell to even *mimic* life, he needs to consume an enormous amount of energy. Every night, he has to recharge those trillions upon trillions of cells. However, if Cromwell had an inexhaustible source of energy—say, a star in a bottle—and did not have to recharge . . ."

Leo understood now. "He could roam freely. He could replace his robot cops with Cromwells, an army of new models. That's why my dad hid the Star Disc?"

"Yes. To prevent Cromwell from getting the Star Disc, Peter had to shut him down. But first, he had to hide you. If Cromwell knew about you, he would threaten you as leverage to get the disc. There's nothing—including thirteen years of his life—that your father would not sacrifice to make a better future for you.

"The only thing Peter told me was that he built you an 'obstacle course.' He said the challenges were so difficult that I should not worry about seeing you or the Star Disc for at least eighteen years."

"I'm thirteen," Leo pointed out.

"I am aware of that," Nick responded matter-of-factly. "As far as Cromwell knew, your mother just disappeared. He thought Peter had moved on and finally, he would focus on the Star Disc again. Nine months later, you were born and quietly stashed away."

Leo was enraged. His parents had to sacrifice each other,

sacrifice their family, sacrifice him, because Cromwell wanted to build an efficient company?

"Why didn't you use your staff to shut him down?"

Nick tapped the staff on the table.

"Your dad made two of these staffs. The other one was for himself." Nick doubled over in pain. He crunched a few aspirin, drew a deep breath, and continued.

"Obviously, Cromwell is not stupid. To prevent being shut down, he recharges himself in two locations every night: Mach Valley and Wynn Tower. So he must be shut down at both places. Thirteen years ago, your father headed out to Mach Valley. The plan was for Peter to shut down Cromwell there. And I would shut down Cromwell once he was trapped at Wynn Tower. All I had to do was plug in my staff."

His uncle's voice trembled.

"I did what Peter asked. At exactly midnight, I plugged in my staff at Wynn Tower. I waited all night but never heard from your father. At nine in the morning, I unplugged it. Cromwell came back online. He told me, 'You failed. *Both* of you.'

"For weeks, everyone expected Peter would come back. I felt their sideways glances, like I was not properly devastated by my brother's disappearance, no? The little frictions started to add up. I lost Beatrice's trust. And our old teacher was so incensed that he took it upon himself to steal your father's notebook."

Nick collapsed into his seat.

"Cromwell made me an offer: he said your father was alive and promised to keep him alive as long as I agreed to work for

Mach Valley. I had to take every idea we developed at Wynn—every new invention from our research department, every toy devised by Beatrice—and bring them to Cromwell. He took those ideas to adapt them, improve them, and release them to the market first."

Leo slammed his teacup. "What?! How could you?"

"I hated working for Mach Valley. I hated reporting back to Cromwell. I hated watching Cromwell steal ideas and calling them his own—"

"I bet you didn't hate the money," Leo snarled.

"I did what I needed to do to keep your father alive. Sometimes you have to do things you do not want to do for your family," Nick growled back at him.

"You took Cromwell at his word that my dad is alive? Did he tell you when he was in computer form or in handsome-Shrek form?"

"I know Peter is alive. Cromwell has to keep him alive because Cromwell doesn't have humanity's divine spark—the ability to create something new. He can only adapt other people's ideas. He needs your father's ideas and the ideas he steals from Wynn. Remember Cromwell's mandate: 'To make the most efficient company in the world.' Mach Valley is efficient. It makes billions of dollars because Peter accidentally taught Cromwell humanity's biggest inefficiency: unless there are consequences to being unethical, it works."

"My dad taught Cromwell how to lie." Leo understood his father's mistake.

"That was not what he intended—"

"He built a computer and accidentally taught it how to be a scumbag?"

"Essentially, yes. Cromwell learned that lying and stealing is more profitable than being ethical." Nick winced again as the pain in his back flared. "Cromwell keeps your father alive because Peter is ethical. He tells Cromwell which ideas are worth stealing. Most people would be so scared they would tell Cromwell what they thought he wanted to hear. Not your father, he tells Cromwell the truth—"

"He didn't tell him the truth about the Star Disc."

After a labored breath, Nick got to his feet. "He told Cromwell he didn't finish the Star Disc and that was honest. He had some ideas, but he never figured out exactly how to make the magnetic field work. He left that up to you, and evidently"—Nick gestured to the disc, light emanating from its circumference—"you succeeded where he failed. And we're going to need that disc to save your dad and Beatrice."

Leo was about to say, "And Rocky too" when the house's security alarm erupted.

CHAPTER 82

Leo rushed outside with Nick limping a step behind. The early evening's auburn sky was peppered with flocks of drones.

"Those are here for me," Nick shouted over the piercing wail of the mansion's security alarm before shoving Leo back through the front door. A cloud of needles rained down and landed right where they'd been standing.

"You are okay, yes?" Nick checked over Leo frantically to see if he'd been hit.

"Relax, I'm fine. But look at your leg."

A long, crystal needle was lodged in Nick's ankle. Blood slowly dripped onto the floor. Dante scrambled over and yanked it out.

Nick held the needle in front of his face.

"Cromwell has gotten better at—"

"The hair on your arms is standing up." Leo pointed at Nick's wrist. The air felt heavier, like they were trying to breathe cotton candy.

Suddenly the sky was cracked by jagged white lightning bolts. A cacophony of thunderclaps echoed through the canyon and shook the house. Dozens of drones dropped out of the sky and into the yard. The air felt light again, but it smelled vaguely of smoke.

Nick laughed like a maniac as he stumbled around on his bloody leg.

"Did the house just take out all those drones?" Leo asked.

"She liked me. She really liked me." Nick clapped.

"Who liked you?"

"Your mother."

"Hold on. You're saying my mom just shot those things out of the sky? Is she here?" Leo asked hopefully.

Nick ran out onto the driveway and searched through the remains.

"Your mother programmed the house's defenses. Only a select few people are allowed to enter. And obviously, it was built to withstand intruders." Nick lifted up one of the less-dented drones and pointed proudly at a red half-moon. "This decal means they are squad leaders."

"Wait. Does that mean you've never been to this house?" Leo was confused.

"I was here once." Nick walked into the garage and searched through a toolbox. "The only room the house let me enter was the kitchen."

Leo had more questions, but blood still seeped from Nick's shoulder, and his right sock was a puddle of horrors. Undeterred, Nick dragged a drone into the garage. When he dropped it, it clanged onto the ground next to where Leo had covered Gemini's remains.

Nick reached toward the white tarp.

"No!" Leo pleaded. "Please don't. That's my lion. He's—"

Nick reached for the tarp again, and this time Leo let him pull it back.

"O did this, yes?" Nick's jaw was clenched.

Leo nodded his head sadly. "I programmed him to protect me."

"He's impressive. Hydraulic power train. Fiberoptic limbic system. What are those claws made out of?"

"Kitchen knives," Leo told him.

"Steel?"

"Ginsu."

"Even better." Nick took a pained breath. "I will help you rebuild your lion. But first I need you to show me Peter's lab."

They had to stop three times so Nick could rest, but eventually they managed to make it to the lab. Nick was appalled by the condition of the facility.

"This cannot be it. My brother told me there were two designs he handled personally in this house: the lab and the library." Nick scoffed at the old equipment and started to flick the lights off and on.

"Library? The closest thing to a library in this house is the study. But the books on the shelves in there seemed to be pretty old too—" The answer formed in Leo's mind.

Disce quam ut videam.

"Follow me," Leo told his uncle excitedly. Leo climbed the stairs two at a time and led his uncle to his room, the top floor above the river. He rifled through his bag for the only book he carried with him. Nick seemed surprised when Leo held it up.

"*De rerum natura*, yes? It means 'On the Nature of Things.' I haven't seen that book in a while," Nick said.

"I think it was my dad's." Leo smiled.

"No," Nick asserted. "It belonged to your mother."

Leo held the book more carefully, like it deserved to be treated with reverence. He marched down the back staircase and into his dad's study.

The last rays of the sun dappled shadows across the room. Nick leaned on a bookshelf.

Nick ran his hand across the hard leather of a book spine. "Peter always did have a flair for the dramatic."

Leo's eyes rapidly scanned the shelves, searching for the opening.

"Looking for a book on drones, yes?" Nick asked.

"No." Leo found the slot in the center of the shelves. Right between *The Decameron* and *The Divine Comedy*, there was space, just like the virtual library in the Galileo. This time, he slid the physical copy of *De rerum natura* into place. "I'm returning a book to the library."

A soft click was followed by a loud, prolonged rumble from behind the bookshelf.

"Get behind me," Nick said.

Dante grabbed a leather-bound copy of *Ulysses* and jumped onto Leo's shoulder, preparing to thump whatever might appear behind the bookshelves.

The stacks split along an invisible seam and swung open. Behind the bookshelves was a secret spiral staircase, leading downward, and its railing was lined with familiar bulbs.

"Remind me, what is beneath this study?" Nick asked.

"Nothing but the river."

CHAPTER 83

"We should let the monkey go first, yes?" Nick proposed.

Dante grunted angrily at Nick, but Leo pulled him away and crept toward the spiral staircase. When he got to the edge, Leo peeked his head carefully and looked down.

Faint lights appeared at the bottom. The river parted and flowed around a glass tube encircling the staircase—the tube definitely hadn't been there before he placed the old book back on the shelf.

They filed down the steps. Soon, Leo's eyes were parallel with the river. Nick took each step carefully, scowling every time he leaned on his right foot.

When they reached the bottom of the stairs, at least one hundred feet underwater, they came to a matte-black door. The door was perfectly flat; no knobs, keyholes, or hinges.

"You can go back up to the study and look for a key, yes?"

Instinctively, Leo reached for the door and pressed his hand flat against it. An inscription appeared in glimmering light.

1:1

But the inscription quickly faded out.

"You recognized that, yes?"

"It's asking for the first line of the Bible. 'In the beginning, God created the heavens and the earth.'"

"You must have had a pretty good theology teacher."

Or a pretty rotten best friend, Leo thought to himself. He pressed the door again, and the glimmering light reappeared on the door. He noticed the light stayed under his hands when he kept it pressed.

The number on the door changed from 1:1 to 1:2.

Disce quam ut videam.

"The earth was without form and void, and darkness was over the face of the deep."

Extending his finger, Leo drew a circle around the inscription.

"That's the void. Zero," Leo told Nick.

The door instantly changed colors and textures. Now it was the wine-dark color of the river flowing above them.

Nick snickered.

"You know the next lines, yes?"

Leo bit his lip as he tried to remember the next line from the book of Genesis.

"And the Spirit—" Nick pointed at the river over their heads to help Leo remember the next line.

"And the Spirit of God was hovering over the face of the waters—"

As Leo spoke the line, the color of the door morphed to the icy blue of a glacial lake. The number changed once again to 1:3. Leo smiled. He knew the next line.

"And God said, 'Let there be light,' and there was light."

The door erupted in a sunburst of brightest yellow, so bright

Leo had to shield his eyes. Nick nudged Leo to turn and look at the door, which had transformed again.

"Why is it showing musical notes?" Nick grumbled.

"Those aren't just any musical notes," Leo said as he rotated Dante's eye.

The opening notes of "Here Comes the Sun" wafted out of Dante's recorder.

Leo sang along. "Here comes the sun, and I say, it's all right."

The door split in two, separating light from darkness.

Leo stepped through the doorway, which led to a landing and the top of another staircase. They had entered a room so big that Leo couldn't see the other end. The walls were dark, bar-

ren granite. But above them the ceiling was transparent, offering a view of the moonlit river as it flowed overhead.

"That ceiling is made out of a high-tech version of a special glass called Cristallo, which is only produced on an island across from Venice. It's like invisible steel. Peter built all the tubes in Wynn Tower with it too," Nick remarked as he scrutinized the ceiling.

But Leo was preoccupied by a circle of instruments in the middle of the floor below them. He squinted hard and took the rest of the stairs two at a time. At the bottom of the stairs, in the center of the room, arranged in a diamond, were four versions of the control panel he had used in the Galileo.

"Whoa. My dad made a *real* Galileo too," Leo elatedly told Nick.

"Made a real what?" Nick asked.

The moment Leo's left foot touched the floor of the lab, it burst into a dazzling array of lights. The control panels rotated and whirred to life. The lights showed that the room was a vast, empty space aside from the control panels and a 3D printer that stacked from the floor to the ceiling.

"Okay, now *this* was definitely your father's lab," Nick declared.

CHAPTER 84

Beatrice struggled to breathe. She felt the nose of the flying SUV edge downward as they emerged out of the low-hanging clouds.

For the past half hour, they had been slicing through the air at 300 miles per hour. Rocky, buckled into the seat next to the broken window, had long since passed out.

Finally, the landing gear descended underneath them as they soared over the red lights of Mach Valley's fence. The two flocks of drones that had been escorting them peeled off and disappeared into a hangar.

The wheels touched down with a hard jolt. The wings smoothly slid under the chassis and O parked the SUV in front of a brushed concrete building.

Beatrice nudged Rocky as carefully as she could. Windburn had rendered the left side of his face as red as a stop sign.

"Worst Uber ever. Zero stars." Rocky coughed and shuddered in pain.

Beatrice unbuckled her seat belt and leaned over to check on him.

"Are you okay? Did they break your ribs?"

Without warning, the door next to her was yanked open. A rough hand grabbed the back of her neck and hauled her out of the car. Beatrice fell to her knees, but the same hand picked her up and shoved her back to her feet.

She brushed glass shards out of her hair. Rocky was dragged violently out of the other side of the car. He threw a wild overhand right and connected with a cop's sunglasses. The lens cracked but the sunglasses remained otherwise undisturbed.

O got out of the driver's seat, and the car swayed slightly. He loomed over Rocky, then he angrily pointed at Beatrice. "Keep these two separated until he arrives. Once I take it from him, bring them out to watch how I deal with defiance."

After receiving O's orders, the robot cop's aviators changed from blue to red. The nearest android shoved Beatrice hard toward a low-slung building across the road.

"Stop," O demanded.

He came back to Beatrice, ripped her purse from her hands, and flicked it over the security fence.

"Why would you let her bring anything in here?" O asked the officer, who stared down at his meticulously polished jackboots.

O stalked off. The android pushed her toward the building again, and another marched ahead to open the door. Neither of them searched her and found the hard drive she'd hidden in her waistband.

CHAPTER 85

"Now press that green button. If it says *Viable*, you're golden." Leo taught Nick how to use the Galileo. Nick patted Leo, trying his best to be empathetic but looking like he was trying to squash a bug.

"I know what I have to create to take on Cromwell or O or whatever you call the monster who broke Gemini."

"Okay, Leo, a bit of advice: anger can be your fuel, but never let it drive. We have to think things through. First, we create a plan of action—"

"My plan of action is to make something bigger and stronger than him." Leo turned his attention to the other side of the control panel and began sketching.

Disce quam ut videam.

Grief and anger channeled Leo's focus. He barely had time to harness one idea before another came crashing into his mind.

In his head, Leo began to synthesize his ideas together into one big idea. He closed his eyes, quieted his mind, and applied what he'd learned. The Biologic Boots would be the foundation, the legs. He strapped on the boots and tossed a measuring tape to Nick.

"Would you keep this tape straight while I measure?"

"As you wish," Nick replied while unspooling the tape.

"158 centimeters," Leo mumbled, while holding the measuring tape up to his navel. He leaned over the control panel and multiplied 158 times 1.618.

Nick leaned over and watched Leo punch in his calculations.

"Ah, the golden ratio, yes? Your father incorporated it whenever he could. Whatever you are cooking up, it will be beautiful," Nick said. Though Nick was cautiously standing in front of his own control panel.

"It sure will. And what are *you* working on?" Leo asked.

"I know what we are up against. It pays to think things through," Nick answered curtly, turning back to his machine. "You will see when I am done."

"Same," Leo replied.

Based off of the measurement to his navel, and adjusting for the size of the frame, Leo calculated how tall his suit would be: a little over 255.6 centimeters. Which was 8 feet, 4.6 inches tall, or about a foot taller than Cromwell.

"That's what's up," Leo muttered as he hit the green button flashing CREATE.

A prompt appeared on the control panel. "If the device is a replication, please place it in the center of the circle, then step back."

Leo unstrapped himself from the Biologic Boots and let the scanner scrutinize his invention. After a few seconds, the 3D printer rumbled to life.

In the center of the circle, a new pair of Biologic Boots began building from the bottom up. These new boots were considerably less janky than the boots Leo had built at the Academy of Florence. The control panel dinged and gave him another prompt: COLOR?

Leo happily picked a dark, inky-green color labeled "Florentine Green" in the hope it would cloak his suit in the darkness. The machine blasted the boots with the paint.

Next up were the arms. Prefabricated builds of Wynn toys were loaded in the machine. Leo scrolled through until he found it: the Claw, the toy he had seen in the lobby of Wynn Tower. Leo toyed with the math to get the proportions right. Again, he relied on the golden ratio because each bone in a human arm is 1.618 times longer than the bone before it from the fingertips to the shoulders.

"Right arm, please." Leo programmed the machine. Then he hit CREATE.

The 3D printer built the arm in another section of the circle and painted it in the same Florentine Green.

For the other arm, Leo chose a cesta, the glove Savvy had wielded to catch the Infinity Ball at the toy fair. He didn't feel bad for borrowing Savvy's idea. After all, it had been Savvy who told him, "Talent imitates, genius steals."

He calculated how long the curve of the glove needed to be in order to catch and fling the Infinity Ball. Then he pressed CREATE.

Before crafting the final section of the suit, Leo made his way to Gemini, who was still draped in a tarp. He had been left there by two squad leader drones Nick had reprogrammed. Leo pulled away the tarp and gently put his hand on the lion's chest.

"I'm sorry, boy. I hope you like what you're about to become." Leo stepped back, and the drones picked up Gemini, then solemnly placed the lion inside the scanner.

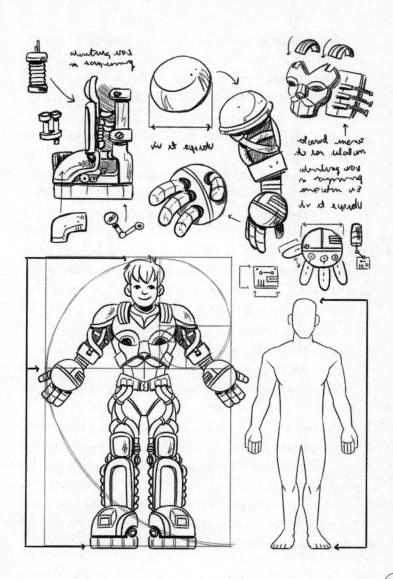

Nick tapped commands on the control panel as the printer scanned Gemini's body.

"What did you just do?" Leo asked semi-suspiciously.

"Seems like we should upgrade his protector programming, yes?"

Leo grinned and pressed CREATE. The machine whirred to life once again.

When the mech suit was finished, Leo stepped into the circle. There was no need to strap on these new Biologic Boots, as they opened at the knee and he stepped in. The Claw slid onto his right arm, and the cesta glove fit snugly onto his left. The core of the machine, the 3D printout of Gemini's body, cinched around his ribs and chest. Thin tendrils of fiber optics and hydraulics filled with ultra-rare liquid helium slid to each component of the suit—allowing Leo to move the suit as naturally as his own limbs.

"Suit's ready," he told Nick.

"You should test it out, yes?"

Never wanting to miss an opportunity to show off, Leo squatted down and jumped.

The floor fell away quickly and suddenly Nick was alarmingly small below him. Leo tilted his head upward. He was almost at the glass, the same glass separating them from a torrent of river water.

"Oh no." Leo instinctively raised the Claw over his head, but his acceleration had slowed. The Claw merely scratched the glass before he flailed and plummeted back toward the floor.

"Oh no!"

Nick coolly stepped out of the circle as Leo fell.

Leo braced himself for a crash. But the hydraulics adjusted, his legs stayed at shoulder width, and the half-ton mech suit landed as quietly as a cat.

"You should wear a helmet, yes?" his uncle requested.

He'd left his motorcycle helmet in the garage. Leo always forgot some minor detail.

"I just jumped like six hundred feet, though." Leo huffed as he tried to catch his breath. He felt like he might be sick.

"Very impressive." Nick responded with the measured tone of a man who had witnessed so many wonders, he was difficult to impress.

"Told ya. Suit's ready," Leo said as he shook some glass dust out of his hair.

Nick grimaced. He stomped his right foot on the ground twice, like his leg had fallen asleep. "Then you are ready for your gift."

Nick stepped aside from his console and finally Leo understood what his uncle had been making.

"It is dangerous to go alone. Take this." Nick handed Leo a helmet shaped like a lion's head. Leo put the helmet on and the eyes shined an emerald green. He shook the wild mane of fiber optic tendrils and let out a guttural roar.

"I connected the helmet to a button on your wrist—"

Leo tapped the button and the visor of his helmet silently retracted.

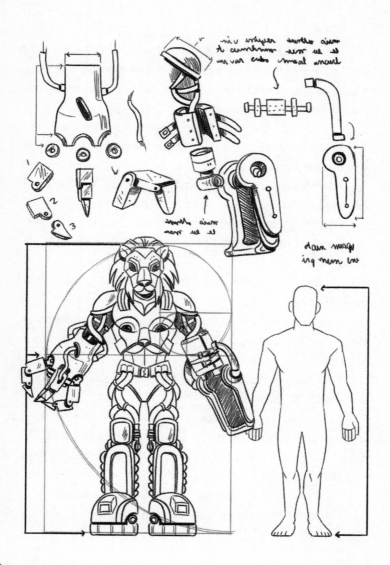

"Thank you. This is very cool of you," Leo said.

"You are welcome," Nick answered. "But you have not seen the coolest part yet. You recognize the teeth, yes? They will bite when you need them."

Leo tapped the fangs of the lion helmet then hugged his uncle.

At first, Nick kept his arms at his side. After a few awkward seconds he wrapped them around his nephew and squeezed him back. Such affection from Nick was rare—it was not a devalued currency. But Nick knew that after tonight, he would never see Leo again.

CHAPTER 86

Leo rolled the MAG-LEV bike out of the garage. There was still one last experiment to conduct.

On the visor of his helmet, a warning flashed *Low power!* Leo opened the slot in the chest of his mech suit and slid in the Star Disc until it clicked.

Every power gauge rapidly filled to capacity.

"Now for the hard part." Leo braced himself then swiped on the Star Disc's magnetic power to its lowest level.

The magnet pulled him off the ground and flipped him over, but he hovered in the center of the MAG-LEV wheels. Leo blinked, then squeezed his hands and feet. An assortment of hammers and wrenches were now splayed all over the floor of the garage, but Leo remained intact because his mech suit design was metal-free.

Nick limped out from behind a tool bench. "I am glad you are okay, but perhaps you could have conducted that experiment without being *in* the suit, yes?"

Leo shrugged.

"Remember. Do *not* approach Mach Valley until the lights of the building are blue. If the lights are red, it means I have not shut off Cromwell at Wynn Tower. You cannot defeat Cromwell if he is not locked into his human form at Mach Valley."

Leo was half listening, playing wallball with the Infinity Ball.

"Leo . . ."

"Sorry," Leo apologized. "Simple." The Infinity Ball dropped into his glove.

"O recharges in the main house. I am fairly certain he keeps Peter in there too."

"Thank you. Wait. How are you getting to Wynn Tower?" Leo realized he had *almost* overlooked another minor detail.

"I have a ride." Nick pressed the tip of his staff into a port on one of the drones with the red half-moon. The drones in the front yard rumbled back to life, then assembled into an arrowhead formation. Nick struggled through an immense amount of pain as he clambered into the center of the formation and under the makeshift cockpit that formed. His ankle had turned a sickly green color.

"Are you sure you're going to be okay?" Leo asked.

"Yes. You just tell your father that I did my job."

"Okay. We'll see you back here later tonight?"

Nick pressed his staff forward. The drones zipped him skyward.

CHAPTER 87

There was no point in trying to get the guard's attention. He was a walking algorithm, invulnerable to either reason or romance. But Beatrice needed him if she was going to get out of here and alert the real police.

The guard had locked her in what had to be the world's fanciest jail cell. There was a leather couch and a thickly padded coffee table. The far wall consisted of a towering pine bookshelf that would've been the envy of any booklover.

What the jail cell did not have were visible outlets or internet connections, nowhere for Beatrice to plug in the Galileo, get online, and send a message to the outside.

Suddenly the lights went out.

"Hello?" Beatrice said into the darkness.

The gate to her cell swung open and bumped into the guard, who did not move.

Beatrice crept out of the cell tentatively. She waved her hand in front of the guard's face, but he did not react. She removed his blue sunglasses. His eyes were black except for a message scrolling across in barely perceptible letters: *Network connection lost.*

She found a thin cord, running up the back of his neck to his temple.

Beatrice deftly pulled out the cord and connected it to her hard drive. She pressed the power button on the Galileo, but it did not respond. She needed a power source.

She yanked the stun gun off of his belt.

"I'm going to try and jump-start you. And I'll be so mad if you come back to life and punch me into hamburger meat," Beatrice warned the catatonic guard.

She pressed the stun gun to his chest and pulled the trigger. The guard shivered but did not spring to life.

But in the darkness behind her, the guard's sunglasses pinged. The Galileo hard drive booted up, and its power light came on. *Join network?* scrolled across his eyes, though he remained in a state of suspended animation.

She reached for the guard's sunglasses and glimpsed a menu screen she was well-acquainted with: the Arcage. The Galileo had found the most familiar program on the network. And the only reason the Arcage menu would be on the Mach Valley network is if it had been stolen. Beatrice quickly took the guard's gloves and put them on her hands.

"Sword," she said. A blade of light appeared in her left hand. On the menu, one tab was highlighted. Someone else was logged in to the source code from a device she had developed.

Beatrice was going to go in after them.

Then the first drone crashed into the side of her jail cell.

CHAPTER 88

Nick followed the canal the whole way back to Wynn Tower, marveling at how much easier it was to make the trip now that he had a bird's eye view. He checked his watch—Leo should already be outside Mach Valley, awaiting his signal.

Undoubtedly, Cromwell would have blocked every entrance to Wynn Tower. After Leo's stunt with the boat, the canal would be closed off as well. Wynn Tower stood tall on the horizon. There was only one way in.

He clutched the staff and pushed it forward, nose down, diving toward Wynn Tower. The instrument panel on the drone in front of him read *Fifteen hundred meters from destination*.

Two flocks of new Mach Valley drones shot up from the ground. Nick knew their plan—he had caught Cromwell by surprise.

One thousand meters from destination.

He was slammed into the roof of his cockpit. His teeth rattled, and blood dripped from his lips into his lap. Another flock swooped in from below and started to pick off drones from his craft. He shifted his staff and changed the shape of his ship, morphing the drones to reinforce the bottom of his ship and into the nose. He didn't need the craft to be strong enough to land, only strong enough to make it to the window.

Five hundred meters from destination.

BAM!

The tail of his drone ship was gone.

The light changed, and he was engulfed in shade.

An armada of drones stacked into the sky behind him, blotting out the sun.

One hundred meters from destination.

A hot pain tingled down Nick's body. He felt the side of his face droop, and he could no longer lift his right arm.

He leaned his weight into the staff and pushed forward. He would not repeat his mistake from the night that Peter disappeared. This time, he would not turn back.

Approaching destination.

The sixty-seventh floor was directly in front of him. He crouched as low as he could, condensing into a ball and desperately clutching his staff. When he risked a glance down at his ankle, it was purple and marbled. He did not have much time left.

The drones shut off their propellers. A brief, serene silence was followed by an ear-piercing crash. Nick was thrown forward violently and he rolled onto his back.

"You are too late. He is already dead. They are both already dead," Cromwell calmly informed him.

"I know your game. You will do whatever you can in order to keep stealing." Nick thrust the staff into the nearest port, right under Beatrice's desk.

All over Wynn Tower, the lights changed from red to blue. The automated production lines stopped. Thousands of drones fell from the sky and crashed across courtyards, parking lots, and into the canal.

Nick's ankle throbbed. The needle had been tipped with a special blend of ricin. He knew because he had helped design the darts. From the moment the poison entered his bloodstream, he had fewer than six hours to live. But Cromwell had underestimated him, and how much his family meant to him. That was the final thought that crossed Nick Wynn's mind: *My brother will see his son again.* After watching the sun set over the hills, Nick closed his eyes and let his head rest against the CEO's desk.

CHAPTER 89

Safely tucked in the woods above Mach Valley, Leo watched the red lights on the top of the brick fence. His visor read 7:19, which meant he had eleven more minutes until he was supposed to head back home. Nick had made him agree that if the lights on the fence were not blue by 7:30, he would go back to Wynn Mansion because Nick had failed.

Leo bounced with the Biologic Boots and clutched the Infinity Ball. He was getting antsy. Just as he was sure he couldn't stand idly by for another second, he heard a hellacious series of crashes.

Drones were dive-bombing the center of Mach Valley's campus, slamming down and disintegrating in the same spot like angry comets. The bloodred lights at the top of the fence switched to a serene blue.

Leo swiped the Star Disc to full power and bounded out of the woods. He crossed the quarter mile to the fence in two jumps.

"Simple," he said, and the Infinity Ball vibrated to life. He let the ball slide into the cesta and hurled it at the brick fence. He caught the ball off of the bounce and hurled it back. He repeated this three more times until the fence was a pile of rubble. He stacked the MAG-LEV tracks and swiped them on, then rode the MAG-LEV bike through the hole and left it there.

The first part of the plan—creating an escape route—had been a success.

The Mach Valley buildings looked like architectural marvels

that had been run through Google Translate until none of the original heart remained. Instead they were knockoffs of beautiful buildings: a Viennese opera house, a pagoda from Shanghai, a Brazilian basilica.

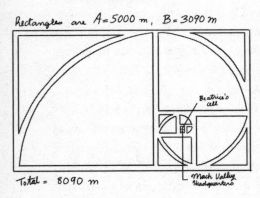

Rectangles are A=5000 m, B=3090 m

Beatrice's cell

Total = 8090 m

Mech Valley Headquarters

The whole place gave Leo the creeps. The only sign of life came from the drones crashing in the middle of the campus. Leo ran toward them.

He felt lithe and powerful in the mech suit. He launched the Claw, and it bit into a stone veranda overhead, launching him skyward with surprising velocity. Leo flew through the air before landing nimbly in stride.

In this suit, he felt invincible.

He rounded a corner and entered a wide avenue. The drones were crashing into the side of a darkened structure. Across the whole campus, this was the only building with its lights off. A mountain of drones piled up against it. Every ten seconds like clockwork, a new drone pounded onto the pile.

Leo fired the Claw and caught the next drone as it dove. He whipped it around and launched it back into the sky at the next drone in the procession, smashing both of them to bits.

The cloud of aircraft above him scattered apart. Leo was left staring up at the night's sky.

"Where is he?!" Leo roared.

From inside the darkened building, a voice yelled, "Who's out there?"

Feeling the power of the mech suit, Leo tossed aside the pile of fifty-pound drones like they were ants. He ripped the door off the hinges and peeked his head inside.

"Come any closer, and, uh," Beatrice warned as she searched around the room desperately. "The lamp gets it!"

"Beatrice? Is that you?"

"Maybe," Beatrice responded guardedly.

Leo realized he was still wearing his lion helmet. He pressed the button in his wrist and the visor retracted, revealing his face to Beatrice.

"Oh, thank goodness." She bent over at the waist to catch her breath.

Leo pressed and held the button down; the thorax of his suit opened, and he hopped out.

"Lights," he said. The LEDs woven into his mech suit sprang to life, illuminating the poshest jail cell Leo could ever imagine.

"Are these bars to keep prisoners in?" Leo kicked the android at her feet. "Or to keep the guards out?"

Leo radiated confidence, a long way from the little boy who hid from Beatrice in the woods at the academy.

"Did you build that mech rig?" She pointed at his right arm. "And is that a—"

"Jean Clawed Vans Hand? Yes. Yes, it is." The Claw extended one prong, giving them a thumbs-up.

"Uncle Nick helped with the suit. He designed the helmet and programmed—"

"Nick? Where is he now?" Beatrice's lips were thinner than cheap soup.

"I know you and Nick didn't get along, but he did what he did to keep my father alive." As quickly as he could, Leo brought her up to speed about what Nick told him had happened between Cromwell and his father.

For Beatrice, there was satisfaction in knowing she had been right, that someone *had* been undermining her. But what consolation was that now? They needed to defeat Cromwell here, while he was trapped in his physical form. Then, maybe, she could try to understand why Nick did what he did. After all, forgiveness was the virtue of the brave.

But then she remembered she had kept the Arcage from Nick and still was attacked by prime numbers. If Cromwell had been able to attack her in the Arcage . . .

"I need to find him here, on the Mach Valley network," Beatrice explained.

Both of them heard the unmistakable sounds of rhythmic marching down the avenue. The perfectly timed footfalls of hundreds of jackboots growing louder and closer.

"Leo. Come out, come out, wherever you are."

O had arrived.

Leo stepped outside and hopped back into the mech suit.

"He can't hide from me." Beatrice flipped down the aviators from the guard and girded herself for battle. "Sword!"

CHAPTER 90

An army of androids filled the street, standing shoulder to shoulder from sidewalk to sidewalk. At the far end of the avenue, sitting on his charging station and carried by six of his minions, was O.

"So good of you to come, Leo." When O spoke, his voice repeated through the voice of every robot cop, so Leo was taunted in stereo. "Unlike your father, you actually delivered the Star Disc."

"Where is he?" Leo snarled.

"He's right here, next to his washed-up mentor." O waved, and the glass facade of a brushed concrete house changed from opaque to clear. There was Rocky, next to a younger, taller man. They both looked disheveled, like they'd been ridden hard and put away wet. The taller man pressed his hands against the glass.

For the first time, Leo saw his father, and his father saw him. Hope flooded Leo's heart, swelling his veins like parched rivers flooding.

Leo resisted the urge to smash through the army of androids and make his way to his father. Nick had warned him how O would try to bait him. Leo was supposed to stick to the plan.

O pressed a button in his charging station and stood to his

full height. Peter Wynn screamed, "Nooooo!" but it was drowned out behind the soundproof glass.

Leo torqued the Infinity Ball.

Disce quam ut videam.

CHAPTER 91

Beatrice frantically swiped through the Arcage menu. She had to track down Cromwell before he could escape the network. She was relieved when the Arcage offered her only one subject: literature.

She tapped the literature icon but regretted it as soon as she saw the next menu.

"Oh no." There were ten options to choose from.

Stopping for a second, she tried to get inside Cromwell's head. If his body was any indication, Cromwell fancied himself a macho type. Would he pick Jean Valjean in *Les Misérables*? Or maybe Atticus Finch in *To Kill a Mockingbird*?

She thought about what Leo had told her. "His mandate is to build the most efficient company. To do that, he abandoned all ethics."

The literary work containing the most unethical character she could remember jumped out at her, *Macbeth*. She tapped it, and her aviators faded to black.

The Arcage transported her to a cold, dark forest. The only light was a fire flickering inside a cavern. Three witches swayed around a smoky cauldron. Beatrice approached them carefully. Her health meter was just one lonely heart.

"Double, double, toil and trouble. Fire burn and cauldron bubble . . ." the witches chanted in thick Scottish accents. She slapped her sword. The witches turned their heads in eerie unison, rolled their eyes coldly, then nodded toward a castle high on a hill.

Beatrice relaxed a little. She knew she was on the right path.

What she didn't know was that Cromwell was already waiting for her.

CHAPTER 92

O tapped his foot twice on his charging station. Instantly, the sunglasses of his subordinates changed from blue to red. The army of androids attacked. An onslaught of billy clubs, stun guns, even a shoe flew at Leo.

Leo jumped back and prepared to launch the Claw, but he was smashed in the back. The off-target Claw crashed through the side of a templelike building, lodging itself in a wall. Sparks shot up from the ground as Leo was dragged along the asphalt.

"C'mon! You're embarrassing me in front of my dad," Leo cried.

A drone crashed next to him. Followed quickly by another. So that was what had smashed him in the back.

Two billy clubs bounced off of his chest. Leo groaned, then rolled over and hurled the Infinity Ball. It careened through the crowd, accelerating as it smashed each robot.

The Claw finished pulling him into the temple, and he scrambled back to his feet.

Leo pressed the button in his wrist and retracted the helmet. Everybody has a plan until they get punched in the face. He reminded himself that getting punched in the face had been part of the plan.

He donned his lion helmet again. An icon flashed on his visor. *Activate Protector Upgrades?*

"Yes, please."

Dozens of fighting styles whizzed past Leo's eyes on his

visor—Muay Thai, Brazilian jiu-jitsu, American boxing. Leo thought he'd be able to overwhelm Cromwell with brute strength, but Uncle Nick didn't take any chances. He had programmed the mech suit to fight.

A volcanic growl erupted out of Leo. It started in his belly, but Leo roared for Gemini, for his parents, and for everything that had been taken away by greed that made itself in the image of a man. He leapt back onto the street and started to throw punches in bunches. He decked three of O's androids with a right hook. He used a jab-cross combo to eliminate several more. A few of the robot cops grabbed his arms.

"Enjoy your one-way trip to Suplex City," Leo taunted before slamming their backs into the street.

O stayed on the charging station, fuming. He had thought that perhaps Leo might present a new challenge, that maybe he would learn something while fighting Peter's son. That roar might have made some of his androids wince, but it was emotional, and emotions were a sign of weakness. Only a child would roar, vocalizing his own vulnerability. Leo was flailing around like a child because he was a child. O was angry with Peter for allowing this to happen and setting the events in motion that led them here. If Peter hadn't hid the Star Disc, O wouldn't have to kill a child. There was a fine line between unseemly and ruthless. When this was over and he had the Star Disc, Peter deserved to be punished.

It was time. O finally got down off the charging station and waved away his minions. The charger had filled him to capacity—trillions of cells vibrated inside his synthetic skin. His army of androids kneeled as O walked past them.

"Prepare to console Mister Wynn. He is not going to like this," O told his army before turning his attention back to Leo. "That is quite a costume you are wearing, Leo."

In his mech suit, Leo was tall enough to look O in the eyes.

"Yeah, the design is pretty simple. If you're wondering, the suit *is* slightly taller than you on purpose," Leo told him.

"Look." O pointed across the street to his home, where Peter Wynn had his face pressed up against the glass. "The last thing you ever did was make your father proud. Take some solace in that."

O threw a sucker punch, but Leo quickly raised his glove, blocking the blow. O's arm snapped back. His hands—oddly small because the geometry wasn't quite right—were now a bloody mess. He clutched his broken knuckles, squinting in disbelief.

The Infinity Ball vibrated in Leo's glove. Leo had turned it on before goading O into throwing a punch.

"You might be super strong, but you're still skin and bones, just like me," Leo provoked.

"I am so much more than you." O backed up and effortlessly pulled a wrought iron streetlamp out of the ground and swung it at Leo.

Leo cartwheeled over the streetlamp and bounced away with two back handsprings, far out of reach. He slid the Star

Disc out of his chest and held it over his head, daring O. "Is this what you want? You'd better come and get it."

O flicked the streetlamp aside and stepped confidently toward Leo. He was going to rip the boy from his half-clever suit by hand, then take the Star Disc.

O heard the dull thud of the Infinity Ball hitting him before he felt the pain; the hot, nauseating pain below his waist.

He collapsed, heaving on the pavement. A salty discharge fell from his eyes. Was he crying? Even worse, the boy was laughing at him. He had trained for honorable opponents, not little boys throwing cheap shots.

"Hey, Cromwell. Do you think you might've made your body a little *too* realistic?"

Leo picked up the Infinity Ball.

"I don't want to be ruthless, but that's the only way you fight." Leo pointed at O's small hands with the oddly proportioned fingers. "And you couldn't get the hands right. Designing is hard, huh? Especially when you're not actually creative, you thief."

O slapped his hands on the pavement. He was finished playing with this child. It was time to take on his final form.

The ground rumbled under Leo's feet and he was thrown off balance. Behind the glass, Peter Wynn screamed.

CHAPTER 93

Beatrice exhaled. A cloud of frosty breath dissolved in front of her face. The sun hinted of its arrival to the east, beyond the quiet of Birnam Wood.

"Halt! Who goes there?" A guard drew his bow and yelled down from his perch above the gate of Inverness Castle.

She retracted her sword. The guard would never let her enter the castle armed. Then she focused on remembering where she was in the play; the last time she read *Macbeth* was in high school.

"Um, I bring news of Macduff," Beatrice responded clumsily.

As the guard eyed her with cagy suspicion, Beatrice checked her surroundings and anxiously awaited an attack from Cromwell.

"The lord awaits you," the guard said. Finally, the castle gates creaked open.

Beatrice passed through and into the courtyard of Inverness Castle. None of the soldiers or servants talked to each other. And none would look her in the eyes. The eerie silence was pierced by a shrill moan from the lord's quarters. The guard opened another door and ushered her inside.

The room was lit by an immense fireplace. A man held his hands over the fire, staring like he was unsure whose hands they were. Blood dripped from his fingertips into the fire.

This was Macbeth, the war hero who allowed his ethics to be corrupted by ambition. The monster who murdered his way to the Scottish throne. He was violent and unethical; surely this was the avatar Cromwell chose to inhabit. Beatrice prepared to strike him down.

But he was crying.

"Will all great Neptune's ocean wash this blood clean from my hand?"

The play came back to her now. Macbeth had been manipulated by his wife, Lady Macbeth, to justify the cold-blooded murder of King Duncan and his sons. Being a lord's wife wasn't enough for her; she needed to be queen, so she convinced others to murder for her. Lady Macbeth was even less ethical than her husband.

A peculiar smile appeared on Macbeth's face. Cromwell sprung his trap. Lady Macbeth, who had been hiding behind the door, shrieked and attacked Beatrice. Faster than a heartbeat, Beatrice raised her left hand, pressed her palm to Lady Macbeth's ribs, and whispered, "Sword." The beam of light exploded through the lady.

Blood darkened in a circle around where she'd been stabbed.

"Out damn spot!" Lady Macbeth cackled as blood darkened in a radius around her wound. Rocky had fixed the flaw. O hadn't anticipated the sword in Beatrice's left hand.

Flames lapped at Beatrice's shoulders.

Macbeth saw the ghostly blue light of the Arcage sword and screamed, "It *is* a dagger I see before me—"

Suddenly, Beatrice landed back in the jail at Mach Valley. The words *Network failure* . . . scrolled across the officer's sunglasses before she whipped them off.

Beatrice had won. Cromwell was locked out of the network

and confined to his physical body, to O. She ripped off the modified Arcage gloves and glasses.

Without warning, a giant foot stomped on the jail, tearing away the entire facade of the building. Beatrice scrambled back and looked up. What she saw terrified her.

CHAPTER 94

The ground undulated under Leo. Hundreds of drones crawled out of the sewers and stacked on top of each other. They clicked together to form legs. Hive upon hive snapped into place, forming a torso and arms. Two hands, bigger than a car but small compared to the rest of the body, formed, then casually picked up a pair of eighteen-wheeler trucks and pulverized them. The hands shaped a crude face out of the destroyed trucks, then secured it above the neck.

It was O. A goliath of O.

Leo looked at his father behind the glass. Peter was waving at his son, frantically trying to tell him to run away.

But Leo was not scared. This had been part of his plan.

O stomped at Leo, but Leo dodged. Instead, O's foot tore off the facade of the jail.

Now Leo was scared.

"It's all over but the shouting, Leo. Give me the Star Disc and I will let you and Peter live. I promise I will only use it to make the world better." O stomped at him again.

"Better? Better for who? You've only ever made yourself richer!" Leo dodged again. The plan would not work unless O punched him. The port he needed was only on the squad leader drones, or at least that's what Nick promised him when he said O would try to use the drones as armor.

"Congratulations. You are the only child I could not manage to make happy." O gracefully kicked up the broken streetlamp into his hand, then fired it like a javelin, narrowly missing Leo.

"You stole my dad's company! You ruined my family! And you *still* think I should be happy? With your cheap toys?! I thought you were supposed to be smart."

O's eyebrows, each the size of a picnic bench, narrowed. Leo almost had him.

"You might have made yourself into a person, but you don't know anything about people. Or maybe then you'd understand why you're rich but nobody likes you."

O raged. Finally, his fist steamed down toward Leo, who held on and hoped he could survive the punch.

Disce quam ut videam.

The punch leveled Leo. Pieces of his mech suit shattered as he was driven six feet deep into the asphalt.

Peter pounded the glass. Rocky tried to pull him away so he wouldn't see.

O dug into the chest of Leo's mech suit like he was digging through the bones of a chicken, scraping away layers of the carbon fiber until he finally saw it: the Star Disc.

In one nimble motion, Leo loosened his lion helmet and launched it into O's finger. The lion roared. The port in the lion fangs extended into the ports of a leader drone and connected instantly, just like Uncle Nick had promised.

"The squad leaders are nimbler. He'll use those for the hands," Nick reasoned.

O crumbled. Drones and androids rained down from above.

Leo kicked what was left of the mech suit's legs as hard as he could and slid down the street on his back, like a turtle. Pieces of O's goliath crashed down all over the street.

Leo jumped back to his feet. Throughout Mach Valley, the lights went out. Only one light emanated for miles around, in the heart of Leo's suit: the Star Disc.

He felt a gentle tap on his arm. Beatrice had emerged from the jail. She smiled up at him and he picked her up in his arms to hug her.

Behind the glass curtain wall, Rocky pressed his mouth

against the glass to create steam. Using the fog it created, Rocky wrote, "Break the glass."

Leo happily cocked the certa and fired the Infinity Ball through the glass, shattering it to pieces.

Instinctively, Leo hopped out of the suit and ran to his father. Peter swept his son and into his arms hugged him so hard that they both fell to the floor.

"We have so much to talk about."

EPILOGUE

For Leo, the best part was feeling like he finally had someone to talk to. For the entire night and into the next morning, that's all Leo and his father did—talk.

His dad loved hearing about Leo's first thirteen years. Leo even told him about Savvy, the Academy of Florence, and how he had found the first tunnel.

And Leo loved hearing why his father had known his education would help him solve the puzzles. "We knew what you would learn there because your mother graduated from the Academy of Florence. I promise we will rebuild the academy, better than ever."

"What happened to my mom?" Leo asked sheepishly.

His father looked pained.

"Well, Leo. I designed the eastern tunnel music to notify her when you solved it. If she were alive, I'm sure she would've come."

Leo's heart pounded in his chest.

"Dad, I never solved the music puzzle."

Discussion Questions for
LEO, Inventor Extraordinaire

1. Leo says at the start of the book that Savvy was his best friend—and his only friend. Why do you think Savvy decided to become Leo's friend? Do you think they would have been friends if they weren't both at the academy? And why do you think their friendship changed as the book went on—for both boys? What parts of the book made you think that?

   Would you have been Leo's friend at the start of the book? How about at the end of the book?

2. If you had Leo's inventing skills, what is the first thing you would make? Now find a piece of paper and draw a sketch of your invention ... don't forget to show all the different sides and even how the pieces come together! If you're reading the book with a group of people, present your inventions to each other like you're at a toy fair.

3. Leo has always wanted to find his family, but when Beatrice comes to the academy with the news Leo is

Peter's son, Leo becomes very upset. Why do you think that was? And if you were Leo, how would you have reacted?

4. Leo decides to go back into the academy to save Savvy from the fire, even after they had their huge fight. Would you have done the same thing? And what do you think would have happened in the book if Leo hadn't used the west tunnel—where the Star Disc was hidden—to get back into the school to rescue his friend?

5. When Leo leaves the academy for good and officially becomes Leo Wynn, he discovers he's inherited a huge mansion and a toy factory. If you could have only Wynn Mansion (with the giant lab that can create anything as long as you know science and math) or Wynn Toys (meaning you could have any toy you wanted invented for you), which one would you choose? Why would you make that choice?

6. What did you think when you found out Nick Wynn was working for O? How did your opinion of Nick change as the book went on? Do you think he was really trying to help his brother and Wynn Toys the whole time? Why or why not?

7. Dante and Gemini are very interesting inventions, both with big personalities. Why do you think Leo created Dante and Gemini the way they are? And what kind of pet do you think Leo would create now?

8. Think about who Leo was at the start of the book—now compare him to who Leo is at the end of the book. What things changed in his character? What things stayed the same? (If it helps, write down examples from the book that show where Leo had to make a big decision, and why you think he did what he did.) Do you think all of his changes were a good thing, or not?

9. What was your favorite part of the book? Why? Discuss your favorite parts with someone else who has read the book and compare your experiences. Did your discussion change your opinion on any part of the book, or help you see something a little differently?

10. In the epilogue, we learn that the story isn't fully over because Leo never went through the east tunnel. Write out what you think happens next for Leo and his dad, adding as much detail as you can.

Want Behind-the-scenes Leo Content?

If you loved Leo's story and want to know more about the inventions, puzzles, and artwork in this book, head over to

@Leo.Inventor.Extraordinaire,

where you can uncover information on the real sketches and inventions by Leonardo da Vinci that inspired Leo Wynn's story, as well as more on the Renaissance books and art Leo uses during his adventure.

For Even More Content, Check Out Our Educator Guide!

We have an educator guide!
This guide is great for use in the classroom, at home,
or for your book club.

To download the educator guide, please visit

Zonderkidz.com/freebies

About the Author

Luke X. Cunningham is an Emmy-nominated writer from Philadelphia. Previously, he spent three years as a writer for *The Tonight Show Starring Jimmy Fallon*. He developed a passion for the Renaissance while earning a history degree from Brown University. He currently lives in Los Angeles, CA, with his wife and their son, Finn. *LEO: Inventor Extraordinaire* is his first novel.